The Pages of Red Diamond

By Gabriella Skory

Chapter One

Hazel is a sixteen year old girl who lives four different lives. Two of her lives are because of her divorced parents. Her third life is her school life. And her last, but favorite, life is when she stays with her aunt and leaves for another world.

◆   ◆   ◆

When Hazel was ten years old her parents got a divorce, splitting the lives she lived into four. The first life she lives is when she is with her dad - David Woodsen. Hazel's dad is a very powerful businessman who you'd never see smiling or laughing unless he was sealing a large deal or meeting with someone very important. Hazel is scheduled to stay with him on Thursdays, though he normally has some excuse to cancel. And, with all of Hazel's after school activities, she has to do her fair share of canceling as well. When Hazel does have the rare chance to stay with her dad she is practically treated, and has to act, like a princess.

There are many maids who live in her father's grand house and part of their job is to make sure that Hazel is always ready to be presented in a manner in which is "socially expectable." Meaning, they make sure Hazel wears the right clothes to the right events - the ones she's forced to attend that is. Even when Hazel's lounging around the house she can't just wear comfortable clothing like sweatpants and a sweatshirt because her father wouldn't want to have someone important stopping by and seeing her in such "distasteful attire." And when *she* looks bad, *he* looks bad (as he likes to say) and David Woodsen's top priority is his image.

Hazel's second life is with her mother, Carol May. Hazel's mother has worked her way up to being one of the most successful and wanted lawyers. Busy as her schedule is, Hazel usually does see her mom more than she sees her dad, but that's only because Carol will always bring Hazel along to all her meetings because she expects Hazel to be a lawyer when she's older. Though try as she might to tell her that being a lawyer is something she is *so* not interested in doing, Hazel's mom never listens to Hazel. Even though Hazel will go with her mom to the meetings, it's hardly mother bonding time, because her mother will constantly be doing work, thinking about work that needs to be done or talking to someone important on the phone. And as much as Hazel wishes she could just stay behind instead of attending the boring meetings, she tags along to make her mom happy - even if that does mean she has to constantly be dressed in uncomfortable business attire.

Hazel's third life, which most kids have, is her school life. Due to the fact that Hazel has two very well-known parents, she is one of the most popular girls in school. Now, Hazel really doesn't like to be the center of attention, so she's not popular in the way where she's running the school and has everybody doing her evil bidding. She more popular in the way that everyone knows of her and wants to have "The" Hazel Woodsen hang out with them or have her come to their parties - which she hardly ever goes to because half the time she doesn't even know the person who invites her!

There are three girls in particular who Hazel always hangs out with at school - The J Girls. They like to be called The J Girls because their names are Jane, Jenna, and Jessica. The J Girls had been the first group Hazel had met when she started high school, they seemed nice enough at first, though Hazel quickly saw that she didn't have much in common with them. The three girls did everything together. They ate the same food, did the same activities, dressed the same way, and even did their school assignments identically to each other. As in, if one of the girls didn't do her homework, none of the others would turn theirs in. Hazel didn't mind The J Girls to much at first, but she really didn't like hanging out with them because they were all so eager to do the exact same thing as each other.

Hazel had always liked to do her own thing and not have anybody tell her how she could or couldn't do it. Unfortunately, Hazel wasn't too happy with the way her life was going, as it seemed like someone was always telling her what to do. Hazel also wasn't the best at standing up for herself, so when The J Girls rearranged their school schedules to get nearly every class with Hazel and signed up at the dance studio Hazel belonged to, she didn't say a word - and she continued to hang out with the J Girls. Even though Hazel did her best to be her own person she usually let the J Girls talk her into doing a lot things she didn't want to do, such as - going to weekend parties, shopping late on school nights, signing up for dance committees, turning in the same school assignments and dressing like a total girly girl.

Now I'm not saying that Hazel isn't interested in fashion – she absolutely loves it! But we're talking high heal, makeup every day, check the mirror between every class to make sure your lipgloss is still on girly-girl. Hazel pretty much did whatever The J Girls told her to do so that she could just blend in, not stand out, and get through the school day, because when school was over she got to go to her Aunt Clair's house and live her fourth life - the only life that truly mattered to her. In that life, no one told her what to wear or how to act. It was the life where not only could she be herself completely, but she could leave for a different world and be a hero.

◆   ◆   ◆

Hazel jumped as the school bell rang.

"Now don't forget class, November Third I want those essays on where you want to be in the next fifteen years on my desk! And don't get so wrapped up with Halloween that you forget about it!" Mrs. Madison said as the kids collected their stuff and left the classroom.

Hazel thought about it. Where did she want to be in fifteen years? She knew she surely wasn't going to be a lawyer like her mom wanted her to be, and she wasn't going to be married to one of her dad's business partners sons like he wanted her to do, and she most definitely wasn't going to be a model like the J Girls wanted her to. Hazel really had no idea what she would write that paper about. Deciding that she had plenty of time to think about it later, Hazel grabbed her book bag and headed for her locker. She wanted to get out of school as quickly as she could so she wouldn't run into the J Girls.

This was her last class of the day and luckily it was one of the few classes she didn't have with them. Usually it gave her just enough time to leave school before they caught up to her, but if she wasn't quick they'd find her, and before Hazel would know it she'd be agreeing to a late night of shopping. Opening her locker Hazel did her normal routine of putting books in she didn't need and taking out ones she needed to study with. Once she grabbed the last of her books Hazel closed her lockers and jumped as she saw The J Girls standing in their usual formation – Jane in the front, Jenna and Jessica right behind her.

"Hey, hey! You just got out of English class, right? I can't believe we have to do that stupid essay, but like, whatevers, just so you know I decided that we're all going to write the same thing - how we're going to become super models, get married to a hot guy and live in a big house with a pool! Got it? " Jane said as the other girls nodded their heads in agreement. Hazel gave a small awkward laugh.

"Yah, maybe…" Hazel said, starting off to the front of the school. She sighed, frustrated with herself. Why did she always let people make decisions for her? It's not like she doesn't have a mind of her own – she does, she just doesn't know how to stand up for herself. She's always letting people tell her what to do, and she never says no. Hazel just wanted to fit in at school and get it over with, so she never argued with Jane. Though lately, instead of just hanging out with the J Girls

Hazel was sort of becoming the fourth J Girl. Just the other day she put lip gloss on right before gym! Something the J Girls do all the time. And Hazel didn't even take gym with them! Hazel was starting to get sick of it, but she didn't know what to do to fix it. She tried hanging out less with the J Girls after school but they didn't seem to be taking the hint. Besides, they were in quite a few classes together. They even took the same after-school dance class, so that didn't help much. Hazel also knew that she didn't have any other friends at school, so if she stopped hanging out with the J Girls, she'd be all alone.

"Do you want to hang out before or after dance?" Hazel heard Jane ask from behind her.

"Oh, I can't today… sorry. I have homework to do before dance and then I have to make dinner tonight because my Aunt has to work late," Hazel said, turning her head so she could see Jane.

"That's fine. We can do homework together!" Jane said happily.

"Sorry, I can't tonight. I'll talk to you guys at dance!" Hazel said, waving goodbye and turning before they could find some way to change her mind. Hazel walked out of the school and headed over to the Pod garage. A Pod was sort of like a motorcycle and a scooter mixed together - almost every kid had one. One of the cool things about them was that they came in every color. Hazel had a light blue Pod because that was her favorite color. Other kids had orange, black, purple and even

9

tie-died. Pretty much every place Hazel went to had a Pod garage because they were so popular with the kids.

Hazel got on her Pod, put her key in, turned it on and headed home. About five minutes later, she arrived at her Aunts house. After putting her Pod in the garage, Hazel headed inside and saw a note on the table.

Sweetheart,

I won't be home until well after midnight tonight. I'm so sorry! For dinner there's steak, mashed potatoes, salad, and corn in the fridge. And don't forget – you have dance at 5:30 pm. Amber's mom is going to take you. For a snack, I bought some popcorn and Fruit Waters. See you when I get home!

Love, Aunt Clair

P.S. Just because I'm not home doesn't mean you can stay up late - it's a school night!!!

P.S.S Don't forget to feed Snowball!

Hazel read the note out loud. Right when she finished, her white fluffy Maltipoo, Snowball, ran into the room. Hazel laughed.

"Are you hungry, girl? Let's go get some food!" Hazel said walking into the kitchen with Snowball trotting behind her. After her dog was happily chomping on her kibbles, Hazel popped some popcorn in the microwave for herself, grabbed a Fruit Water from the fridge and headed to her room to wait for the popcorn to be done. They really needed to get a new microwave as the one they had took twice as long to cook everything because it had trouble heating up. Right when Hazel walked into her room she went over to her bookshelf, took a couple books off and saw a sticker of a big tooth with the words "I went to the dentist!" written on it.

Hazel gently pushed on the sticker and a square panel of the bookshelf slid aside to reveal a keypad. When you typed in the correct password, it would open a hidden compartment.

Hazel's Aunt Clair had bought the bookshelf for Hazel when she was ten, though she had no idea about the keypad. Hazel didn't know about it either until she was eleven and decided to put her dentist sticker on it. When she pressed the sticker to the shelf, she saw the key pad appear. She figured that you were supposed to put in a password. Not sure what to do, and being only eleven years old, she typed in the word "KITTY" on the keypad. Being much older now, Hazel seriously regretted it, but she had no idea on how to change it.

The secret compartment was just big enough to fit a book in it, so Hazel kept a special one there that her dad had given her when her parents got their divorce, he told her it would be good to write down her feelings in it. Though, as much as Hazel cherished the book, she never once put a pen to it. The book was a beautiful deep purple with different sized mirrors and colorful sequins on the front, and its thick pages were a cream color with sparkled streamers pressed into them.

For about a three years Hazel didn't even look at the book because she was so angry with her dad and her mom for breaking up the family. But when she finally opened it, much to her surprise, it took her to another world, a world called Red Diamond, where they had been expecting her.

Legend spoke of a girl with eyes of hazel brown, who would travel to Red Diamond, with the help of magic book, from a distant land to help Red Diamond when it was in need. It was said that the girl would be kind hearted and brave. Hazel met all of the requirements. It was a lot for her to take in but she got used to it. Now, whenever someone in Red Diamond needed help, whether it was getting a cat down from a tree or stopping a bank robbery, she did what she had to do.

Hazel had only told two people about Red Diamond - her Aunt Clair and her best friend Amber. Neither of them believed Hazel until she grabbed the book and disappeared right before their eyes. From then on they believed her. Her best friend Amber always joked that Hazel was an undercover-secret-agent-ninja-thingy, which was actually pretty close. One day Hazel came home with a scrapped knee, from clumsily falling on the sidewalk, and her Aunt freaked out and said that Red

Diamond was becoming to dangerous and she didn't want her going back.

After much compromising they decided Hazel could go back if she took selfdefense lessons and karate classes. With only a short time of taking classes, Hazel was already a brown belt in martial arts, as she quickly excelled through all the classes, and was soon to be moving up to black belt. Her teacher was very impressed with Hazel's natural talent, she was progressing through the belt ranks faster than anyone else in her classes. Even though Hazel never let her aunt know, the classes have been very helpful because at time things did get a bit rough in Red Diamond.

Hazel typed "Kitty" on the keypad. She heard a click and then the keypad swung up to revel a spot just big enough for her beautiful book. Hazel took it out, opened it and saw the word *Trouble*.

Whenever there was a problem in Red Diamond, the word "Trouble" would appear in big red letters on the first page of her book. A paragraph underneath would then describe what was wrong. Hazel sighed and looked at the clock. It was three fifteen.

"I've got time," she said quickly getting up and running over to her closet. She walked in and pulled on her black stretch pants, a baby blue tank top and a black jacket which held her gadgets. She slipped on a pair of black sneakers, pulled her hair back into a pony tail, quickly looked in the mirror and smiled. This was the outfit that she wore every time she had to go to Red Diamond. She liked it because it was comfortable and she could easily move around in it. Her Aunt and Amber called it her crime fighting outfit. Hazel headed over to her book and read more about what was going on.

"Trouble! The Gold Room key has been stolen. Location: Hotel Clarisse," Hazel read aloud the message, then sighed. The Gold Room was where the Queen and King kept all of their money, gold, and priceless jewelry. There was only one key that you could use to open the only door to the room. Hazel had told them multiple times that they needed to get better security.

Without thinking about it any more, Hazel closed her eyes, held the book to her chest and thought about Red Diamond. She felt a cool breeze, and when she opened her eyes she was in the woods that she had grown so familiar with - the spot the book always took her. Theses woods were just outside of the main town, but remote enough that no one ever really wandered through them - making it Hazel's personal spot. Hazel smiled at the familiar scenery and turned around. She took the book she was holding and put it in the chest that was in front of her. She pressed the top down until it clicked and watched as the trunk sunk into the ground. She kicked some leaves over it so no one would see it. Making her way through the trees Hazel stopped just as she reached the edge of the forest and looked out into the beautiful city of Red Diamond.

In the center of the city was its shopping center surrounding a beautiful park. Beyond the shopping center, against the brilliant blue sky, stood the grand castle. Over to the left, Hazel spotted Hotel Clarisse. It was about a mile away and was the only hotel in Red Diamond. A lot of people had weddings or parties there. Remembering that she wasn't in Red Diamond for pleasure, Hazel took a deep breath and started running towards the hotel. The city of Red Diamond blurred past as she ran. She could hear kids playing in the distance, and although she could hear their laughter, Red Diamond seemed to feel empty.

After what seemed like forever, Hazel finally ran up to the golden steps of the hotel and took a minute to catch her breath before pulling open the grand glass doors. Hazel walked inside but didn't see anyone. She grabbed a pair of glasses out of her jacket, put them on and clicked a button that was on the side. They were her x-ray glasses. She could see through anything with them on. Hazel looked up and saw two figures. She counted how many floors up they were.

"Ugh, of course they are on the one-hundredth and twenty-sixth floor!" Hazel grumbled, taking off her glasses. She walked over to the stairs and started running up them. Once she reached the twenty sixth floor, she sighed. "I can't take it any more!" she said out loud as she walked over to the elevator. Walking inside she clicked the button with the "126" on it. She closed her eyes and leaned against the wall to catch her breath. Hazel knew it was risky taking the elevator since the two people would hear that she was coming - but she wasn't about to run up another hundred flight of stairs.

She heard a ding. "Floor one-hundred and twenty-six," the elevator said. Hazel opened her eyes and moved over to the side where the buttons were as the elevator doors opened. Holding the "open" button, Hazel peeked her head out. She didn't see anyone so she slowly walked out of the elevator and looked around. Off to the side, she saw two people against the wall. Each was wearing all black, with big black hooded sweatshirts, huge green sunglasses and yellow bandanas over their mouths. Hazel screamed. Hearing the scream made the two hooded figures scream as well.

"You scared the heck out of me!" came a muffled voice from one of the hooded guys. Hazel couldn't tell which one it came from.

"Yah, you scared me too," Hazel said, slowly taking a step backward as they took a step forward. She tried to see who they were, but she couldn't.

"So um, uh...what are you doing here?" asked the man in the front.

"Well, I could ask you the same thing," Hazel said taking another step back.

"Well, we're just here because we have to–"

"Don't answer her!" the guy in the back said as he hit the one in front on the head. He turned to Hazel. "We asked you first, and you're going to answer us!" he said, pushing the guy in front to take another step.

"I'm just looking for someone," Hazel said. But right then they lunged at her - and she was ready. Hazel jumped back and started running, leaving the two men on the ground.

"Get up and go after her!" one of them yelled. Hazel hopped onto a side-table, knocking over a little lamp and letting just one foot touch the surface before she jumped off and headed for the stairs. While running up the steps she turned her head. She could hear the guys catching up. Hazel started to run faster. She came to a door, pushed it open, and found a huge room with the tallest ceiling she'd ever seen. The whole room was filled with hundreds of tables. Scanning the room she saw a bunch of chairs stacked up in front of the exit door. Knowing she wouldn't have time to move them, Hazel looked around the room again and saw an elevator with a sign that said "Out of Order" on it.

"I see her!" one of the men yelled. Hazel looked back and saw their hoods. They were about twenty feet away. She jumped on to one of the tables and ran from one to the next until she got to a table that was at the back of the room. She dived off and rolled under it. With the table cloth covering her, she knew they wouldn't find her. Breathing heavily but quietly, Hazel tried to get her breath back. She had to think of a plan, and fast. All she had to do was get the key, but she was making things way too complicated.

"Yah, nice one Hazel. I'm just looking for someone?! Why not just ask them for the key!" she mumbled to herself. She held her breath as she heard the two guys enter the room.

"Come out, come out, wherever you are," she heard one of them say. His voice was clearer. Hazel figured they must have taken off their bandanas.

"Wait, Richard, I have a great idea!" the other one said. *Ok, one of the guys name is Richard,* Hazel thought. Then it suddenly hit her. She'd dealt with these two before. Their names were Richard and Steve. They were both stupid when it came to the whole criminal stuff, especially Steve. But lately, for some reason, they've been getting a lot better. I mean, the whole disguise thing? They would have never thought of that themselves. They must be getting training, or working for somebody, but Hazel had no idea as to who would want to help or hire them.

"Oh, and what great idea would that be, Steve?" Richard asked. Hazel could hear him lift up a table cloth. "There must be five hundred tables in here!" she heard him mumble to himself.

"I'll say Little Robin, Little Robbin, and then she'll tweet! And then we'll see where she is! It's perfect! Everybody loves that game!" Steve said, excitedly thinking about his plan. It took Hazel a moment to realize what in the world Steve was talking about before she remembered what he was referencing. Little Robin, Little Robbin was a game the children of Red Diamond played. One kid would have his eyes closed and yell out "Little Robin, Little Robin!" and the other kids would "tweet" as they ran away. The point of the game was to catch someone who was "tweeting." It was very similar to Marco Polo, Hazel thought.

"Wow that's...that's a great idea, Steve! Except for two things," Richard said sarcastically.

"What?"

"One, we're not at a park! Two, we're after her! She's not going to give away her position! She's not stupid...like that idea! Now, do you still have the key?" Richard asked. Hazel smiled to herself. Stupid mistake number one, they just told her who had the key.

"Yes, I have the key. It's right here on my key chain," Steve said, jiggling his key chain. "But it's really heavy. Why can't you hold it?"

Hazel looked through a small hole that was in the table cloth and saw Steve's key chain on his waist. The Golden Room key looked funny because it was so big compared to the other keys. With the way he had it on the chain, she would easily be able to take it off. If only she could get him closer.

"I'm telling you, Little Robin, Little Robin will work," Steve said, forgetting about the heavy key. Hazel laughed a little. Then she had an idea, the perfect way to get him over. But she had to act fast. Hazel quickly pushed a button on her shoe. Though they looked like normal shoes, they could actually stick to anything when activated. They worked almost the same way spider legs did. Hazel then grabbed her gloves out of her jacket, pressed the button on them and slid them on. She would only have one chance to do this.

"You know what? I'll make you a deal. If your whole Little Robin thing works then I will give you my earnings for our next three jobs," Richard said. *So they are working for someone!* Hazel thought. "but if it doesn't work, then you have to give me *your* earnings for the next three jobs!" Steve thought about it.

"Well, one hundred gold coins would be a lot. That would be as much as we got from the last four jobs the boss gave us, " Steve said, pausing to think about it. "but I'm pretty sure my plan will work... so... you're on!" Steve said shaking Richard's hand. "Now step aside and watch how it's done," Steve said cracking his knuckles. He cleared his throat. "LITTLE ROBIN, LITTLE ROBIN!" he yelled nice and loud.

This was her chance. Hazel put her feet on the top corners of the table. They stuck like glue. Then she grabbed the bar on the table and lifted herself up so her body was flat against the bottom of the table. She took a deep breath.

"Tweet, tweet!" she yelled loudly, feeling incredibly silly. Steve started clapping his hands. "Yah, baby! I told you it would work! Don't forget, you have to pay up!" Steve said as Richard grunted.

"I didn't think she was stupid," he mumbled.

"LITTLE ROBIN, LITTLE ROBIN!" Steve yelled again.

"TWEET! TWEET" Hazel yelled even louder, trying to shake the table.

"Perfect," Steve said in a hushed voice. He stared to walk towards Hazel's table.

"Little Robin, Little Robin," Steve said more quietly.

"Tweet, tweet," Hazel said matching Steve's tone. Sensing that they were near the table, she tried to push herself up as much as she could. She could hear them breathing. Steve signaled Richard to get on the other side of the table.

"On three," Steve whispered. "Ready? One, two, three!" They both lifted up the tablecloth. Hazel held her breath hoping that they wouldn't see her. They peeked their heads underneath the table, but they didn't see anything. They let go of the tablecloth.

"That's weird," Richard said as Hazel slipped one hand out of her glove. She felt for the ground with her hand. Once she felt it, she lowered her other hand to the floor, arching her into a back bend.

"I know! I mean, you saw the table move, too!" Steve said turning his back to the table. Hazel quickly but quietly reached her hand out from underneath the table and grabbed the key. She slid her hand back under the tablecloth, but right when she did, she felt her shoes suddenly turn off and her feet came unstuck from the table. She fell with a loud thud to the floor.

She gasped as she landed on the ground, confused as to why the shoes had stopped working. That had never happened before.

"Did you hear that?" Richard said flipping the table over. They stared at Hazel who was lying on her back.

"Stupid shoes," Hazel muttered standing up. "Hello," she said with a little wave.

"Hi!" Steve said as if he was at a tea party. Richard hit him over the head.

"Look, just hand over they key and nobody will get hurt," Richard said. Hazel, realizing that she still had the key in her hand, quickly put it in her jacket pocket. She looked around to see if there was a way that she would be able to escape quickly and easily. She looked around and saw a window that was about fifty-five feet up on the wall.

"Well, I shouldn't have to give it to you, because it's not your key. So, you can't tell me what I can or can't do with it. So ha!" Hazel said while putting her hands behind her back. She grabbed onto the charm bracelet on her left hand.

"Well, I don't think that it's yours, either. So you can't tell us what we can or can't do with it either, therefore neither of us can do anything with it, so ha to you!" Richard said.

"Point well made. But you know what? I am getting sick and tired of people telling me what to do and when to do it! What to wear and how to act!" Hazel found herself yelling now. "I'm getting sick and tired of following rules that aren't even rules! I mean, who said you have to be a lawyer or be a model and marry a rich guy! No one! It's just stupid! Stupid, stupid, stupid! So, for now, I have the key and I'm going to keep it! Okay?!" Hazel finished with a sigh. Steve and Richard looked at each other shocked, taken aback by Hazel's outburst. Hazel smiled to herself. She had never thought that she would be venting about her life problems to two criminals. Steve's eyes were starting to water.

"I know just how you feel!" he said wiping his eyes. Without anymore hesitation Hazel put her hand out in front of her, aimed it for the metal fire alarm that was above the window and pressed the ballet shoe charm on her bracelet. The dance shoe went shooting towards the fire alarm, leaving a trace of the smallest and strongest string you would ever find. The ballet magnet stuck to the fire alarm. Hazel knew that it would support her because you could hang a house by this magnet and string. Richard and Steve, realizing what was going on, lunged for Hazel. Before they could grab her she clicked the tap shoe charm that was also on the bracelet and started flying toward the window.

Forgetting that her shoes were not longer working and wouldn't allow her to stick to the wall, like she had planned, Hazel changed her plan and went for the window. She quickly reached her arms up and covered her face as she smashed through the large glass window, her bracelet slipping off her wrist. As she flew through the window, Hazel gasped as the shattered glass cut against her skin. She felt a rush of wind as she flipped over in the air, falling from the one hundred and twenty-eighth floor. Hazel quickly reached into her jacket and pulled out what looked like a finger sized skateboard with a chain on it. She pulled the chain off and it turned into a full sized jetboard.

Hazel put her feet on the board as she continued falling and pressed the button on the back of it. Nothing happened – she was still falling.

"No! No! NO!" Hazel yelled over the roar of the wind. "COME ON, WORK!" she yelled, clicking the button over and over again. Hazel closed her eyes, knowing that it was going to be a painful landing. If she didn't die from the fall, she would certainly suffer. She felt a sudden jolt. Hazel opened her eyes and saw that she was hovering inches from the ground, standing on the activated jetboard.

"Thank you!" Hazel said, sighing deeply. Getting her balance, she leaned forward and lowered the board to the ground. Hazel looked up and saw Richard and Steve yelling out of one of the windows on a lower floor. Hazel smiled and gave them a wave.

Chapter Two

Hazel cruised along the streets of Red Diamond on jetboard and headed to the palace. About five minutes later she arrived at the castle gates. She saw the royal family, along with the king's six guards, waiting for her. She hopped off her jetboard and walked over to the family.

"Your Highnesses," Hazel said bowing before the royal family. "King Bilimora, I believe this belongs to you," she said, taking out the large key from her jacket and handing it to the King.

"Thank you so much, Hazel! Who knows what could have happened if someone had gotten into the gold room!" the King said, taking the key.

"No problem. It was easy," Hazel said, not mentioning the part where she almost got splattered on the ground.

"Easy? My goodness child, what happened to you?!" the Queen asked. Hazel looked down at herself. At first glance she looked fine, but she then realized that there were cuts on her hand from when she flew out the window. Nothing major, but they were still bleeding.

"Nothing. Just a scrape," Hazel said, putting her hands behind her back so that the queen couldn't see them. The King, seeing that Hazel was fine, put his hand on the Queen's shoulder who still looked worriedly at Hazel – she was always concerned that they were putting Hazel in too much danger.

"I hope that this teaches you two not to play with something that doesn't belong to you!" the Queen said, scoldingly to their twins, James and Emily. The twins were nine years old and caused quite a bit of trouble in Red Diamond.

"Sorry, Mom," the twins said at the same time, looking at the ground.

"Hazel, you must come inside and join us for some tea! After all the trouble you went through, it's the least we can do!" the Queen said. Hazel looked at her watch. It was four forty-five. The time had gone by quickly.

"Oh, I would love to! But I have to get home for my dance class and I have to stop by Calvin's quickly. Some of my stuff isn't working," Hazel said.

"Ok. Well, then another time," She said, a look of concern still in her eye.

"Of course!" Hazel said, giving the queen the same smile she gave her aunt whenever she was worried about her. Jumping onto her board Hazel waved goodbye and headed over to Calvin' house.

Calvin is a citizen of Red Diamond and the one who makes all of Hazel's gadgets. He was seventeen, only a year older than Hazel, but quite the genus! His house was about a block away from the town center. He lived with his Aunt and Grandma (who was very old and close to dying) since his parents passed away when he was twelve. He never told Hazel how, though. Hazel neared the small house that looked like a cottage. They always had a fire going, and with the big willow tree in the front yard of the house always looked so welcoming. Hazel hopped off her board, tucked it under her arm and walked past the big tree and smiled. It was perfect for climbing, and it was so nice and quiet when you were up in it. Calvin liked to sit up in the tree when he had to think about something.   Sometimes when Hazel came over, Calvin would be up there, so she would join him and they would both just sit and think. Or sometimes they would talk and watch the wispy branches sway in the wind.

Hazel knocked on the big wooden door. She took in a deep breath, smelling the cherry-wood fire, the flowers...and it smelt like someone was making chocolate chip cookies. The door swung open.

"Hello there! I heard you were out saving the world. I was hoping you would stop by!" Calvin's Aunt, Page said as she hugged Hazel and pulled her inside.

"I didn't save the world. I just had to get back the key for the Gold Room." Hazel said with a smile as she hung her jacket up and took off her shoes.

"Pish Posh," Page said with a wave of her hand. "Saving the world, getting a key for the Gold Room, they're all the same thing!" she said taking a step back and placing her hands on her hip. She looked Hazel up and down and gave a tisk. "Come here," she said grabbing Hazels wrist and leading her into the kitchen. As a stop a Calvin's was pretty routine with Hazel's trips to Red Diamond, Page was always ready with first-aid for any mishaps Hazel may have encountered. As Page pulled Hazel into the kitchen, the smell of chocolate chip cookies became overwhelming. On the counter was a tray of giant chocolate chip cookies and two glasses of milk. After rinsing off Hazels cuts, putting some sort of blue liquid on them that stung, Page wrapped Hazel's hands in a soft cloth and deemed her better.

"Ok, now that we've got you all fixed up, try one of these!" Page said, taking one of the giant cookies and handing it to Hazel. "They're fresh out of the oven!" Hazel took the cookie, realizing just how hungry she was, as she left right before having her snack. She took a bite and it melted in her mouth. It was chewy, crunchy, gooey and the best cookie she'd ever had!

"How are they?" Page asked excitedly.

"They're de-lish-us! I don't think I've ever had a better cookie!" Hazel said, taking another bite. Page smiled.

"Perfect! Now, why don't you take these down to Calvin. He has been locked away all day!" Page said laughing. Calvin had turned the entire basement into his work room. He was always making new gadgets and stuff, but he could get so wrapped up in what he was doing that he wouldn't come up for hours. Page handed the tray to Hazel. "I have to take his grandma to the doctor. Will you two be ok just hanging out here?" she asked, starting to walk over to the hallway.

"Yup," Hazel said making her way to the basement door. "And thanks for the cookies, Ms. Page!"

"No problem. I'll see you later!" she said walking into one of the bedrooms. Hazel walked to the far end of the kitchen and came to a door which led to the basement. She liked to call it Headquarters. Luckily the door was unlocked so Hazel didn't have to deal with the alarm system. Calvin, worried that someone might try to steal his stuff, had made an alarm that took about five minutes of typing and scanning just to get into the basement. Hazel used her foot to pull the door all the way open and walked down the stairs. It was dimly lit compared to the brightens of the kitchen, so she squinted to see as her eyes adjusted. Hazel walked over to Calvin's desk and put the tray down but didn't see Calvin anywhere.

"Cal? Are you down here?" Hazel yelled out while looking around. She laughed. The place looked like a mad scientist's lab. There were boxes, unfinished projects, computers, desks, papers and wires everywhere!

"I'm right in front of you," Hazel heard Calvin's voice say. She put her hands on her hip.

"I'm looking straight ahead, Calvin, and you are not in front of me," she said peering around the basement again. All of a sudden one of the cookies lifted up into the air.

"Did my aunt make these?" Calvin's voice asked as a bite disappeared from the cookie. "She really is good at baking stuff." Hazel lunged toward the spot where the cookie was but hit nothing. The cookie had disappeared.

"I'm here! You just can't see me." Calvin said, his mouth obviously full of cookie.

Hazel tried again to lunge toward his voice but got nothing. She was looking around the room when she felt a hand push her on the back and send her flying forward. Hazel put her hands out in front of her as she rolled into a somersault and flipped over, but because there was so much stuff in the basement, she hit her foot and tripped over a box which started leaking some sort of green smoke to as she fell on her back.

"Ow," Hazel said as she looked up and saw Calvin standing above her with a smile on his face. "I hate you!" she said as Calvin helped her get up. Hazel was going to ask what was in the box but Calvin started talking first.

"Well, if you hate me so much then I won't give these to you!" he said holding two black bands with a blue ornamental C on each one. This was on everything Calvin made for Hazel. Of course the C stood for Calvin. She reached out and snatched them out of his hands just as he tried to pull them away.

"You will always be smarter than me, but I will always be faster than you," she said slipping the bands on. She looked down and didn't see her body. "Oh, my gosh! Calvin, these are way cool!" Hazel said.

"Great! Now take them off so I can see you," Calvin said reaching out for where Hazel was, but she swiftly stepped aside. "Ohh no, it's payback time," Hazel said as she poked him in the stomach, and then the shoulder.

"Ok, ok, ok I'm sorry!" Calvin said laughing. Just as Hazel was about to poke him again Calvin reached out and grabbed her hand. He slid the bands off her wrist.

"Hey! You are such a fun ruiner," Hazel said grabbing a cookie and gulping down some milk.

"I know. That's what I live to do, ruin your fun!" Calvin said smiling. "But you can't have them just yet because I have to work out a few kinks," he said putting the bands on his desk.

He looked back at Hazel and noticed the bandages. "You ok?" he asked, the concern apparent on his face. Hazel rolled her eyes.

"I'm fine! It's just a scratch!" She laughed. Though it could get a bit tiresome having to always convince people that she was ok, Hazel was actually very touched about how much everyone in Red Diamond cared about her. "So, if I can't take the bands, do you have any other fun gadgety things for me to take home?!" Hazel asked, wanting to the change the subject.

"Well..." Calvin said as he reached into his pockets and pulled out a pack of mints and handed it to Hazel.

"What do these do?" Hazel asked looking at the mints.

"Makes your breath nice and minty!" he said sarcastically, and then started laughing as he reached back for the mints. But Hazel closed her hand.

"Sorry, but these could come in handy," she said putting the box in her jacket pocket.

"Fine," Calvin said with a chuckle. The thought of the mints seemed to remind him of something, as he became slightly nervous and moved over to one of the tables that was behind him and leaned against it as if he was hiding something.

"What's on the table?" Hazel asked suspiciously.

"Nothing!" he said defensively.

"Calvin! If you didn't want me to know that there was something on the table you should have just stayed where you were and not have been so obvious about it! But since you you didn't, tell me what's behind you!"

Calvin grabbed whatever was behind him and held it in his clenched fist.

"Nothing, it was just my fist," he lied. Hazel went over and grabbed Calvin's fist and squeezed his wrist.

"Ow!" Calvin said as a pack of gum fell out of his hand and into hers.

"This is what you were hiding from me? A pack of gum?" Hazel looked at the gum. It had a strange electric feel to it. "This isn't just gum, is it?! It's supper cool gum that will be able to do something totally awesome, isn't it?!" she asked. The look on Calvin's face told her she was correct. "It is, it is, it is!!" Hazel said jumping up and down excitedly.

"Ok, it is, but there is no way you are going to be taking it home today, or the next day, or the next! There are so many kinks I have to work out! And I don't know if I'll ever even be able to work them out at all!" Calvin said as he ran his fingers through his hair. He did that whenever he was frustrated, and he always got frustrated when he couldn't get something to work, or didn't know how to make it work.

"Ok, then can you at least tell me what it does?" Hazel asked with her best puppy dog face. Sometimes when Calvin created something he wouldn't even give her the slightest clue as to what the gadget was going to be able to do, as he didn't want Hazel to get too excited incase he never actually got it to work. Calvin sighed.

"Well, if I can ever get it to work... you'll put the gum in your mouth and chew it for about five seconds, then when you take it out it will be really stretchy, but it will be thick like rope. However, you'll only have about fifteen seconds to use it because after that anybody or anything that touches it gets a near-fatal shock." Hazel stared at Calvin.

"That is freakin' awesome! I'm so taking this home!" she said wide eyed.

"No!"

"Yes!"

"No!"

"YES! Pleasssse?"

"Hazel, NO! If you chew it right now you get a huge... and I repeat...*huge!* shock in your mouth. And if you held if for more than three seconds it would probably kill you! So I repeat, you may not take the gum home, understood?"

"But if I just-"

"Understood?" he repeated. Hazel sighed and handed the gum back to Calvin.

"Understood," she mumbled, putting on her best pouting face. She hated how Calvin would get her excited about something when she wasn't even allowed to use it. Well, she knew it was her fault for asking about something that he didn't want her to know about, and that's why he often refused to tell her about anything,...but still! He could at least hide stuff better or not be so obvious about it! Hazel knew that if she put on her pouting face with Calvin she would at least get something cool. But realizing what time it was, Hazel knew she wouldn't have time to goof around anymore. She had to get home for dance.

"So, I don't have a gadgety thing to take home?" Hazel asked with deep sigh.

"Well... how about this?" Calvin asked, reaching into his pockets and pulling out a tube of lipstick.

"Calvin, come on, I have to go soon," Hazel said folding her arms.

"No, I'm not kidding – this is it."

"What am I supposed to do? Make my enemies look like girls?"

"No. Watch," Calvin said as he went over to a piece of wood he had laying on the ground. He held it up in one hand and with the other he took the lipstick and drew a circle on the wood. Then, after a second, he gave the circle a push and it fell out of the board. Hazel gasped.

"That is so cool!" she said.

"I know! So if you ever need a door or a window, you can draw one!" he said handing it to Hazel. She put it in her jacket pocket. Then she hit Calvin on the shoulder.

"Hey, what was that for? I just gave you a gadget! What more do you want from me!?" Calvin asked backing away with his hands up.

"I just remembered why I came over here! Because of you I almost got captured and almost died!" Hazel said.

"Well you didn't, so what's the problem?" he asked jokingly with a nervous little smile.

Hazel picked up a glass of water that was on the table and held it threateningly over his head while glaring at him.

"Ok, I'm kidding! I'm kidding!" he said quickly as Hazel put the glass back down. "I'm sorry you almost got captured and... died?" he said uncertainly. Hazel sighed and rolled her eyes. "Now, how is *almost* getting captured and *almost* dying my fault exactly?" He asked. Hazel picked up the glass and threw the water at his face. She crossed her arms and raised an eyebrow as if to say "what do you think?" Calvin spit out the water that got into his mouth.

"What's not working?" he asked as he grabbed a sweatshirt that was on his chair and used it to wipe his face.

"My shoes just stopped being sticky when I was on the bottom of a table, and I fell to the ground revealing were I was. And since they weren't sticky, I was thrown out the window when I was using my bracelet – which, by the way, I'm going to need another one. Then, I was falling out of the window on the one-hundred and twenty eighth floor and my jet board didn't start until I was inches away from the ground! So, to tally up all of your gadgets that did not work, I need new shoes, a jet board and and a new pair of those sticky gloves because I dropped them. My shoes and jet board are upstairs." Hazel said.

Calvin opened up his mouth to say something but decided against it and just smiled.

"Ok, well I can fix them in about an hour," he said, already pulling stuff out from his desk drawer. "Stick around?" Hazel looked at her watch. It said 5:15 pm.

"Shoot! I have to get back home in fifteen minutes!" Hazel said as she ran over to the dresser that was in the corner of Calvin's basement. She kept some of her stuff in it, like a change of clothes in case something happened to the ones she was wearing. Hazel grabbed a pair of tennis shoes and slipped them on.

"Calvin, I would love to stay, but I really have to go. I have dance class," she said.

"Oh yeah, no problem. I can give you a lift," he said grabbing his jacket and a couple cookies and handing them to Hazel.

"Thank you!" she said as she ran up the stairs with Calvin following behind her. They quickly grabbed a bag for Hazel's cookies then headed for the door. Calvin grabbed his keys from the key box that hung on the wall. It was a burgundy box with a glass door with the words, "As far as you go, you'll always find a way back home," painted around the edges. Hazel ran over to Calvin's car as he locked up the house. They hopped in and were off.

"Thanks again, Calvin, this is a big help," Hazel said as Calvin drove towards the woods.

"No problem," he said with a smile. They sat in the car for a bit, neither one saying anything. That was one of the things Hazel liked about Calvin. You could just sit with him and not feel the need to start talking. Hazel drifted off in thought and started to think again about how she let everybody run her life. It must have shown on her face because Calvin looked over at her, worried.

"What are you thinking about?" Calvin asked.

"What do you mean?" Hazel asked.

"Well, you're frowning with your arms crossed," Calvin replied with a soft smile. Hazel looked down and saw that her arms were crossed. She let them fall to the seat.

"It's nothing…" she said. Calvin looked over at her and raised an eyebrow. Hazel sighed. "It's, just… all day I've been thinking about how I let everybody run my life! I swear, it's as if have no life of my own! I feel like such a fake person! I mean, I only hang out with the J girls because... I don't even know! Maybe because they were the first people I met on my first day at the school. When I saw the way they acted, I didn't want to act any different because I was afraid they would tell me that I couldn't hang out with them, then I would have to eat lunch all by myself. I guess I liked the way they looked, and they were already so popular. And then they sucked me into the black hole! A don't even get me started on my parents! My mom, she keeps saying, 'Oh you're going to be a great lawyer!' and I don't even want to be a lawyer! And no matter how many times I tell her, she just seems to ignore me and pretend she didn't hear me!

"And my dad keeps saying, 'Oh, have I got plenty of men lined up for you to marry. All rich! You'll love the French diplomat's son. Can you imagine how good that would be for my career if you married him?'" she said, mimicking his deep voice. "I'm sixteen years old, for goodness sakes! I don't want to even think about who I'm going to marry! I don't even date! And my dad's talking about how he's going to pick the guy I'm going to marry!

"Aren't dads supposed to tell you you're not allowed to think about guys until you're thirty? Why does everyone want to plan my life out for me! And why can't I ever just look them in the eye and say, 'Enough!' The only time I'm allowed to have my own life is when I'm staying with my aunt and when I'm here! I mean, ugh!" Hazel started hitting the dash board. "It's so unfair!" she yelled as she kept on hitting the dash board. Then she stopped when she realized how childish she was acting. "Sorry," she mumbled as she crossed her arms again.

"Me too," Calvin said gently.

"I didn't mean to vent on you. It's actually the second time I've vented since I've been here," she said with a small laugh. Calvin gave her a questioning look.

"Don't ask," Hazel said with a small smile.

39

"Too bad you have to go to dance, you really need to spend some time in the thinking tree!" he said with a smile. Then his face got serious. "Look Hazel, I know you have some messed up things going on in your life but I really think you should try your best to fix it. You really don't know how good you have it till it's gone." Hazel gasped.

"Ugh! Calvin, I'm sorry I didn't mean..."

"It's ok, I know you didn't," he said with a weak little smile.

"You must think I'm such a selfish, egotistic, spoiled brat! Here I am complaining about my life and how stupid my parents are and... you don't even have parents," Hazel said sadly.

"It's ok. I just know from past experience how things aren't always what they seem. Sometimes, people need second chances," Calvin said as he pulled his car off of the road and stopped at the edge of the forest. "So, just do your best to try and change things. Not just with your family, but your friends too."

"Calvin, has anyone ever told you how fantastic and amazing you are!?" Hazel asked.

"I could hear it more often," he said with a smile. Hazel laughed.

"Have I ever told you that you are one of the best friends in both your world and mine?" Hazel asked.

"Oh, so I'm not your only best friend? I'm just one of them! Well then..." he said jokingly as he crossed his arms.

Hazel gave him a playful shove. Calvin knew all about Amber and how she was Hazels best friend back home.

"Ok, I'll see you later!" Hazel said getting out of the car.

"Ok. Oh, wait! I almost forgot," Calvin said reaching into his pocket and pulling out a Keyflip 3. The Keyflip was the phone Hazel had always wanted. It looked like a normal touch screen phone, but when you clicked a button, the phone flipped around to reveal a super thin keyboard. She had one but her current phone service wouldn't allow it. She had given it to Calvin so he could convert it for her.

"I hacked it and unlocked it for you. And...I made it so that I could call and text you in your world. Don't ask me how but I found a way. Also, don't freak out if you find out it's a thousand times cooler than when you gave it to me," he said with a wink, tossing the phone to Hazel.

"Calvin, you are the best!" she said catching the phone. Hazel waved goodbye and headed into the woods. She put the cell phone in her jacket as she reached the spot where she kept her book. Hazel kicked back the leaves and found the top of the trunk. She twisted the red diamond that was on top of the chest in a full circle. Clockwise, then counter clockwise. Then she pressed the diamond down. Hazel heard a small click and the chest rose up while the top opened. She grabbed her book and thought about being home. Hazel felt a slight breeze, opened her eyes and was back in her room smiling.

Chapter Three

Snowball barked and jumped off of Hazel's bed as she appeared in the room.

"Hey there, girl! Did you miss me?" Hazel asked, ruffling the hair on Snowball's head. She then quickly grabbed her old cell phone – which had a cracked screen, was five years old, and missing a few keys – took out her sim card and put it in the new phone that Calvin unlocked for her. She couldn't believe that she finally had her dream phone! Hazel realized the house phone was ringing. She had no idea where the phone was and knew she wouldn't make it in time to answer it, so she decided to let it go to voice mail.

"Hey! You've reached Page and Hazel! We can't come to the phone right now... so, yeah....leave us a message!" Hazel laughed at the greeting she had recorded several years ago. She heard the beep and then heard Amber's voice.

"Hey there, girly-girl! I'll be at your door in one-hundred and twenty seconds! Better be ready or you're gonna be walk'n!" Hazel laughed as she quickly ran into her closet. She peeled off her clothes which were ripped and dirty and put on a blue sparkly leotard and black shorts. Then she grabbed her dance bag and headed to the kitchen. Realizing she had left her cookies in Calvin's car, Hazel put the microwave on to warm up her popcorn. She put on her shoes, went and un-locked the door, then walked back into the kitchen to grab her popcorn. She heard a knock on the door just as she was trying to transfer the popcorn into a plastic bag.

"It's open!" Hazel yelled out. She didn't hear the door open, but just as she was about to repeat herself, she felt someone tap her on both of her sides. Hazel screamed and jumped into the air, spilling some popcorn on the ground. She turned around to see a smiling Amber.

"Oh my gosh, you scared me!" Hazel said, putting a hand to her pounding chest. Amber bursted out laughing.

"The look on your face! You jumped so high!" Amber said while still laughing, trying to catch her breath. "If you could jump that high in dance class you would be a star! Why are you so jumpy...and in a hurry?" Amber asked as she took a hand full of the little bit of popcorn that was left in the bag.

"Um, hello! Anyone would be jumpy if they didn't hear their door open and then someone poked them in the sides! And, I just got back from Red Diamond and I really don't want to be late for class," Hazel said as Amber walked over to the fridge and took out a Fruit Water for herself. Hazel laughed. That was one of the things she liked about Amber, she made herself right at home and would just help herself to something to eat when she was hungry.

"You're such a time freak!" Amber said. She put her hands on her hips and puffed out her chest and spoke in a deep voice as she pointed her finger sternly, "I've got to be here at this time, then there at that time, and here, then there!" She laughed. "I mean, have you ever been late for anything?" Amber asked taking a sip of her drink. Hazel thought about it.

"No, not really. My mom and dad have to be everywhere on time, so that means I have to be on time. I've been on time since birth!" Hazel said as they started laughing. "It just stuck with me. Once on time, always on time! I just have to make sure that if I'm going somewhere with my Aunt, we get there on time. She's not as tight with time as me and my parents," Hazel said taking the popcorn back from Amber so she would stop eating it. Hazel zipped up the popcorn then shoved it into her dance bag.

"Soooo, what's new in Red Diamond? What'd you have to do? Who did it? Why'd they do it? Did you get any new cool gadgety things?"

"Nothing's really new. I had to get the key back for the Gold Room. Steve and Richard, the guys I told you about last time I was there. Don't know why they did it. And I got this lipstick that can cut through almost anything. Oh, and Calvin unlocked my Keyflip 3!" Hazel said walking toward the door.

"Oh my gosh! Now I can't rub it in your face that I have a Keyflip!" Amber said jokingly as she followed Hazel out the door. Neither Hazel nor Amber had their driver's license, but they were planning on getting them soon so they wouldn't have to keep having someone drive them around all the time. Both the girls hopped into Amber's mom's car.

"Hi, Mrs. Lambert. Thanks for taking me to class," Hazel said buckling her seat belt before taking out her popcorn.

"It's not a problem at all, Hazel! Did you have a good day?" Mrs. Lambert asked.

"It was ok," Hazel said with a smile because Mrs. Lambert didn't know about Red Diamond.

Hazel and Amber chatted the whole way to dance, ignoring all of the threats of being thrown out of the car if they didn't both stop talking at once.

"All right ladies, I'll be back to pick you guys up at seven thirty!" Mrs. Lambert said as she pulled up to the dance studio. The girls said their goodbyes as they exited the car.

"Finally! Peace and quiet!" Mrs. Lambert jokingly yelled out the windows as she drove away. Hazel and Amber started to giggle. As they made their way inside, Hazel winced as hot pain shot through her ankle.

"Whats wrong?" Amber asked.

"My ankle just started to hurt really badly," Hazel said rubbing it, although it was not hurting quite as much anymore. Amber looked at Hazel's ankle.

"It looks all right to me. Does it hurt right now?" she asked as Hazel rolled her foot in a circle, testing it.

"Just a little, but I think I'm fine now," she said.

"Maybe I should have my mom come back and look at it, her being a doctor and all. If something is really wrong her office is right around the corner," Amber said getting her phone out.

"No, no it's fine. Really, I don't need her to look at it." Hazel started walking again, trying not to show that it still hurt. "I really don't want to see a doctor," Hazel mumbled to herself. The reason why Hazel didn't want to see a doctor was because her mom and dad would find out. Then her mom would want to know where and how she hurt her foot and try to find a way to sue the place. And Hazel had a feeling that she didn't hurt her foot in this world.

"Ok, it's *your* foot," Amber said as she started walking again. "But if it starts hurting again then let me know and I'll call my mom," she said. Hazel smiled.

"Ok, thanks," Hazel said, her foot barely hurting anymore.

"How did you hurt your ankle anyway?" Amber asked as she opened the door.

"Hmm, let's see. It could have been when I fell from underneath a table, or when I flew out of a window that was higher than one hundred stories," Hazel said sarcastically, but she knew that none of those were the reason. She thought about it more. She knew that she didn't hurt it at the hotel, even though she had been through a lot there. If not at the hotel, then where did she hurt it? As they walked inside, Hazel suddenly remembered. "Ughh! When I was at Calvin's we were goofing around and I hit my foot on a box and—" Hazel began, but stopped short as she saw three blond girls making their way over to her. "Oh no, hide me!" she mumbled to Amber.

"Hazel!" Jane said with Jenna and Jessica trailing behind her. She ran up and gave her a hug. Amber cleared her throat.

"Oh, um, hi Amber," Jane added, not trying to hide the annoyance in her voice.

"Jane," Amber answered, rolling her eyes. Jane and Amber had never gotten along, but they both tried to stay polite towards each other for Hazel's sake. Though neither of them were good at it.

"Where have you been?" Jane asked as Amber and Hazel put their dance bags on the shelf. "We tried calling, texting, tweeting, we even tried e-mailing you, but you didn't respond to any of it! It was like you disappeared from the world!" Jane said as she shot an annoyed look at Amber, as if Amber was the reason Hazel wouldn't answer the phone.

"She did," Amber mumbled so only Hazel could hear. Hazel gave her a small kick in the leg.

"I don't think I got any text messages," Hazel said. She took out her phone and saw that it was blinking. There was a small box that read, 'You have 50 unread messages.' Hazel quickly shut her phone and put it back. "Hmm," she said with a shrug as she started to put on her dance shoes. She noticed that her foot didn't hurt any more. Hazel smiled in relief and followed Amber into the dance room and joined the other girls who were stretching before class.

"Ok, class! Let's do some stuff across the floor. Hazel, you first, toe touches!" Ms. Tory, the dance teacher, said as she sat down at her table and started writing down the attendance of the students. The girls got in line. Hazel did her prep walk then jumped in the air and kicked her feet out. But instead of landing on the floor with both feet as she had planned, when her right foot hit the ground she collapsed and toppled over onto the hard dance floor. Hazel's ankle was suddenly throbbing with pain. She tried to get up but she couldn't. It hurt too much.

"It's ok, we all fall sometimes," Mrs. Tory said, looking back down at her papers, not seeing that Hazel wasn't getting up. Hazel tried to hold back the tears coming down her face and grabbed her ankle, which was hurting more by the second. She winced quietly. Seeing this, Amber ran over to Hazel.

"Oh my gosh! Hazel, are you ok?" she asked kneeling down next to her. Hazel, not wanting to talk, shook her head "No." Finally seeing what happened, Ms. Tory gasped and ran over to her student. She gently took off Hazel's Jazz shoe. Hazel's ankle was now a deep purple color. Hazel almost screamed when she saw her ankle because she knew it did not look like that five seconds ago. Amber headed out of the room to grab her cellphone.

"Oooh, oh dear, it looks like you may have broke your ankle," Ms. Tory said. "Someone, go get me a cold water bottle from the fridge." before she had even finished her sentence, someone had handed her one.

"Thank you," she said as she put the water bottle on Hazel's ankle. "Now, Hazel," she said looking very serious, "this doesn't look like it just happened right now. It looks like it happened earlier in the day. This is serious. You just can't ignore something like this! How did it happen?" But before Hazel had a chance to answer, Amber came back into the room.

"My mom said that she'll be right here," Amber said sitting down next to Hazel. Hazel gave a small sigh, glad that she didn't have to answer Ms. Tory's question.

"Let me go call your parents," Ms. Tory said starting to get up.

"NO!" Hazel said a little too quickly and loudly. "I...I..mean you can't. My mom's in court and my dad's at a big banquet, and my aunt's at a really important show and might get promoted because of it. So tonight Amber's mom is watching me." It wasn't a lie, really. Everyone *was* someplace important, even though technically she could call them if it was something urgent. But the real reason she didn't want to call them was because she knew that her ankle was not broken. She did not hit her ankle that hard on the box. Something else had to have happened. Ms. Tory and Amber helped Hazel out of the dance room and into a chair just as Amber's mom was running down the stairs with her big doctor bag.

"Oh, my gosh! Are you ok? What happened? I leave for ten minutes and you do something to your ankle?" she asked as she kissed Hazels forehead. She leaned down to Hazel's foot as she put down her bag with her doctor supplies in it. Luckily one of the girls had called Ms. Tory over and away from Hazel, because suddenly her ankle wasn't swollen any more. It looked just fine, although the bone looked a little funny. Amber let out a gasp but covered it quickly with a cough.

"Ok, it looks like you sprained your ankle," Amber's mom said cooly as she reached into her bag and took something out that looked like a roll of stretchy bandage material.

"I'm going to press on your ankle a bit to see how bad the sprain is. It's probably going to hurt," she said as she pressed on Hazel's Ankle. Hazel closed her eyes, ready to feel a rush of pain, but she didn't feel anything.

"Is that all?" Hazel asked, opening her eyes. Mrs. Lambert looked at her.

"Yah, I'm surprised you didn't think that hurt," she said as she started wrapping up Hazel's foot with the bandage. Hazel gave a wince so Mrs. Lambert wouldn't think she was crazy, but Hazel did wonder why she hadn't felt any pain or why her foot was no longer purple.

"Ok, so it shouldn't hurt too much to walk on it, but I want you to stay off of it and put as little pressure as possible on it for about one week. And then you can take the wrap off and it should feel brand new!" she said. Once she was done wrapping up Hazel's foot she put the extra material into the bag and stood up. "Ok, I think that we should call it quits for today. Hazel, I can drop you off at your aunt's house and Amber can stay with you until she gets home."

"Ok. Thanks for all the help, Mrs. Lambert," Hazel said standing up and feeling no pain in her foot at all. Mrs. Lambert gave her an odd look. "Owww! Forgot not to stand on it," Hazel said, quickly sitting back down. Mrs. Lambert gave her a smile.

"Ok, then I'm going to talk to Tory," she said walking into the classroom.

"Oh my gosh! You scared me! Are you ok?! I told you we should have called my mom!" Amber said once her mom was out of earshot.

51

"I'm fine, but the real weird thing is, it doesn't hurt at all anymore!" Hazel said in a whisper.

"What do you mean?" Amber asked.

"I don't know! And you saw that my foot doesn't look the same! And look!" Hazel got up and started running in place, then quickly sat back down before anyone could see her.

"Ok, so did it ever really hurt?" Amber asked in a whisper.

"Of course it did! But we'll look at it later. For right now, everybody still has to think that it still hurts," Hazel said as Amber nodded her head in agreement.

"Ok, can you hand me my bag?"

"Why? You can walk," Amber said sassily.

"Yah, but if someone sees me walking then I'm toast! And you would be, too!" Hazel said.

"Fine," Amber said as she walked over and found Hazel's bag and threw it at her with a giggle. They both headed outside and went to their car to wait for Mrs. Lambert. Hazel stared down at her wrapped ankle, wondering what was going on.

◆　　◆　　◆

The girls got out of Mrs. Lambert's car with the pizza she bought them, yelled goodbye over their shoulders and headed towards Hazel's house.

"Do you want me to hold the pizza while you open up the door?" Amber asked, but Hazel didn't answer because in the window she saw her aunt pacing.

"No, No, No!" Hazel said pushing the door open. "Aunt Clair! I didn't mean to have you leave your show! I didn't even know that Amber's mom called you! I didn't even really hurt my ankle that bad."

Hazel's Aunt sighed in relief as she saw her. "Uhh! As long as you're ok, sweetie!" Clair said as she gave Hazel a hug. "And don't worry about my show, we ended early and I was on my way home when Mayla called me. I've been sitting here praying that she wouldn't call me saying I needed to meet you guys in the emergency room!" she said laughing. Clair saw the pizza boxes and realized that the girls were probably starving by now. "Why don't we have some pizza and you can tell me about your ankle. Where did Amber go?"

As if on cue, there was a high pitch excited squeal coming from the kitchen. Amber came running out with two outfits hanging on hangers. The one in her left hand had a white button-down shirt that had a stylish wrinkled look to it and blue buttons. It also had a blue high-wasted skirt with sparkly studs and and a black bow belt. The outfit in Amber's right hand was the same thing but in pink.

"Are these ours?" Amber asked jumping up and down before Clair even answered.

"Of course! Who else would I give my designs to other than my two favorite models!" Clair said with a smile. Clair worked as a fashion designer and had her own store. She was always making clothes for Hazel and Amber to wear. "The shoes are in the kitchen, but first we're going to eat. Then you can try them on," Clair said smiling as Amber ran over and hugged her.

"Thank you, thank you, thank you!" she said running back into the kitchen and coming out with plates and napkins. Hazel laughed and went into the kitchen to look at the outfits a little closer.

"These are really cute, Aunt Clair!" Hazel said as her aunt pulled some lemonade out of the fridge.

"Thanks, sweetie, I like them too. They're going to be part of our new mid fall fashion line. Coming out in two weeks, if anybody at your school asks," she said with a laugh.

Hazel heard her phone buzz and figured it was one of the J Girls checking in on her. She went over to her bag and grabbed her phone to see that she had twelve unread messages. She sighed. As Hazel scrolled through the list. She didn't recognize the number. She opened the message and read,

"Hazel! Your foot is going to start hurting really bad, if it hasn't already. Cal."

She rolled her eyes. She should have known this had Calvin written all over it. The next one said,

"HAZEL! Do not go the hospital! Cal."

And the other ones were him asking why she wasn't responding, how her foot was doing, and not to let anyone see her foot. And then the last one said,

"Hazel, your foot won't hurt anymore. When you were over at my house, you hit your foot on a box. Apparently neither of us realized that there was green smoke coming out of it."

Hazel stopped reading because she did recall seeing something coming out the box. She felt bad for forgetting about it but kept reading,

"I was working on something that temporarily makes someone's feet stop working. But so far, it only makes them start hurting really bad! Talk more later!"

Hazel scowled.

"Are you going to eat?" Amber called from the dining room. Hazel put her phone on the counter and sat down at the table.

"So, what's up with your ankle?" Clair asked as Hazel grabbed a piece of pizza and some lemonade. She told them about Calvin's text messages. Clair sighed. "That boy is a load of trouble! Sometimes I wish he wasn't so smart! But then I would feel worried every time you opened up that book of yours," she said with a soft smile. Hazel smiled in return. She knew that neither of her parents would understand about Red Diamond and was glad that she had her aunt.

"Hazel, is your Kung Fu tournament still tomorrow?" Amber asked as she chopped the air.

"No... my karate tournament is, though," Hazel said with a laugh. "You both can come, right? Because I'm so nervous – this is big! I could win a trip to China where I get to study with the greatest martial arts masters!"

"Do you really think I would miss that?" Clair asked. Hazel smiled. Her aunt hadn't missed even one of Hazel's events, no matter what it was – science fairs, talent shows, plays, dance recitals, even trips to the dentist.

"As long as your aunt keeps making me clothes and you keep your fridge full of food, I'll be there too!" Amber said jokingly. Hazel smiled. She loved her aunt and best friend. She couldn't imagine life without them.

"Are your parents coming?" Clair asked. Hazel nodded.

"Yah, I've been checking with them every week since last year to make sure they were going to be there. And they both promised and put it on their calendars," Hazel said. Her parent's rarely came to any of her events because there schedules were too busy, so she was super excited that they were actually going to attend her tournament.

After finishing dinner, Clair told the girls that she would clean the kitchen and that they could call Amber's mom to let her know that Hazel was ok and that Amber was spending the night. After doing so, the girls tried on their outfits and modeled them for Clair in the family room.

"I can't wait to wear this to school tomorrow!" Hazel said spinning around so that her aunt could see the entire outfit.

"Oh, it looks fabulous! I love it!" Clair said as she snapped pictures of Hazel. "Amber come on out!"

"Next is our top model, wearing the new divine fall-outfit designed by Clair Woodsen…" Amber said introducing herself from around the corner. "...please welcome, Amber Lambert!" Amber came around the corner walking just like a model, flinging her hair from side to side. She stopped and posed as Clair snapped pictures. Then Hazel joined in, posing in over the top and silly positions with her best friend as Clair continued taking pictures.

"These are going to look great in the scrap book!" Clair said. Every time the girls got a new outfit they took pictures and put them in a scrap book they had.

"Ok, Hazel, we're going out somewhere tomorrow just so we can show off our outfits together!" Amber thought for a moment. "I've got it! We'll go to Club Sizzle!" Club Sizzle was a club for teens to hang out at after school and on weekends.

"Did you forget that soon? My tournament's tomorrow!" Hazel said grabbing Amber by the shoulders and shaking her.

"My tournament's tomorrow," Amber said sounding almost exactly like Hazel. "I'm not stupid! I'm actually very smart. Now stay with me on this. Your tournament's at eight-thirty. You'll need to be home at six so you can get ready, eat and all that fun stuff. You get out of school at three thirty. By the time you have your books, you get on your pod, drive to Club Sizzle, it'll be four o'clock and I will already be there. We'll be like an advertisement for your aunt. We'll bring some catalogues and some coupons to hand out, and we'll show off our outfits! We'll leave Club Sizzle at five forty-five, get home at five fifty-five leaving you five minutes to spare 'till it's six o'clock. You'll get ready and do some homework to ease your nerves.

"Your Aunt will get home at six thirty, we'll eat at six forty five, and then we'll leave at seven thirty. We'll get there at seven forty-five. We'll buy our snacks and find your parents and sit with them, you'll be checked in and with your group, and it will be eight o'clock by then. You'll warm up, go through practice stuff and you'll start the tournament at eight thirty. You'll win by nine thirty, and we'll be eating ice cream by ten.

"You'll drop me off at home by ten thirty – I can't spend the night because I have to clean the house for my mom's meeting on Saturday – and you will be right back here at ten forty-five sharp." Amber put her hands on her hips. Hazel stared at her shocked that she had just come up with that.

"What if my aunt hits traffic on the way home from work? It will throw the whole schedule off!" she said sarcastically.

"There won't be any traffic," Amber said flatly.

"What if one of our pods gets a flat tire on the way home? I'll be late."

"I always keep a repair kit in my pod," Amber said matter-of-factly. Hazel tried to think of something that could go wrong with the plan. Both girls stared at each other then burst out laughing.

"Fine! You win, there is nothing wrong with that plan! But I am so sure that it's not going to be exactly the same timing," Hazel said.

"Oh trust me, it will," Amber said turning to Clair who, it turns out, wasn't in her seat. Clair came back into the room just as they were about to call for her. She was holding two shiny bags - one pink and one blue.

"Here are some bags, and there are already catalogues and coupons in there. All you have to do is pass them out! There's also some money in there so you can grab a snack," Clair said handing the bags to the girls.

"Guess I don't need to ask if I can go!" Hazel said as they all started laughing.

A little latter Hazel did some homework while Amber watched TV. "Do you know how lucky you are that you're homeschooled?!" Hazel asked as she put away her finished homework.

"I know! I just wake up every day and look in the mirror and say, *Amber you are the best looking and the luckiest girl in the whole wide world!*" Amber stretched herself out on the bed. She had been homeschooled her whole life. Once, when she was in 8th grade, her parents thought it might be a good idea if they put her in school so she could get the school experience. But they pulled her out after a week because they didn't like the way the school taught and how much homework they gave out to the kids. Hazel's Aunt wanted Hazel to be homeschooled as well, but her parents sure couldn't teach her, and with her job going so well, Clair couldn't either. Hazel wanted to be homeschooled, but she didn't mind going to her school. She liked the teachers that she had.

"I'm really glad you're my friend, though. Because after spending all day everyday at my house with my dad and four siblings, I like to just get away! Don't get me wrong, I like homeschooling...and it's certainly better than that jail you go to everyday! No water in class! You have twenty minutes to eat your disgusting food that's in the cafeteria! Oh, and make sure you do your seven hours of home work after you get home from seven hours of school!" Amber said mimicking a teacher's voice. Hazel laughed.

"Yeah, it is crazy how much homework they give you, but it's not all bad! Some of the teachers are really nice. There wasn't one teacher you liked when you were there for the week?" Hazel asked.

"Well..." Amber said as she thought about it. "there was this one teacher who was really nice. I couldn't open up my locker and he did it for me. I saw him throughout the whole day and he was always smiling and whistling. He always wore all blue, though. Must have been trying to start a new fashion trend or something. He was really cute too – had to be in his twenty's," Amber said as she turned off the TV and yawned.

Hazel tried to think of which teacher Amber was talking about. Then Hazel started laughing hysterically.

"Ambeeerrr yyyoouu heee," Hazel said, gasping for air.

"What are you laughing at?!" Amber demanded.

"Ammmbeerr." Hazel couldn't stop laughing. After a moment she took in a deep breath. "Amber, that wasn't a teacher!" she said taking in more air. Amber looked confused.

"What do you mean he wasn't a teacher?" she asked as she snuggled up in Hazel's bed.

"That was the janitor!" Hazel managed to gasp out. Both girls immediately fell into a fit of laughter. Hazel's Aunt came in half an hour later to tell them to quite down and get some sleep. Amber climbed back into the bed which she had fallen out of while she was laughing and Hazel climbed in too. Soon, they were both fast asleep.

Chapter Four

Much too soon after having fallen asleep, Hazel heard the
alarm clock's BEEP! BEEP! BEEP! BEEP!

"Oh my gosh, Hazel! Could you have gotten a more
abrupt alarm clock?!" Amber asked, her voice heavy with
sleep. Hazel searched for the clock with her eyes closed and
then heard a crash. The beeping stopped. Amber, without seeing what occurred, knew what had happened and started
laughing.

"Good! Now we don't have to worry about that anymore!"
She said as she got out of the bed and stretched. Hazel, who
was not a morning person, opened one eye and saw her alarm
clock on the floor, broken in to about a dozen pieces.

"Shoot, that's never happened before," Hazel said with a
small laugh. She closed her eyes and turned around to go to
sleep again.

"Don't you have to go to school?" Amber asked from Hazel's closet where she was picking out an outfit for herself.

"Ughhghg." Hazel rolled over again, covering her head
with the pillow. "Whe tine whi it?"

"What was that?" Amber called from the closet.

"What time is it!" Hazel yelled back taking her head out
from under the pillow.

"6:00 AM," Amber said as she walked out of the closet wearing a pair of jeans with stud hearts and stars on them and a pink tank top. She plopped an outfit on the bed which Hazel couldn't see.

"That's for you," she said as she walked over to Hazel's desk and took out a pair of scissors and some different colored ribbons. She tied them to her shirt straps.

"Why do you have to be such a morning person?!" Hazel asked as she slowly got out of bed and rubbed her eyes. Hazel picked up the outfit that Amber picked out for her. It was jeans that had pink flames on the bottom of them, with a black tank top that had a sparkly smiley face on it, and a white button down shirt. Hazel was going to tell Amber that she doesn't normally wear those types of clothes to school, but then she stopped. She realized that she didn't ever wear what she wanted to wear to school! She only wore what she thought people would like, and what the J Girls would like! Just so she could fit in with them! And she liked the outfit Amber had picked out for her. She was going to wear it.

"I love it, but weren't we going to wear the outfits that my aunt made us?" Hazel asked as she started to put on her clothes. Amber gave a little snort.

"Please, you expect me to let you wear the outfit to school? It's the first time you're wearing it, you'll just be destined to spill food on it at lunch, or get water on it at the drinking fountain! What if someone starts a food fight?!" Amber asked as she walked back into Hazel's closet to find a jacket for herself. "Do you know how lucky you are to have a walk - in closet with so many clothes?" Amber asked as she came back out with a black jacket.

"Don't you mean we? You wear my clothes as much as I do!" Hazel laughed as she finished putting on her clothes. She looked in the mirror. She really liked the way she looked. "I should really dress the way I want to more often!" Hazel said, frustrated that she was letting more and more of her life get taken out of her hands.

"That's what I've been telling you! You should wear what you want and what I tell you looks good!" Amber said jokingly. She handed Hazel a pair of black boots. "And, if you want to, you should wear these boots. They would just look fabulous with your outfit," Amber said excitedly as she handed them to Hazel who liked them just as much. Amber loved fashion as much as Hazel's Aunt did.

"Amber, I'm serious! I only do things so I don't disappoint people. I do whatever I want when I'm with you and my aunt and with Calvin, but with everybody else… I act the way they want me to act, dress the way they want me to dress – I'm like a robot! I mean I have to dress right just to be in the presence of my parents!" Hazel said as she plopped herself on the ground to put her shoes on.

"Hazel, it's your life and you can do whatever you want to do with it! I know it's tough with your parents and, well – I mean, they're parents, so you kind of have to do what they say, but you can talk to them about it. Tell them about your life – what you like to do, what you like to wear – tell them what you want to be when you're older! And as for The J Girls.... why *do* you always let them tell you how live your life?" Amber asked softly.

"I don't know!" Hazel said, and she really didn't. She remembered that Calvin had told her yesterday that she really needed to try to get her life back in her own hands. She decided that today was going to be that day.

"Girls! Breakfast is done!" Clair yelled from the kitchen. Clair, like Amber, was a morning person. Amber hopped up and pulled Hazel with her. But Hazel was still thinking about what Amber had said. Why did she always let people tell her how to live her life? As the girls walked into the kitchen they saw that Clair had made the girls chocolate chip muffins, bacon and fresh squeezed orange juice.

"Yummy!" Amber said as she sat down.

"Hey! I thought you guys were going to wear the outfits I made!" Clair said as Hazel sat down and grabbed a muffin.

"Amber said that I'm such a klutz that I'm not allowed to wear it at school. So, we're just going to put them on at Club Sizzle. But the time I'll need to put on my outfit will put us off schedule..." Hazel said giving Amber a nudge under the table.

"It will not! I swear on it! You're just jealous that I can come up with a perfect schedule and you can't!" Amber said as she took a bite of her muffin. Hazel finished up her breakfast and said goodbye to her aunt and Amber. She got on her pod and headed off for school.

Outside at school, Jane, Jenna and Jessica were sitting at a table doing their makeup and fixing their hair. Hazel realized that she wasn't even wearing makeup today, and had just put her hair up in a simple high pony tail. She looked, and felt, really good - even without the hours of primping.

"Hazel!" Jane said as Hazel walked over to the picnic table where the girls sat. Jenna and Jessica looked questioningly at her outfit. Not in a bad way, but kind of a confused way. Jane however, looked less than pleased. Hazel looked at their outfits too. They were all wearing skirts, similar colors with white leggings and gold flat shoes, with a long sleeved shirt to match their skirts. Hazel realized she used to dress just like them; in fact, she had probably even gotten the text message with the day's wardrobe plan from Jane. She had let their ways become her ways. Hazel then thought about the essay and how they wanted her to live the same life as them – marry a rich guy and have a lot of expensive stuff. They said nothing about a family or falling in love or having a job they enjoyed. And with how rich all of their parents were, they probably never worked a day in their life and never would!

"Hi guys," Hazel said with a wave.

"I like your outfit," Jenna said. Hazel looked at Jenna. She looked so pretty with her long brownish red hair, and just the perfect amount of freckles on her cheeks, though you could hardly seem them through all the makeup.

"Thanks, Jenna. Amber helped me put it together," Hazel said with a smile.

"Did you not have enough time to put on any makeup? We can do it for you," Jane said making some room for Hazel on the bench. Jane looked almost mad at Hazel.

"I don't really think she needs it today," Jessica said with a smile.

"Yeah, she already looks really good!" Jenna said looking at herself in the mirror as if she were thinking about taking some of her own makeup off. Jane looked like she was going to explode.

"A little could never hurt," she said through clenched teeth. Hazel just smiled.

"You know what, no thank you, Jane. I think I'll go without the makeup today. See you guys later!" Hazel said as she turned and started walking toward the school not even bothering to see their reactions. As she walked away Hazel felt as if she had a weight lifted off her shoulders. Though she was glad to have been able to walk away from The J Girls, she was also a littler nervous as she realized that she didn't have any other friends besides them at school! As Hazel made her way into the school she made sure to wave and smile at people who she hadn't talked to in a long time. They were a little confused at first but returned her wave with a friendly smile. Hazel decided that even though she still had fifteen minutes before class that she would get there early. She stopped by her locker first and got some books and then headed to her homeroom. Hazel walked into the class and saw that she was the only one there. The teacher wasn't even there yet. In homeroom it was whoever came first got the seat they wanted, so she decided that she would sit in the middle row instead of the back where she normally sat with the J Girls. Today she wasn't going to get distracted by their note passing.

Hazel sat down in the seat by the window because it was such a nice day for October. She noticed that the homeroom was decorated with paper candy, ghosts and pumpkins. She took out her phone to see what day it was it was. The 10th – a little early for Halloween decorations, she thought. But then she smiled. There was no rule that said when you could or couldn't start decorating for Halloween. She realized she hadn't even started thinking about Halloween. Hazel tried to remember if Amber had even begun to talk about what they were going to do that evening. Hazel thought back on the previous week, remembering something about Amber mentioning halloween costumes. Still, she couldn't remember what it was exactly. Suddenly she recalled that it was around last Friday, which had been a particularly bad day for her.

There was no school because it was a teacher conference, so she had stayed the night at her dad's house on Thursday and intended to stay all day Friday. Hazel woke up

Friday morning hoping that she could actually talk to her dad as he hadn't been there the previous night. When Hazel arrived, her dad's assistant Sam looked embarrassed and gave Hazel an apologetic smile which she was very used to getting. It was the "your-dad-isn't-here-and-isn't-coming-back-anytime-soon-and-I-feel-really-bad-that-you-have-to-put-up-with-this-time-after-time" smile. Both of her parent's assistants were pros at that smile. So, without having it to be voiced by Sam, Hazel knew that her father was out for the evening. Sam was more fatherly to Hazel than her own dad ever was. Sam would remember that she was coming over and send a car to pick her up and he always got her a present on her birthday and on holiday. Sam would often personally drive Hazel around places when she asked him to. He would always ask how her week was and genuinely listen when she talked with him. Hazel really liked talking with Sam, but of course he also had a bunch of work he had to do, so he couldn't exactly spend all of his time talking to her when she was there.

Sam helped out Hazel's dad with a lot of things but primarily he would help him with remembering names of people at parties, made sure his dry cleaning was picked up, important packages, contracts were delivered and so on. He did almost everything for Hazel's dad but keep his appointments. Hazel's father was very strict about his appointments and said he could handle that himself. Although Hazel often wished that

Sam was in charge of his appointments so her dad would remember once in a while that she was coming over.

When Hazel's dad did come home on Thursday night, he stopped by her bedroom.

"I forgot you were coming," he said simply. Then he stood in the doorway not sure what to say next. Seeing that he wasn't going to say anything else about it, Hazel sighed and moved on to a different topic.

"Dad, you're still coming to my karate tournament, right? It's next Friday," Hazel said. Her dad thought about it.

"Yes. Well, good night," he said and left the room. Hazel felt so angry at her dad! He didn't even apologize for forgetting that she was staying with him! After he left, Hazel rolled up in her bed, too angry to even cry. Her own father didn't remember that his own daughter was coming to stay with him... like she did every Thursday! Hazel tried to shake it off. It wasn't the first time that he had forgotten or canceled – or more accurately, that Sam had called and canceled – but he at least canceled more than he forgot. *At least he'll be coming to the tournament,* Hazel thought as she fell asleep.

When Hazel woke up, her father was gone. Sam said he had left for a very important trip and wouldn't be coming back for a couple of weeks. Sam had said that Hazel's mom's chauffeur had called to say that she was coming to pick her up within the next few minutes. Hazel wasn't sure why she was being summoned by her mom, but didn't really care. All she really wanted to do was go home, but she didn't really feel like being alone. Her aunt was gone all day at a fashion show and wasn't going to be back until late at night.

Reluctantly, Hazel had gotten into the black shiny car that pulled up in to her fathers driveway. Hazel was surprised, however, to see her mom in the car. She was going to ask her what she was doing but her mom quickly held up a finger. Hazel got in and buckled her seat belt. As the car started moving, she saw the ear piece in her mom's ear and knew that she was on the phone.

"No, no, no, NO! I will not work with that! It's not my fault! Uh huh...hmm, yes, no, no, you're going to have to pay me a lot more if you want me to get you out of this!" Hazel rolled her eyes. She knew her mom was on the phone with a client who wanted her to be their lawyer for a case.

"Well I am sorry but I do not see that as my problem," Hazel's mom sighed and gave Hazel a small apologetic smile and mouthed "one minute." Hazels mouth dropped open in shock. She was very confused about how her mom was acting right now. First of all, Hazel's mom never came to pick her up. Secondly, she never even looked at Hazel when she was on a phone call with a client, let alone mouthed how much longer she would be!

"I am one of the best lawyers, and you want to pay me how much?!" A disgusted look came across Hazel's moms face. Hazel looked out the window so she wouldn't laugh.

"Yeah?! Maybe next time you should think about getting the money for a good lawyer to defend you before you break the law! Yeah, well you know what? Have fun in prison!"

Hazel's mom sighed dramatically and she hung up the phone. Hazel laughed but then covered it up with a cough. Sometimes her mom could say some really weird things. Like what she just said. She should have told the person they shouldn't have broken the law. But instead she practically told the person 'Hey, it's ok to break the law! Just make sure you have the money to hire me first!' It kind of bugged Hazel how her mom cared more about the money she was getting than the person she was defending.

"How was your day with your father?" Hazel's mom asked as she started flipping through business papers that were on her lap. Hazel sighed. There was no point in lying and saying she had a good time, because her mom could tell when anybody was lying.

"Dad forgot that I was coming over so he was in a meeting when I got there after dance, and he left today for some trip or something." Hazel's mom sighed.

"He never was good with that kind of stuff." Hazel wasn't sure how her mom could be blaming him, seeing as how she's forgotten many times that Hazel was supposed to be coming over. She started talking again. "Anyway, I thought that you and I could grab a bite to eat. I haven't had any breakfast yet so I thought we could try this new little place down the street.

Sound good?" Hazel's mom asked without looking up from the paper she was reading. Hazel knew that no matter what she said they would still go, but she thought that it did sound nice. Hazel wasn't sure why her mom was acting so motherly, but she was going to enjoy it for however long it lasted.

"Sure," Hazel said with a smile. A few minutes later they pulled up to a restaurant with people walking in and out wearing nice business suites. Hazel looked down at her outfit. Since her dad had forgotten that she was coming over, while getting dressed Hazel had decided to wear something that would annoy him. So rather than wearing one of the nice skirt and shirts that one of the maids had left out for her, Hazel had settled for wearing torn jeans and a t-shirt that had Sponge Bob's face on it. But her dad wasn't even home to see her outfit. Now Hazel wished she had put on something nice because she was really under dressed for this restaurant. Her mom, however, didn't seem to notice. Hazel followed her mom out of the car and into the restaurant. The hostess led them to a nice big black leather booth and handed them both a black leather menu with gold writing on the front. Hazel couldn't quite make out what the writing said but figured that it was the name of the restaurant. She noticed that her mom hadn't even picked up her menu. When the waitress came back, Hazel ordered pancakes, bacon and orange juice. Her mom just ordered coffee.

"Aren't you going to eat?" Hazel asked.

"I will, just not yet," she said with a smile. Hazel was starting to wonder why her mom had taken her out for breakfast. She'd only stuck a couple of folders in her purse and she wasn't even looking at them!

"Mom, you're still coming next week to my karate tournament, right?" Hazel asked. Her mom smiled.

"Of course I'm coming! I wouldn't miss it for the world!" she said with a smile. "Oh Hazel, I can't wait until you become a lawyer! You'll be just great at it. I can tell."

Hazel sighed. "About that...Mom, I don't really think a lawyer is what I want to be when I'm older," Hazel said. Her mom just looked at her as if she had spoken a different language. But before she said anything Hazel's Mom hopped out of the booth.

"Sarah!" Hazel's mom said, waving someone down. The woman, who was apparently Sarah, turned around spotting Hazel's mom and waved. Hazel turned around and saw that 'Sarah' was a lady who was dressed from head to toe in red and heading straight towards them. Hazel's mom walked to meet up with her. The woman was holding a large red bag in one had and little boy, who was about seven, was holding her other hand. The boy looked like he was going get his picture taken for a family portrait. He was wearing a red sweater vest with a white t-shirt under it and khaki pants with little brown shoes. His little hair was jelled and parted to the side. Overall,

he looked really cute but Hazel could tell he was super uncomfortable in the getup.

"You remember my son, Nathan," Hazel heard Sarah say.

"Of course I do!" Hazel's mom said, kneeling down so she
was level with Nathan. "How are you sweetie?" she asked in a
voice Hazel had never heard her use before. Nathan stared
blankly at her. Hazel could tell the little boy did not want to be
at the restaurant. "You remember my daughter Hazel," her
mom said gesturing back to Hazel, who was still sitting in the
booth. Sarah smiled and waved before she set her brief case
on a table, which Hazel's mom has sat down at, then started
walking towards Hazels booth with her kid in tow. Then it
clicked. Hazel wasn't here to have breakfast with her mom,
she was here to babysit the little boy while her mom had
breakfast with a client! That's why she was being so nice! She
was manipulating her! Hazel felt like stomping out of the restaurant right there and then. But she didn't know where she
was and she wouldn't be able to find her way home, so that
wouldn't work. And Hazel knew the driver wouldn't just take
her home without her mom. She thought about calling Sam,
but she figured that he was already off to meet her dad wherever he was.

After a moment, Hazel began to calm down. Yes, her
mom hadn't even asked if Hazel could watch the little boy, but
she was taking off work to come and watch Hazel at her tour-

nament. So Hazel decided that she was going to let her mom off the hook... just a little.

Nathan sat down in the seat across from Hazel. His mom told the waitress that her son wanted a bowl of plain low fat yogurt with a side of broccoli and tomato juice. The waitress looked like she might throw up but she walked away with the order. Then Sarah went to go and join Hazel's Mom at the table that was across the room. When the waitress brought the food, she gave Nathan a sympathetic look as he gazed longingly at Hazel's food. Hazel smiled.

"Does your mom drag you to a lot of things, Nathan?" Hazel asked.

"Yah," he said with a sigh.

"And does she always make you eat weird things?" Hazel asked looking at the broccoli, yogurt and tomato juice.

"She says that I can't eat sugar or I might get hyper and not take a nap or go to bed on time. But I know that she just wants me out of the way so that she can work. And I have to have a vegetable with every meal so that I can be strong. Well, that's what Corkey the Dinosaur on T.V. said." The little boy sighed again and Hazel laughed.

"Kid, I know just how you feel," Hazel said with a smile. Hazel took the tomato juice and dumped it into the yogurt. Then she put the broccoli in the bowl. Nathan laughed. Hazel asked the waitress to take away the dishes and to bring a new plate and cup. The waitress smiled and came back with a new table setting. Hazel put some bacon and pancakes on Nathan's plate and split the orange juice. She looked at Nathan's face. He was smiling like it was Christmas.

"Thanks!" he said as he drowned his pancakes with syrup and enjoyed the best breakfast he'd had in ages while his and Hazel's mother finished up their meeting.

After they had left the restaurant, Hazel and her mother sat in the car in silence. "I can't believe that you signed me up for babysitting without asking!" Hazel said.

"Sweetheart, look I'm sorry! I didn't think you would mind. It really was a last minute thing."

"Mom, I wouldn't have minded if you would have just asked me! I minded because you didn't ask me!" Hazel said as she crossed her arms.

"Sweetie, I really wish you wouldn't cross your arms like that. It doesn't look professional." She stared at Hazel with a stern look. Hazel rolled her eyes and let her arms fall to the chair.

"Look, I'm sorry. I see now that you thought we were going to have breakfast with just the two of us, so why don't we do something else? We could get our nails done or—" Hazel's mom stopped and picked up the phone. Hazel hadn't even heard it ring.

"Hello, yes, yes, yes, ok, no problem, ok, ok, I'm on my way." Hazel sighed and looked out the window.

"That was Martha. There's a big case in Thailand that I need to help with. I have to rush to the airport, so I guess we'll have to reschedule."

"Whatever," Hazel said crossing her arms again.

"Hazel, there's nothing I can— what did I say about the arms? You really need to learn how to conduct yourself in a matter that is-"

"Just take me back to Aunt Clair's house," Hazel said interrupting her mom.

"Anna," her mom said to the driver who had obviously heard about the Thailand case. She, like Sam, was quite familiar with the routine of Hazel being tossed around. As soon as the car pulled up to the house, Hazel got out without saying goodbye to her mom and slammed the car door shut. She marched up to her aunts house and opened the door, then slammed it shut, startling Snowball who was in front of the door waiting for her to come home. Snowball let out a little yelp.   Hazel mumbled an apology and called Amber over to spend the night so she didn't have to be alone waiting for her aunt. Shortly after, Amber came over with a sketch book.

"I can't wait to show you what I designed for our Halloween costume! They're so cool! I've been working on them forever!" Amber said once she was at Hazel's house, holding out the sketch pad proudly. Hazel, still in a foul mood, snapped back at Amber without even looking at her designs. "Who said

I was even going trick-or-treating? Don't you think it's a little bit childish?" Amber looked startled.

"Don't you want to go? I mean it's not that childish. I think it's fun. My mom and her friends went till they were like eighteen and they always watched scary movies afterwards. As long as we dressed up and stuff–" Amber said but Hazel cut her off.

"Well I don't want to! And I don't like how you just decided for me that we were going trick-or-treating! I can make my own decisions, you know!" Hazel said.

"Ok, I'm sorry," Amber said quietly and put her sketch book back in her bag. Neither of them said much that night. Hazel was surprised that Amber had stayed. She hadn't meant to snap at Amber, she was just fed up with both of her parents.

The school warning bell rang and Hazel jumped as she came back to reality. She made a mental note to apologize to Amber as soon as she saw her next. Hazel looked around the class room and saw that kids were taking their seats now.

"Doing some deep thinking?" A voice asked.

Hazel jumped and saw a girl sitting in front of her. She had twisted around in her seat so that she was facing Hazel. Hazel looked at the girl

"Alice?!" She said recognizing her friend from when she was little.

"That's me!" Alice said with a smile.

"Ok, I know I haven't been hanging out with anybody else but the J Girls, but you haven't always gone to this school have you?" Hazel asked. And she knew that if Alice said "yes" she was going to start crying because she'd been such a zombie. Alice laughed.

"No, I just transferred over like two weeks ago. It took me a couple of days to recognize you because you looked so... different. After I figured out that it was you, I asked around about you and everybody knew you. They said that you didn't hang out with anybody else but the J Girls. Some people said that you were stuck up because your mom and dad are so well known, but I knew you weren't stuck up," Alice said with a smile.

"Uggh! I feel like such a jerk! And every person who said I was stuck up, they were so right! I have been stuck up! I have let the J Girls run my life! I've let everybody run it! But now, that's going to change." Hazel started laughing.

"Just like old times, huh? See you for five seconds then you just spill your guts out!" Alice said laughing. When they were much younger, whenever Alice would play with Hazel, Hazel would always tell Alice her problems and then Alice would give her advice.

"You're just too easy to talk to!" Hazel said laughing. "I can't believe we lost touch like that! I haven't seen you since we were like ten!"

"I know! I don't want it to happen again!" Alice said smiling.

"Me neither!" Hazel said. "I know I should have totally recognized you, but how come you never came up to talk to me once you recognized me?

"Ha! I tried! If I got within fifteen feet of you, Jane looked like she was going to kill me! Later there was a note on my locker from "you." I could totally tell that it wasn't your hand writing but it said that the J Girls were your only friends and the only friends you needed and that I should just go away. Like I said, I knew it wasn't from you. I just figured I would have to get you alone. But I just got so busy with schoolwork and after-school actives, and I didn't feel like dealing with Scary Mary!" She laughed but Hazel was shocked. She couldn't believe that Jane would do that! Well, she could, but still!

"So anyway... you were talking about how you were thinking about your life and how you're parents are oh so controlling and how you're going to fix it," Alice said with a smile.

"You know, you are so scary how you do stuff like that, listen and give advice! It's not even funny," Hazel said laughing. "And I can't believe Jane did that! She's probably done the same thing to other people! No wonder the whole school thinks I'm a stuck up jerk!"

"But you're not a stuck up jerk!" Alice said. "Jane is just jealous of you! I mean, you're like a princess for goodness sakes!" Hazel looked at Alice confused.

"Oh come on Hazel, you're the only one in the whole fourth grade who got to be what they said they wanted to be on career day! About ten girls said they wanted to be a princess, and you got to be one! Who knew your dad was serious when he was always saying 'my little princess!'" Alice and Hazel laughed. Hazel never thought of Jane being jealous. But it made sense. Jane had always made sure that at school Hazel never looked better than her, and made sure Hazel didn't get a lot of attention. Hazel sighed.

"Yah, but a princess is supposed to meet a prince who sweeps her off her feet and have two parents who love her and give her some attention. Not just make her their little puppet! And if I could trade with Jane, I sure would."

Alice gave Hazel a comforting smile. And she didn't say what everybody else says – 'I'm sure your parents love you very much, they're just busy'. She just sighed and said, "I'm sure it can be really tough, Hazel."

Hazel smiled. She was glad she had stepped out of the little bubble she was living in. The J Girls walked into the class room and when Jane saw Hazel wasn't in the back row and was sitting – and talking – with Alice, she looked like she was going to scream. Alice ended up being in almost every class with Hazel, and Hazel apologized over and over for never seeing her and felt terrible about it. She had lunch with Alice, and a couple of Alice's friends joined them, too. All throughout the day, Hazel gave polite smiles and waves to the J Girls as she passed them in the halls or while they were in the same classes, but that was it.

School let out at three thirty on the dot. Hazel invited Alice to Club Sizzle but she said she had to babysit for her little sister. Hazel waved goodbye and got on her pod and headed to meet Amber. She got there right at four. Hazel thought about making Amber crazy and sitting outside for a bit but then remembered she still had to apologize to her and hurried inside. Hazel went to the check in at the front desk, showing her Club Sizzle ID, then went inside. Hazel loved the way Club Sizzle looked. Everything was so futuristic and modern looking! There were tall silver chairs with a silver table that looked almost like glass waves. At the end of the room was a dance floor with cool lights above it. But no one was dancing because most people only danced on the weekend evenings. Lining the club were big booths that fit lots of people in them and scattered around the room they had high top tables that were orange and blue that glowed in the dark when the lights were low. TVs set up in one corner were where some kids were playing video games. And there was a mini snack bar in the back, and even a stage for when they had live performances. It was about the coolest place a kid could hang out!

Hazel saw Amber sitting at one of the high tables and ran over to her, but before she could say anything Amber handed her the bag her aunt had given her last night.

"Quickly go put this on," Amber said with a smile.

"But..."

"No talking, go put it on then come back!" Amber said as she pushed Hazel in the direction of the bathrooms. Hazel looked around Club Sizzle and saw that the place was starting to fill up pretty quickly. She ran into the bathroom and put on the outfit her Aunt had made for her and headed back to Amber.

"Amber! Please, please, please, please ten thousand billion million times forgive me! I didn't mean to! I was having such a bad day, I was so angry that I just snapped! I couldn't...I was just so... aghhh!" Hazel sat down in a chair and banged her head on the table.

"Gessh, what did you do? Rob a bank?" Amber said with a smile.

"No! Worse! I was so rude to you! All you wanted to do was show me the costumes you designed! And you always make the best ones in the whole world! And I really do want to go trick-or-treating because it's fun and I want to get a bunch of free candy! I was just so mad at both of my parents and ghhhuuu! Please forgive me!" Hazel said as she started hitting her head on the table again. Then she started laughing and so did Amber. "Was that a good finish?" Hazel asked after they finished laughing.

"Very good! And of course I forgive you! I just figured that you were having a bad day and you didn't want to talk about it so I didn't make you. I thought that maybe you didn't want to go trick-or-treating and you just yelled it out instead of saying it," Amber said reaching over and giving Hazel a hug. "I have them right here in my bag! You know I always have my sketch book with me! I thought this year we could go as Disco Girls! I have some great ideas!" But before they had a chance to look at the book they noticed that there were a couple of girls standing next to them at their table.

"I really like your outfits!" the one girl said.

"Me too!" the second one added.

"I'm Fiona. And this is my sister Monica," Fiona said.

"Thanks! It's nice to meet you! We're just trying on the latest fall fashion from No Strings Attached. They're starting this great new mid fall fashion line. You should really check it out!" Amber said as she took out a catalogue from the bag and handed it to Fiona.

"And here's a gift card for $10 off your next purchase!" Hazel said handing them each a card. Amber and Hazel loved advertising for Clair. It was really fun because they got lots of complements and got to talk to lots of cool people. They continued to spend their time talking with people and handing out more magazines. Everyone really seemed to be enjoying their outfits, which was good news! At exactly five forty-five Amber grabbed her bag.

"Let's go!" she said with a smile. Most of the kids around the club were starting on their homework to get it out of the way before the weekend, or looking at the catalogue that they had gotten from Amber and Hazel. The girls left the club and got on their Pods and headed back to the house.

"How is it that you planned everything out perfectly in a matter of seconds?!" Hazel asked as they let themselves into the house at exactly six.

"I'm just that perfect!"Amber said laughing.

"I can't wait for tonight! I think I'm going to throw up!" Hazel said grabbing her stomach trying to calm her nerves.

"Not in that outfit!" Amber said laughing. "Hazel, you are the best Kung Fu master I know! You're going to be fantastic tonight, so stop worrying!" she said as she shook Hazel by the shoulders. "Now, I'm going to watch TV while you go do some homework to calm your nerves." Hazel sighed.

"You're right, I just need to settle my nerves... but oh my gosh I'm so nervous! What if I mess up? You know they take points off if you forget to go "HI-YAH!" when you do something! And what if I can't break the board? What am I going to do?!" Hazel asked as Amber pushed her into her room.

"Sit," Amber said pointing to the chair at Hazel's desk. Hazel sat at her desk obediently. Amber took out Hazel's homework and put it on the table. "Do," Amber said as Hazel got out some pencils. "Good girl," Amber said, smiling as she patted Hazels head. Hazel chuckled. At the sound of 'good girl' Snowball came running to the room and sat down in front of Amber. Both girls started laughing at the little dog wagging its tail. Hazel tried to concentrate on her homework for about fifteen minutes but couldn't. She was too excited, so she watched some TV with Amber instead. At six thirty they heard Clair come in.

"I'm home!" she yelled to the girls.

"Right on time!" Amber yelled back as Hazel got up.

"I'm going to shower then get dressed," Hazel said to Amber. "Do you want to feed Snowball? Then, while my Aunt gets ready, see if there is something in the fridge to feed us?" Hazel asked laughing as she headed to the shower, half hoping that it would rinse off her nerves. When Hazel was done, she went into her closet and sighed. Now she wasn't so much nervous as she was excited.

"I founnndd sommeee bagels!" Amber sang from the kitchen. Hazel smiled as she heard her friend. She tried to smell what Amber was making – popcorn, hot chocolate – Hazel laughed and wondered what kind of meal Amber was planning on making.

"Amber?" Hazel yelled from her bedroom as she tied her brown belt around her waist. "What the heck are you making us for dinner?"

"The perfect comfort nerve-calming dinner!" she yelled back. Hazel heard her Aunt burst out into laugher as she walked into the kitchen. Hazel put her hair up in a high pony tail and pinned up the extra pieces so that she wouldn't get distracted by hair tickling her neck. She walked into the kitchen and laughed. Amber had made big mugs of hot chocolate, popcorn, and sandwiches with ham, turkey and cheese on plain bagels.

"Oh yes! Definitely the perfect comfort food!" Clair said laughing. "Bet you won't have a nervous nerve in your body once you're done with this meal!" Hazel couldn't agree more. She looked at the perfect meal and smiled.

"Ha! See Hazel, it's six forty-five on the dot! Nothing is going wrong with my perfect plan!" Amber said with an over-the-top evil laugh. The girls laughed and started eating. They finished at seven fifteen just as Amber said they would. Clair cleaned up while Amber went to go watch Hazel finish her warm-ups.

"HI-YAH!" Amber said as she kicked. "HI-YAH!" she said again as she punched the air. "HI-YAH, HI-YAH, HI-YAH, HI-YAH," She said punching with both fist. Hazel grabbed onto Ambers arms and kicked her legs out from underneath her and dropped her softly onto the ground.

"HI-YA! Now shut up! I can't hear myself think!" Hazel said as she dropped a pillow on Amber's face. Amber got up grinning.

"I think I'm really good. Maybe I could be like a secret last minute entry," Amber said laughing.

"How do you think I'm supposed to calm my nerves with you HI-YAHING!?" Hazel asked. Amber rolled her eyes.

"Ok! Let us go," Amber said as she stood up. "Seven thirty on the dot, on the dot! On the dot! Seven thirty on the dot, I'm so great! Cha cha cha!" She sung the words to the tune of London Bridge is Falling Down. They all go into the car. Hazel sat bouncing her leg excitedly as they drove to the tournament.

Chapter Five

Hazel, Amber and Clair got to the karate gym at seven forty-five. Once they were inside, Hazel gave her Aunt and Amber a hug.

"Good luck, honey! I know you're going to win that tournament! You could do it with your eyes closed and your hands behind your back!" Clair said.

"Thanks, Aunt Clair," Hazel said hugging her again.

"Look, I'm counting on you!" Amber said. "If you don't get those four tickets to China, how do you think I'm going to be able to study other countries' fashions?" Amber asked giving Hazel a hug. "You're going to do great! We're going to get our snacks then go to our seats. We're row eight, seat G or something like that. Your parents got seats right next to us. So, count up eight rows and you'll see us!"

"Ok! Go get your snack or you're going to throw the whole schedule off!" Hazel said. She turned to go get in line for check-in. After checking herself in, Hazel went to go sit with her group. They did some warm ups and stretches. It was almost overwhelming with more than five hundred kids yelling "HI-YAH!" at the top of their lungs.

"If everybody could please take your seats, the competition will start momentarily. If the students could please get in your ready position," the announcer requested. Hazel counted eight rows up and saw her Aunt and Amber sitting in their seats. Hazel felt her heart drop when she didn't see her parents next to them, their seats empty. Her aunt had her head turned and looked like she was on the phone but Amber gave her a thumbs up. *Don't jump to conclusions,* Hazel told herself. They could be getting snacks, or they could be in the bathroom. But her parents were time freaks! They would have done all of that stuff before they sat down. Hazel held back her tears. They weren't coming. Hazel felt more angry than she did sad. How could they not come?! They promised her for the past year that they would come!

"Hazel!" Hazel turned around and saw her friend Ryan signaling her over. He was her partner for the board breaking.

"Coming," Hazel said making sure her voice wasn't shaking.

"Still want me to break first?" Hazel asked as she ran over to where Ryan was standing. Hazel looked around the room. Everybody was with their partner – one person holding the board, the other in their ready position.

"Yah, we're doing the foot board first," Ryan said getting in his ready position – holding the board an arms-lengths away from his face so Hazel wouldn't kick him. Hazel looked around the room again. Coaches were going around the room giving students last minute advice. Hazel's coach reached her last. He put both arms on her shoulder.

"You ok?" he asked.

"Fine," Hazel said a little too fiercely. "Just nervous," she added quietly. Her coach smiled.

"You just need to calm yourself. Take a deep breath. You seem a little angry. Don't use bad energy to break the board. Just take deep breaths." Hazel took a deep breath.

"Yes sir," she said as he turned to talk to Ryan. Hazel tried to calm herself but she couldn't. How could they not show up!? She wasn't even angry any more, she was now furious!

"READY POSITIONS!" someone yelled. Hazel wasn't sure who – probably the person who ran the competition, but Hazel didn't care. She just wanted to get this whole thing over with. She got in her ready position.

"ONE... TWO... THREE!" the person yelled. On three, Hazel thrust her wrist forward and snapped the board in half in a perfect line. Ryan looked amazed at first, and then gave her an apologetic smile.

"What?" Hazel asked quietly so no one could hear but him.

"We were doing a kick board! I can't believe you broke it with your hand! It's so much thicker!"

"Dang it!" Hazel said angrily as she put her hands on her head.

"What am I supposed to do now!?" Hazel said looking around the room. The judges were writing down on the paper. Hazel franticly looked around the room and found her coach. He signaled her to breath, and then he motioned her to do the hand break again. Hazel took a deep breath.

"Hey, they might have been so impressed with how you broke the board that they won't take off points," Ryan said as he wrote Hazels name on the board and picked up another one.

"READY POSITION!" the announcer yelled. Hazel looked up at the seats again. Every seat in the room was filled but the two seats next to Amber. Clair still had her phone to her ear even though everybody had been asked to turn them off a while ago. Amber was yelling, "GO HAZEL!" and throwing pop-corn in the air. Hazel turned her attention back to the board.

"ONE, TWO, THREE!" Hazel broke the board again with her hand. It felt like a twig compared to the last board. Ryan wrote Hazel's name on the board as Hazel went to go get one for Ryan.

For the rest of the competition Hazel couldn't fully con-centrate. She kept on looking at the seats to see if her parents were there, and with the annoyed look on her aunt's face she knew it wasn't something bad that happened to them that was keeping them from coming. Hazel did alright with the rest of the competition. She was good enough to get her black belt, but she could have done much better.

"Ladies and gentlemen! Our first place winner is..." The announcer stopped while a fake drum roll played on the speakers. Everybody crossed their fingers.

"Please, please, please," Hazel mumbled under her breath.

"Joshua Heart!" the announcer said. Joshua jumped up and threw his fist up in the air. The rest of the room clapped. Joshua stepped up on the little block while someone put a medal around his neck Hazel felt herself shaking. She couldn't tell if she was angry at her parents or if she was upset and mad that she didn't win. She held back tears and closed her eyes. She stood there and didn't pay any attention to anything and didn't even hear what the guy was saying. A couple of seconds later Hazel felt someone pushing her.

"HAZEL!" the girl who pushed her yelled.

"What?" Hazel snapped at the person, who luckily didn't seem to notice Hazel's attitude.

"Go up there!" the girl said again, pointing to the blocks where four other kids were already standing. Hazel didn't recognize the person but they sure knew her.

"What?" Hazel repeated again, but people were grabbing her and she obediently walked as they lead her over to the blocks. She stood up on the remaining one. A man came up and handed her a medal. She looked at it – it said fifth place. She sighed. At least she ranked. She gave a small smile when she noticed people were taking pictures and clapping.

"We want to thank everybody who participated in tonight's event!" the announcer said. Everybody in the room clapped again. Hazel politely thanked everyone who congratulated her. She grabbed her bag and headed to the door when her coach stopped her.

"Good job, Hazel" he said with a smile and pat on the back.

"I...I could have..." Hazel stopped talking in fear that she was going to start crying.

"I know. It's very hard to concentrate when your mind is somewhere else. I know that you were looking forward to having your parents come, but at least you have your Aunt and best friend here!" he said with a smile "And you're lucky. I didn't even have one person to cheer me on at any of my biggest tournaments!" He gave a sad little smile. Hazel gave a small smile back. "There will always be next year!" he said as he gave her a pat on her shoulder. Hazel nodded and went to go find her Aunt and Amber. She looked around at all the kids with their friends and family, laughing and hugging. Hazel sighed. She wasn't going to let her parents ruin her night any more than they already had. At least she had placed and that was good enough for her.

"AHHH! That is just about the coolest medal I've ever seen! And out of like five hundred kids, you coming in fifth place is like amazing! And not to be rude or anything, I thought you totally blew it when you did the hand break instead of your foot kick! I mean, that was awesome!" Amber wrapped her arms around her and hugged Hazel.

"You're not mad at me for not winning us the tickets to go to China?" Hazel asked as she poked Amber in the stomach.

"Of course not! I mean, these things are always rigged anyway! And that Joshua was pretty cute, I'm sure I can work something out with him!" Amber said with a wink, causing Hazel to truly smile for the first time that night. Amber went over to a garbage can to throw away her wrappers, leaving Hazel and her aunt to talk.

"You did great!" Clair said as she gave Hazel a hug.

"Thanks. And my parents?" Hazel asked quietly. Clair rolled her eyes and sighed, then gave Hazel a hug again.

"They missed a great karate tournament," she said as Amber came back.

"Come on you guys! We're going to be late!" Amber said as she grabbed Hazel's hand and dragged her to the car with Clair following right behind them. They pulled up to the ice cream store, parked the car and got a table outside. It was a beautiful autumn night.

"Don't you think it's just a perfect night to eat outdoors?" Amber asked as Hazel and Clair sat down on the wooden bench. "Ok, I'm going to get the ice cream, because I want it to be a surprise!" Amber said, trying to lighten up the mood that was obviously grim.

"Alright, but I don't think I'm going to have any ice cream tonight," Clair said. "And tell the lady that I'll come in and pay once you're done. And go wild with the ice cream!" Without needing another word Amber excitedly went inside. This was Hazel's favorite place to get ice cream. You got to pick your flavor, and then you got to pick whatever toppings you wanted to put in it. They had everything from candy bars to fruit. Hazel and her Aunt sat without saying anything. Amber finally came out holding two chocolate-dipped waffle cones with so much ice cream in them that it looked like it was going to fall out.

"The lady thinks I'm pretty crazy, so you better go in and pay quickly!" Amber said laughing. She sat down next to Hazel and gave her a cone and a spoon. Hazel looked at her ice cream. She couldn't tell what kind it was but she saw Oreos, sprinkles, cookie dough, peanut-butter cups, Milky Ways, some other chewy chocolate bar, caramel and chocolate sauce and just a little bit of whipped cream on the top. Hazel laughed.

"What are you trying to do? Give me clogged arteries?" Hazel and Amber started laughing. Hazel took a spoon of her ice cream and tasted the creamy flavor. It was her favorite – cake batter.

"Look, I'm really sorry your parents didn't show up," Amber said after a moment of silence. "your Aunt and I called them like crazy, but they had their phones turned off," she added with a sad smile.

"Don't worry about it; it's not your fault. It's my fault for thinking they'd actually come. I should have known that they wouldn't show," Hazel said taking another bite. She didn't really want to talk about it and Amber could see that. Hazel looked in through the window and saw her Aunt grabbing the receipt from the lady at the cash register. Then she took her cell phone out, and after a moment she started yelling into it. Hazel knew she was trying to call again but had gotten one of her parent's answering machines. Clair shut the phone and said something to the girl at the counter who looked slightly frightened. Clair came back out and sat down without saying anything.

The two girls slowly ate their ice cream in silence. At ten thirty they finished eating, left, and then pulled up to Amber's house at ten forty five.

"Thanks for bringing me!" Amber said as she got out of the car.

"Thanks for showing up." Clair mumbled quietly under her breath.

"No problem, Amber! Thanks for coming and getting the great ice cream!" Hazel said and watched as Amber quickly ran up to her door step and was greeted by her mom who waved at Hazel. Of course Mrs. Lambert didn't know that Hazel was at a karate tournament because she still thought that she had a sprained ankle. Mrs. Lambert gave Amber a hug and then led her inside with one arm around her. Hazel felt her stomach shift. She wanted her mom to be the one hugging her once she was done with the tournament. Her aunt drove in silence. They pulled up to the house and went inside.

"Hazel, I am really sorry your parents didn't show up. I tried calling them both but their phones went straight to voicemail. They both must have got caught up in a meeting or... I don't know." Hazel sighed. She hadn't thought about that. Maybe they were caught up in a meeting and were looking at the clock every second to see if they had enough time to make it. But she doubted that.

"It's not your fault. You're the best, Aunt Clair," Hazel said as she hugged her aunt. "Well, it's been a long day. I'm going to go get some sleep," Hazel sighed.

"Ok. I'm going to go to bed, too. I was thinking about going into the shop early to work, but if you want we can go out for breakfast instead." Hazel thought about taking her up on the offer, but she didn't want to ruin her Aunt's plans. She knew how much she loved working at the store. Hazel smiled.

"No thanks. I think I'll be ok here. I've got some homework to do anyway. Good night," Hazel said. She gave her Aunt another hug and went to her bedroom. Hazel shut the door and put her back to it and slid to the ground. She wasn't sure how long she'd been sitting there, but after a while she heard her Aunt close her own bedroom door.

Maybe I should call them, Hazel thought. *No, because then I might find out where they really were, and it's much better to just think that they got held up in a meeting.*

"Ugh," Hazel said out loud. She knew that it would drive her insane if she didn't know where her parent's really were. Hazel tried to think where they could have been. Did they say anything about meetings when she was with them last week? She thought about it. She didn't talk to her dad because he forgot she was there and then left for a trip, and she didn't talk much with her mom because her mom had signed her up for babysitting and then left for her trip. Hazel let out a deep sigh, then gasped as realization dawned on her. All of a sudden it felt like someone was dropping boulders on her. Trips! She remembered. Last week they both left for trips! They probably weren't even back yet! Without thinking, Hazel grabbed her phone from her bag and dialed her dad's cell phone. Sam picked up the phone. He sounded tired.

"Hello this is—"

"Where is he, Sam?" Hazel demanded, interrupting him.

"Hazel?" he asked sleepily. She must have woke him up but she didn't care; she was far too angry to care. Her body was shaking in anger.

"Yes, Sam! It's Hazel! Where are you and where is my dad?"

"Well, after you left last week, I flew to meet your dad in Spain," Sam said confused. "But you do know that there's a time difference and it's like—"

"Put him on the phone," Hazel said through clenched teeth.

"But he's sleeping, and he gets really mad when—"

"Put him on the phone NOW!" Hazel yelled. She heard quick footsteps, a door opening, then her father grunting.

"Who is this?" Hazel heard her Dad's sleepy voice on the phone.

"Dad," Hazel said trying to keep herself from yelling at him.

"Hazel?! What do you need? Can't it wait until the morning?" That did it – Hazel couldn't hold it in. He forgot! He totally forgot! He's never late or forgets anything when it's an important client, but when it's his own daughter, he forgets.

"*HOW COULD YOU!?*" Hazel yelled into the phone. "You both promised! You said you would! Out of all the things! Why?! Why are you so selfish?! I can't believe you! Do you even care that this was one of *THE MOST* important things to me? That because I was distracted by you not being there I lost my tournament?! I NEVER ever want to talk to you or see you again!" Hazel furiously hung up her phone and dialed her mom's number. She knew that she was acting childish but she didn't care.

"Carole-Anne May," Hazel heard her mom say. She didn't even recognize Hazel's phone number.

"MOM! You promised! You signed me up for babysitting and I did it 'cuz you promised me! You and Dad both missed it! And I lost because you didn't come! How come you always miss stuff of mine but when someone offers you money you never miss a thing? Is that what I need to do to get your attention!? Pay you?" Hazel had angry tears coming down her face.

"Hazel, what on earth—" Hazel didn't let her mom finish.

"*MY TOURNAMENT, MOM!*" Hazel yelled into the phone.

"I told you I wasn't coming," she said plainly. Hazel was shocked. She almost felt like throwing up.

"You... you never did such a thing," Hazel said through

clenched teeth, her body shaking.

"Yes, I did. I told you that I was going to Thailand," her mom said. Hazel heard her start flipping through papers.

"THAT'S NOT TELLING ME, MOM! That's saying you're going to Thailand! What you should have said was 'Hazel, I'm not going to be coming to your karate tournament because someone is going to pay me money. So even though I told you one year ago that I would be coming to your tournament, I'm not coming anymore, because money is WAY more important than you! Always has and always will be!'

"Well congratulations, Mom! You and Dad can focus on your money and your perfect careers all you want! Because I am done! I am so done with waiting for either of you to care! I'm done with having this crazy dream that one day you'll actually support me! That you'll actually act like my parents. But you know what? Don't even worry about it anymore because I am no longer going to consider myself your daughter! I'm going to live with Aunt Clair for the rest of my life. I'm not going to have you and dad shove me around and forget about me anymore. I am never going to think about you or talk to you again!" Hazel hung up the phone and let out a scream as she threw it across the room.

Hazel stomped into her closet, tears streaming down her face, ignoring her ringing phone. She grabbed three suit cases that her parents had bought her and went around her room throwing everything her parents had ever given her into the suit cases. Anything that couldn't fit she just threw out into the hallway. When Hazel finally finished, she sighed, tears still running down her face. She looked around the room. She had thrown out her laptop, iPod, books, pens, makeup, clothes, shoes, pictures, hairbrushes, headbands and jewelry. Her room felt empty but she didn't care. Hazel took off her Karate outfit, put on her pajamas and curled up in bed with the small bear her grandpa gave her when she was younger, and fell asleep.

◆　　◆　　◆

Hazel woke up at the feeling of a hand rubbing her shoulder.

"Hazel," Clair said.

"Hmm," Hazel said without opening her eyes.

"Do you want to go for breakfast?"

"Not really." Hazel stretched, remembering last night.

"I talked to your dad last night." Hazel sat up and rubbed her eyes. They felt puffy, probably from all the crying she did last night.

"What did you say to him?" Hazel asked curiously.

"Well... some things I probably shouldn't have," Clair said with a small smile. "I heard you talking to them last night."

"Yah, I wouldn't really call it talking. More like me letting out five years of bottled up emotions," Hazel said with a embarrassed smile.

"Well, I knew you let most of it out on your mom, so I let *my* sixteen years of bottled up emotions out on your dad. I told him he was a poor excuse as a father and a brother, stupid, selfish...I think you see where I'm going with this."

"But it's all true," Hazel said with a sigh.

"That may be, but perhaps he didn't know it. Same with your mom." Hazel thought about it, but her thoughts went back to what her Aunt had said before.

"You said that you had sixteen years of bottled up emotions. Are you mad at my parents for dumping me on you?" Hazel asked a lump forming in her throat.

"Hazel!" Clair said shocked. "Why on earth would you think that?"

"Because they did! They didn't want me to be with them all the time so they just dumped me on you like a sack of potatoes! They should have taken care of me, but they didn't because they're selfish, so they gave their problem to you. That's what I am – just one big problem!" Hazel started to cry again. She hated being this emotional. Clair got onto the bed and snuggled up with Hazel. She stroked her hair.

"Hazel, I don't ever, ever, ever want you to think that you're a problem! Sweetheart, your uncle died a couple months before you were born. We'd only been married for a few years and he made me so happy. When he passed away I thought that I would never be able to feel that happy again. A few months later, when your dad called and told me that they were on their way to the hospital to have you, I was there in a heartbeat. Your mom and dad told me that they wanted me to be your Godmother."

Clair blinked a couple times, trying to keep herself from crying. "And that made my day, year, life! And when I held you in my arms, you were just a little thing! I looked into your big hazel eyes and you smiled! You were so beautiful! And for the first time in a long time, I was truly happy again. I came to visit you every day. People at work noticed that I was always smiling, and it was because I was alway thinking of things to get you, or just *thinking* about you! I spent more time with you than your parents did and I guess that it upset me a little because they let me!

"I was always waiting for your parents to tell me to go home, or to stop being with you so much, or to let them hold you. But then they started *asking* me to watch you – and of course, I didn't mind. I had a whole room set up for you here! They would go on business trips or meetings and I would get you twenty-four seven until they came back. I guess it was no surprise that your first word was Clairy! And let me tell you, I started crying when you said it!

"When you got older, I still got to see you – you spent the night all the time! I was glad when your parents finally started doing stuff with you too – not as much as they should have, but I thought they were heading in the right direction. Then, when you turned ten, your parents told me that they were getting a divorce. I wasn't that shocked – I mean, they never really spent that much time together anyway. They didn't fight, they just didn't have time for each other.

"When they were trying to figure out who got you and when, I was shocked how they were just so casual about it! Your mom said she couldn't take you on these days because she had this, and your dad had that and blah blah blah! I was so angry that they weren't going to rearrange their life just the teeniest bit for you. So I said you would come and live with me and that you could stay with your mom after school on Mondays and Tuesdays, and your dad would do the same on Thursdays and Fridays.

"Every time they canceled I would get so mad... not mad that I had to watch you, but because they weren't making time for their own daughter. I just got so angry at them for missing events of yours, and angry at how they just tossed you back and forth." Clair had tears in her eyes now. "I felt so bad because every time I had to explain that they weren't coming, I could just see the devastation written across your face. And it's something I still see you having to deal with everyday.

"Hazel, you were the best thing that could ever happen to me! And you are far from a problem or a sack of potatoes. And I think I've done a pretty good job of raising you, don't you think?" Clair poked Hazel in the stomach. They both giggled.

"I think you have done a fabulous job!" Hazel said, feeling so incredibly grateful for her wonderful Aunt. "And I love you so much, Aunt Clair."

"I love you too, sweetheart. More than you will ever know." She squeezed Hazels shoulder. "So, what do you say we go and get some breakfast?" Hazel smiled.

"It's ok, Aunt Clair, you can go into work today. I'm going to be fine," Hazel said as Clair took her arm off of her.

"Are you sure?" she asked. "I would love nothing more than to hang out with you."

"Yeah, I'm sure. I have homework to do and I think I just need a little alone time."

"Ok. That sounds good. Though, I do think you should talk to your parents," Clair said softly. Hazel sighed. She was working on forgetting about last night.

"I don't want to! And I don't think I should have to. They're the ones who missed my tournament," she protested.

"I'm not going to make you call them, but just to let you know, they called the house and your cell phone last night. They kept calling until I picked it up and yelled at them. But I think we should both apologize for yelling at them and tell them that we're sorry for *how* we said the things we did, but that it was the way that we felt." Clair got up and headed for the door. Hazel wanted to say she would apologize after *they* did, but she bit her tongue.

"I love you, sack of potatoes! So just do whatever you want!" Clair said as she left the room. Hazel laughed.

"Bye," Hazel called after her. Hazel lay back down on her pillows and sighed. She replayed last night in her head thinking about what her aunt had just said. She was still angry at her parents, especially her mom, and she didn't want to apologize or talk to either of them for a long time. She felt that they deserved it. Hazel got up and went to look at the clock but noticed that it was still broken on the floor next to her bedside table, so she got a watch off of her shelf and saw that it was eight thirty. She heard her Aunt shut the door and Snowball barking her goodbyes. Hazel looked at herself in the closet mirror. She was a mess. Her eyes were red and puffy, her hair was frizzy, and her face was blotchy. Hazel went to the bathroom and took a long hot shower, letting the water warm her body. She tried not to think about her parents but the more she tried the more she thought about them. And the more she thought about them, the more she became upset.

Hazel got out of the shower and got dressed. She went into the kitchen but didn't feel like eating anything. She went back to her room, ignoring the stuff that was in the hallway that she had thrown out last night. Hazel decided that she would do some homework but realized that her mom and dad had bought all her school supplies and she wasn't going to touch them. She looked around the room for her cell phone but didn't see it. It wasn't in the hallway either. She had tried to remember where she had thrown it last night. Hazel went into the kitchen and used the house phone and called her cell phone. It was ringing in her aunt's room.

Hazel hung up the phone and went to the room and saw her phone on the ground by the door. Her aunt must have either dropped it or thrown it once she was done talking to Hazel's dad. Hazel picked up the phone and went back to her room. Finally, she opened it up. "You have 15 unheard messages," the phone said.

"Don't listen to them," Hazel said aloud. "It's only going to make you more mad and you don't need that right now." Hazel sighed. She sat there with her legs crossed on her bed looking at her phone. She wasn't sure how long, but it felt like forever. She picked up the phone and put it to her ear.

"Hazel, it's me, your father. Look, I think we just need to talk about this. I think maybe you're over reacting about-" Hazel pressed seven to delete the message.

"Hazel, it's your mother, I didn't appreciate that tone you were talking to me with, and I—" Hazel deleted that message too, starting to get angrier. She knew it would happen if she listened to the messages but she did anyway. Knowing she would regret it, she listened to the rest of them but deleted each before it finished because every message made it sound like she was the bad person, like they were so disappointed in her.

"UGHHH!" Hazel felt tears coming again. She didn't want to repeat last night. She needed to get some air but she didn't want to take a walk in her neighborhood. Too many people knew her and she didn't want to have to talk to anyone. Then she smiled, hopped off of her bed, ran into her closet and slipped on a jacket . She grabbed a piece of paper and a pen and wrote:

Went to Red Diamond to hang out with Calvin. I'll be back before dinner.

Love, Hazel

P.S. I didn't want to talk to my parents so I never called, just thought I'd let you know. You don't have to call them either if you don't want to. Love you!

Hazel put the note on the counter in the kitchen and ran back to her bedroom. She put her cell phone in her pocket and grabbed the earpiece from her desk and put it in her ear. She then took out her book from the book shelf. She closed her eyes, opened the book and thought of Red Diamond before she had a chance to see the bright red "TROUBLE" printed across the pages.

Chapter Six

Hazel felt a chill run down her back. When she opened her eyes she was in the forest. She put the book in the chest and closed the wooden top. Hazel walked out of the forest and stopped. It was quite. Too quite. Nobody was in sight, not even an animal. She stopped walking and looked around. It was a nice day but there were no kids playing outside and no cars driving. There were no lights on in the houses either. Something didn't feel right.

"Hello?!" Hazel yelled pulling her jacket around her neck so she wouldn't feel the cold wind blowing. Feeling as though someone was watching her, she started walking. Hazel thought she heard someone breathing, so she quickened her pace. She heard a twig snap. She started running. Looking over her shoulder Hazel saw someone who was coming out – or going into (she couldn't tell) the forest. She started running faster and faster until she was running as hard as she could, her legs and lungs burning with pain. Hazel looked back but couldn't see anybody. Maybe the person wasn't even there. Just as Hazel was wondering if she had imagined the the person, she heard a voice in her ear.

"It would be a lot easier if you just stopped running," the unfamiliar voice said hauntingly, sending a chill down her spine. Hazel yanked her cell phone's ear piece out of her ear. She wasn't sure if that's where the voice had come from, but it didn't matter. She had to get to Calvin's house. Running faster than before, her lungs feeling as if they were on fire, Hazel finally saw his house on the horizon. She sprinted faster, filled with joy that she was almost there and that Calvin would tell her what was going on. Hazel jumped over their small little fence then came to a sudden stop. Something was very wrong.

The front door was broken off of the hinges and most of the windows were either shattered or cracked. Hazel slowly started walking again, but when she got closer to the willow tree she gasped. There was blood on it. She slowly approached the tree hoping that it was just red paint, but as she ran her fingers across it she knew it wasn't. Thankfully it wasn't a lot. Hazel kneeled down on the grass to wipe her fingers when she saw a piece of blue fabric. She felt her heart stop. It was a piece of Calvin's shorts. She remembered because she had gotten him the shorts for his birthday. Clair had specially designed them for him. Hazel quietly stood up and grabbed a heavy stick that was on the ground and slowly made her way to the house. She peeked into one of the broken windows but didn't see anyone inside. Chairs were tossed around the room, side tables were broken, picture frames were either on the floor, shattered, or were crooked on the wall. She saw that the fire wasn't going either, and there was always a fire going. It was one of things Hazel found so comforting about Calvin's house. Hazel hoped that whoever had done this to the place was long gone. She quietly stepped into the house.

"Calvin?" she whispered, but only silence answered.

Walking over to the fireplace, she poked it with her stick. She pulled the stick out and touched it. It was wet but still hot. Someone had poured water on the fire to put it out quickly. Hazel stuck the stick back into the glowing ashes so the tip would get hotter, just in case there was still someone in the house. She walked slowly into the kitchen and saw broken cups and plates. Drawers were opened and on the ground. Then Hazel saw two plates on the dining room table. They had bagels, eggs and muffins on on them. One plate looked as if someone had already started eating, the other looked untouched. There were two cups – one was a mug that still had warm coffee in it, and the other was tipped over with orange juice pooled in front of it and dripping onto the floor.

Hazel ran down the hallway into Calvin's room and saw that the clock said nine fifteen a.m. She looked around the room. There were books on the floor, drawers out of his desk, stuff was opened and thrown around – it looked like someone must have been looking for something. Hazel sat down on his bed, trying to piece together the little bits of information she had. It just didn't make any sense. It was nine fifteen, Calvin and his Aunt must have been having breakfast because the food was still on the table and the fire was still hot. All of the mess that happened couldn't of have been done any longer than twenty minutes ago. But what she didn't get was who would have done this to the house and taken Calvin and his family! And what were they looking for? Hazel saw a newspaper on Calvin's floor. She picked it up and started reading.

"Over the past few days even more officials and citizens of Red Diamond have gone missing!" the headline read.

Hazel set the paper down. What exactly was an Official? And why were they missing? Hazel heard a noise that broke her thoughts. She heard it again. It sounded like a cough. Hazel slowly stood up. With her stick clenched tightly in her hand she walked across the hallway to another room which belonged to Calvin's aunt. She slowly opened the door. It looked just like Calvin's – books were off the shelves, stuff was thrown around everywhere. She heard the coughing again. Hazel came to the last door in the hallway. She was slightly afraid because she couldn't remember what room was behind that door – but she was pretty sure that was where the coughing was coming from. She put one hand on the door handle and with the other she clenched the stick. Hazel held her breath and swung the door open. She gave a frightened scream. There was someone in the room holding a box up threateningly, but the box was covering the person's face and Hazel couldn't tell who it was. The person lowered the box, getting ready to throw it at Hazel, and Hazel gasped as she saw who the person was.

"Ms. Molly?" Hazel asked dropping her stick. Hazel stared at Calvin's grandma. She was wearing a night gown.

"Oh, thank heavens you're here, Hazel!" she said looking at her with sad blue eyes. She sat down on her bed.

"What happened?" Hazel asked looking around at the room that looked much like the others.

"I, I really don't know who the people were, b-b-but Page and Calvin were eating some breakfast and then I heard a scream and I heard..." She stopped and coughed for a little bit, and then cleared her throat. "I heard stuff breaking...and yelling and fighting...and then doors were slamming open and closed. I heard stuff falling." She stopped and coughed some more.

"Do you want me to get you some water?" Hazel asked worriedly, she knew that Calvin's grandma wasn't in the best of health.

"No, no, I'm fine. Five large men barged into the room with guns in their hands. I was lying on the bed and they started going through the drawers and the closet. They were talking about how they needed to find the papers. I knew what they wanted but I didn't say anything. When they noticed I was in the room, one of the men called out into the hallway and someone brought Page to the room and asked who I was. Page said that I was her sick mother.

"They started talking to each other and I heard one of them ask if they should take me with them, but the other one said that I looked as though I was going to die soon, which is true, he said I would only slow them down." She stopped and started coughing harder. "They grabbed Page and then they left. I heard some more fighting and yells. Once I was sure they were gone I got the box I keep hidden in the wall." She handed the rectangle box over to Hazel. As Hazel went to open the box, Molly shook her head. "Now is not the time to open it. But it will be up to you to make sure that things are set back to normal once again." Hazel looked at her, confused about what she meant.

"What do you mean set things back to normal? What's going on? Where is everybody? What papers did they want and why do you have them? And what is that newspaper talking about when it says missing Officials and citizens?" Hazel asked the questions all at once, trying to figure things out. Molly coughed before answering.

"It's a king's feud, Hazel. King Bilimora's brother, Abaddon, is trying to overthrow him."

"Why would he want to do that?" Hazel asked, not even aware that the king had a brother.

"Well, both sons wanted to be the king. They were very close in age so they both had a chance. When their father died he had barely left a Will and Testament saying who got what. It only covered a fraction of his possessions and wealth. It didn't address at all who was to succeed him as king. According to tradition, it is assumed that whoever becomes king inherits anything not specified by the king. And it is tradition that the eldest son is often chosen by his father as the future king. But some kings don't always pick the eldest son, they pick the most capable.

"Since their father never said who would be king, the advisers assumed that it would be best if they just picked the eldest son, which Abaddon was never happy about. So to answer your question, Abaddon wants to overthrow his brother because he wants what every man wants... power and wealth. And you're going to have to have to be the one who fixes this, Hazel."

"Um, how? It's not like I can just pick which one of them gets to be king!" Hazel said.

"Everything you need to know is in that box," Molly said pointing to the wooden box in Hazel's hand. "But you mustn't open it until you are safely away."

"And how am I supposed to know when I'm safe?" Hazel asked, worried.

"I think you'll know," Molly answered with a smile. "Now bring me that map that's on the floor, along with that pen." Hazel went over and picked up the items. Molly unfolded the map and Hazel let out a small gasp.

"I never knew that Red Diamond was this big," Hazel said in amazement. Molly smiled at Hazel.

"This is not just a map of the city of Red Diamond, this is a map of our world, which happens to also be called Red Diamond." she said.

"Your world?" Hazel asked confused. Molly gave a small laugh.

"You thought we would have a king for just a small town of no more than five hundred people?" Hazel shrugged.

"I guess I've never given it much thought," she said, feeling stupid for having not realized it. The map Molly was holding looked not that much different from the maps she was used to back home. Red Diamond was almost a perfect circle, surrounded by ocean on all four sides. The circle was sectioned into smaller squares and rectangles, Hazel realized that they were all cities with their own names.

"You see Hazel, Calvin tells me that your world is called the United States, right?" Hazel nodded, figuring it would be easier to say yes than to have to go into details about her whole entire world.

"Well, Red Diamond is the name of our world. It is also the name of the city where the king lives, which is where we are right now. All over the world of Red Diamond there are large cities, and within each city there are individuals called Officials. To answer your other question, Officials are the King's representatives.

"They let the citizens know of new laws that will be implemented and other things the king would like the city to know." Molly cleared her throat. "That newspaper you saw is actually a few weeks old. Since then, every Official and pretty much every citizen from the city of Red Diamond has gone missing." Molly paused for a moment. "Now, I'm fairly certain that Abaddon is taking everybody from the city of Red Diamond captive to a secret place where he thinks only *he* knows about. But that's not accurate. I know about it, and soon so will you."

"Why would Abaddon take everybody in Red Diamond captive? Don't you guys have an army to protect you? Or police?" Hazel asked franticly.

"There hasn't been a war in Red Diamond for over two hundred and eighty years! We don't exactly *need* an army on guard at all times. However, the King does have about a hundred men in reserve who are highly trained and would help recruit an army if ever needed. In the meantime, they simply go about with their day to day business. But as I said, there hasn't been a war in a long time, and even what's happening now couldn't be considered a war!"

Hazel wasn't entirely satisfied with that answer. "Besides the army, doesn't Red Diamond have any protection? Like police or guards or something!? How could someone just come and kidnap a city of five hundred people? And why would they only take the people in the City of Red Diamond? Why wouldn't they take the whole world?"

Molly smiled. "Ah, so many questions." Molly stared into the distance as if thinking about which question she was going to answer first. "Well firstly Hazel, I think it is much harder to kidnap a full world than a small city," she said, causing Hazel to blush at the silliness of her question. "secondly, everybody who lives in the City of Red Diamond is either highly involved in royal politics, which ends up affecting the entire world, or they own a major company. Most of our worlds resources come from only a couple of large companies which are owned by people who live here in the city." Molly paused. "All together, as the City of Red Diamond, we are the influencers of this world. We influence the voting on new laws, the pricing of food...and in addition to many other things, we help make sure everything runs fairly and smoothly. You see, Hazel, if someone wanted to overthrow the King, a good place to start would be with the 'influentials' of Red Diamond. I'm sure whatever Abaddon's plan is, he has taken that into consideration."

Molly sighed and looked off into the distance again. Hazel took in a deep breath and tried to register everything Molly had just told her. There was so much more to the city of Red Diamond, let alone the entire world of Red Diamond, than she had ever imagined!

"As for security," Molly said suddenly. "In the city of Red Diamond, for the most part, it is quite a peaceful place. We have law breakers here and there from simple things as going too fast on the road, or for something as big as stealing, or very, very rarely, murder. So each city will have a couple of small police stations with a few officers who do large casual sweeps around the city to make sure everything is alright. But for our city, it's a bit different." Molly looked as if she was trying to find a way to put this so that Hazel would understand. Then she took the map she was holding and flipped it over so it was only a map of the City of Red Diamond. "We do have officers, but we now also have you. Have you ever really thought about why you're here? What you do? And why you do it?" Molly's question took Hazel aback. She never had thought about it. It was just something she happened to come upon.

She figured that in some way she was supposed to stumble upon that book, but she never gave much thought about *why.* Why was she the one who was chosen out of all the people in her world to come across that book? Why were the things she did in this world as important as helping the Queen and King, and as simple as helping a family get their cat out of the tree? Why did she keep coming back to Red Diamond, rather than throwing the book away and running, screaming, like any other person would probably do?

"I, I don't know why. I guess it's because since the first day I came to Red Diamond it has been my second home. I've become best friends with Calvin, and everyone here just accepted me for who I was. They didn't expect me to be anyone but me. Yes, they also expected me to help them when they needed it, but that was who I was. I love Red Diamond and the people in it so much, I don't even think twice before opening my book and coming here!" Hazel said. Molly Smiled.

"Hazel, we may never know who made the book that brings you here to Red Diamond, or why they made it, or if it was one person or thousands of people, or even if it was a *person* who made it. But we will always know why they picked you to find the book." Hazel stared in shocked at Molly while she stopped to cough several times.

"What do you mean you know why they picked me?" Hazel asked.

"Hazel, Hazel...if some *one* or some *thing* had the knowledge to make a book that could transport you from your world to ours, I am certain they knew, or at least suspected, that all of this was going to happen!" Molly said gesturing her arms around the room. "They also knew that you were going to be the brave, kind hearted and loving girl that you are, and that from day one you were going to fall in love with Red Diamond.

Hazel, they knew that when all was lost, Red Diamond would have you! That's probably why the book will have you doing things for the King one day and for a family the next, because you have a bond with Red Diamond that I don't think even the greatest king will ever have, Hazel."

Hazel felt tears coming to her eyes as she tried to even her breathing. It was all beginning to become a bit much to take in. Molly coughed and gave Hazel a sheepish smile. "However, I do think the book underestimated the danger a bit. You don't have to do this, Hazel. Despite everything I just said, you can back out now," Molly said looking slightly guilty over the fact that she had just told Hazel that she was responsible for making sure that everybody got home safely, without even asking her if she wanted to do it.

"Because, there is one thing I think you should consider..." She paused to cough. "You will not be able to travel back and forth through the book until this is over. Abaddon is almost as smart as Calvin when it comes to technology stuff. I overheard one of the guards talking about how they knew exactly where your book spot was, and how they were planning to ambush you when you next arrived in Red Diamond. I'm not sure what happened to the ambush, but I am sure that by now your book is in Abaddon's possession. I'm certain he has someone guarding it. He would let you leave, Hazel and you wouldn't have to deal with this. But you would never be able to come back to Red Diamond again."

Hazel didn't know what to say. She wouldn't be able to see her family or friends ever again if she didn't do everything just right. And if she did just walk away, she would be letting everybody in Red Diamond down and she would never be able to see Calvin again. Either way, she would loose people that she cared for and loved.

"I would risk everything to make sure that Calvin, Page and all of the other families in Red Diamond get home safely," Hazel said, knowing that her first and for-most duty was to the citizens of Red Diamond. Molly smiled, her eyes looking tired.

"It is going to be a long journey, but I know you can do it. Now, to get to where Abaddon has taken everybody, you're going to have to go through the woods," Molly said as she took the map and looked at the City of Red Diamond side. She grabbed the pen and with shaky hand she drew a line from where they were to a thick patch of trees.

She started coughing heavily. "Now it may look simple on the map, but the woods will be a difficult journey. They're forbidden to the public and unlike anything you've ever encountered. After you've made it through, you will come to something, I can't tell you exactly what it is, but let me tell you this – the first thought that comes into your head is the right one. And you will not die, trust me." Molly paused again. Hazel stared at her wide eyed. "I know that sounds odd and confusing, but it will make more sense as you go along," Molly said, her voice fading as she lay back in her bed. Hazel was far more than confused. Did this mean that the thing she was going to see could kill her? It wasn't making any sense! But she stayed quiet so that Molly could finish talking.

"Hazel, I am going to die very, very soon. I have never feared death. I have had a long and happy life. But I was afraid that I was going to die knowing that my baby Page and Calvin were in danger. But now, I know that they will get home safely because of you." She reached out her hand and Hazel grabbed it. "Now take as many supplies in our house that you can for you journey, and..." She started coughing, her voice fading even more. "... I forgot to tell you, Abaddon found a way to hack all of your gadgets and put tracking devices in them. Calvin found this out just the other day and he made you some new versions of the gadgets you already have. He didn't get a chance to do all of them, but you must destroy the gadgets you have immediately." Her voice was almost a whisper by now.

"Please don't go," Hazel begged, tears slipping down her face. " I...I'm afraid. I need help. I don't think I can do this by myself," Hazel said, but Molly hushed her with a smile.

"Hazel, it's good for everybody to be afraid of something sometimes. Just don't let your fear overcome you. Now make sure you don't open the box until you are safe in the forest. Please tell Calvin and Page that I love them very, very much, and that I will see them again someday." Molly started to cough and her eyes began to close, but she mustered up the strength to lift up her shaky hands and take off the necklace that was on her neck. She handed it to Hazel. It was a golden key with small red diamonds placed around the elaborated top, hanging from a gold chain.

"This will open the box. I wish you good luck. Goodbye Hazel," she said with a smile while grabbing Hazel's hand again. Suddenly, she looked up and chuckled softly. Her voice no longer sounded as if she were talking to Hazel, but instead sounded as though she were speaking to herself.

"Always remember, what goes down, will go up!" She smiled as if she had finally remembered something she had long since forgotten. Then she closed her eyes and passed away with a smile on her face. Hazel squeezed the hand she was holding and then slowly put it down. She took the map off of the bed, then picked up a blanket that was on the floor and laid it over Molly's body. Hazel smiled knowing that Molly had died happy. She wiped her eyes, picked up her box and went back into Calvin's room to find something to hold all the stuff she was going to bring.

Chapter Seven

The first thing Hazel knew she had to do was go get her gadgets, so she put the map and box on the counter and headed to the door that was in the corner of the kitchen. It looked as if someone had tried to break the massive metal door open but didn't succeed. Hazel put her left hand on the door and held it there for ten seconds. Calvin had made it so that he, Hazel, and Page were the only ones who could get into the room. Calvin decided that it should be everybody's left hand, because normally the right hand was used for stuff like that. If someone, like today, tried to open the door, they would get a nasty shock on their hand. And if they tried it too many times, it would give them a painful burn.

A patch of the door slid over to reveal an eye hole. Hazel pressed her eye against it and let the light scan her eye. After five seconds she backed away and waited for the door to open. But unexpectedly, another part of the door slid over to reveal a touch-screen keypad. Hazel's heart stopped. That was definitely new. Unlike Hazel's keypad, this one was all numbers, no letters. Hazel tried to think of things that Calvin would use. She tried typing in "1,2,3,4" onto the key pad, hoping that Calvin would go obvious as it wouldn't be obvious to others, and it gave a beep. "Incorrect, two more tries," the voice said. Hazel tried to think. Why would Calvin do a number pad!? Then she remembered that Calvin had once taught her a secret way to write notes. Every letter in the alphabet had a number. A was one, B was two, C was three, and so on. It was one step closer, but she still had no clue what word Calvin would use. And she knew that after three tries the alarm would sound and only Calvin's hand could turn it off. That was it! Maybe he used his own name. Hazel thought about it for a minute then typed in 3, 1, 12, 22, 9, 14. Hazel waited but the door beeped, "Incorrect, one more try."

"UGH!" Hazel said frustrated. What else would he use for the password? She only had one more try left, and if she didn't get it right then she would have to do everything without any gadgets! She wished more than anything that Clavin was standing beside her. Then Hazel knew – well, hoped – that she figured out the word. She took a deep breath in and typed on the key pad, 8, 1, 26, 5, 12. The door clicked and swung open. Hazel let out the breath she had been holding in and ran down to the basement, glad to see that everything seemed to be untouched. Hazel saw that her new gadgets were on Calvin's desk. Unfortunately she did have that many to work with, but she'd have to make do. Before gathering them up, Hazel put all of her old gadgets on the floor, found a board and started to smash them - every last one of them. When she had to smash her cell phone she closed her eyes. She had waited so long for that phone.

Some of the gadgets started to spark and Hazel hoped that they wouldn't catch on fire. Once she was sure they were good and broken she went over to Calvin's desk and started putting the new gadgets in her jacket. Right when she was about to leave she saw something on a separate table. It was a pack of gum. But Hazel knew it wasn't just any kind of gum, it was the gum Calvin was telling her about. It didn't look any different from when she was last there, so she knew that he hadn't had a chance to work on it. Hazel went over to the table and saw that there was a note.

Hazel. If for some reason you are down here without me (if I go to the bathroom, if my aunt needs me, it doesn't matter WHERE I am) DO NOT TAKE THIS GUM! I was not joking when I said it could kill you! I haven't had time to work on it so DO NOT TAKE THE GUM! DON'T TAKE IT! And if you do, I will realize that you did the second I come back from wherever I am... so there is NO point whatsoever in even trying. Please! I'm asking you as a friend, DO NOT TAKE THE GUM! Cal

Hazel took the note off of the gum, threw it in the garbage and put the gum in her pocket. Then she went over to her dresser to see what clothes she had in there. She only had two tank tops and a pair of shorts. She sighed but took the clothes out any way. Hazel then went back upstairs, shut the door and pushed it until she heard the click and knew that the door was securely locked.

Hazel went into Calvin's room to see if he had anything else she might need. Grabbing a couple of backpacks so she would have something to put her stuff in, Hazel looked under his bed and found a box that said "Camping Gear," but the box was hardly bigger than a shoebox. When she opened it, Hazel saw a bunch of little tubes. There were duplicates of most of the tubes but some said "sleeping bag" another one said "pillow" another said "fire set" and another said "blankets."

"Jackpot!" Hazel said as she put them in the front pocket of her backpack.

About fifteen minutes later, Hazel had packed all the camping gear, a few of Calvin's clothes, food, a first-aid kit, the map, Molly's box, some pens, notebooks, and a few other knick knacks she thought might be useful. Hazel sat down in one of the chairs so she could look at the map. Molly had drawn a red line from Calvin's house to a huge forest. Not the forest she had come out of, though. It was ten times bigger – at least it looked like it on the map. Hazel sighed. It would be at least an hour walk. She looked out the window to see if she could see the forest, but all she could see was, well...nothing, really. It was all open fields and the city in the distance. She thought she might have seen something brown in the horizon, but that was it. Then, as she looked out the window, she noticed that Calvin's car was in the driveway, and his keys were in the box hanging by the door.

Hazel, she thought to herself, *what are you thinking? You can't drive a car. You don't have your driver's license. But, then again... you have have driven a car before with Aunt Clair, Sam and Amber's Mom. You do know what to do... so it couldn't hurt if you just drove to the forest. After all, maybe the law is different here...*"

Hazel put the map in her backpack and went over to the key box. She reached her hand out to grab the key but then stopped. What was she doing! She could crash Calvin's car! And he would never forgive her. He built that car himself and it took him a long time to finish it. But there weren't even any other cars she could crash into. She was in a completely empty city! Hazel tried reaching her hand out again but it didn't seem to want to move. She had no idea why she was so nervous. Hazel sighed, she turned around and took one last look at the house, quickly grabbed the keys and walked out of the house straight for Calvin's car.

After unlocking the door, and shoving her bags into the passenger seat, Hazel slid into the driver's seat, put her seat belt on and adjusted her mirrors. She put the keys in the ignition, held her breath and turned the key. When the car started with a low grumbling sound the radio came on as well, blaring a song from one of Calvin's favorite stations. Hazel jumped, then sighed.

"Hazel, pull yourself together!" she said out loud "You've started a car before and you've even driven a car before. You're starting Driver's Ed soon. This is no biggie. And it's not like you can get caught!" Then Hazel noticed what the announcer on the radio was now saying.

"This is Alison from Aderdale, bringing you further news trickling in on the City of Red Diamond situation. It seems as if the entire city of Red Diamond has been abducted! This disturbing news has caused an uproar among citizens across the nation! A straggler who survived the abduction said that the whole thing was masterminded by King Billamore himself! This is truly disturbing news! What is Red Diamond going to do without our king? And if this is true that King Billamore is behind this, what could his motives be? We'll be back with more questions, and hopefully some possible answers, after this commercial break, sponsored by–"

Hazel turned off the radio, cutting off the female announcer. She had to hurry. Hazel took in a deep breath and pressed the gas pedal lightly, but the car shot backwards breaking the fence. She screamed and let go of the pedal. "No way am I doing this! What is wrong with this freak'n car?" Hazel turned off the car and looked at the dashboard.

Calvin had made it way more complex than any other car she had ever seen! She took in a deep breath and turned the car back on. She managed not to jump this time when it started. The dashboard lit up like a Christmas tree with too many lights. She couldn't remember if it had done that the first time, but it didn't matter. Hazel studied the dashboard. There was a red button that was glowing that said TURBO. She clicked it and it stopped glowing. There was another button that was lit up that said AUTO. She wasn't sure what it meant so she just clicked it so it would also turn off. Other than that, everything looked good. With her hands firmly on the steering wheel Hazel slowly pressed her foot down on the gas pedal and let the car start moving backwards. Pulling out of the driveway and onto the road, Hazel began driving toward the forest. The longer she drove the easier it got. After fifteen minutes Hazel felt like she had been driving for years. She loved driving! She made a mental note to make sure that if she lived, to drive more when she got home.

After about twenty minutes – without seeing a single soul – Hazel got to the woods. She pulled the car up closer hoping she could just drive through the woods to save time. But once she got nearer, she saw that there was no way she was going to get the car through the dense trees. Seeing a small clearing in the trees, she decided that this might be a good place to park and hide the car. She slowly backed the car up into the small opening in the woods, but as she moved the car backwards she heard a long screeching noise as a branch scraped the side of the car. Her heart stopped. Hazel turned the car off and went to see how badly she had messed up Calvin's car. With her eyes closed she walked over to the others side of the car. When she opened them she saw that there was a big thick long scratch going across the whole right side of the car.

"Nice," Hazel said out loud. Maybe Calvin wouldn't fully kill her, maybe he'd just sort of kind of kill her. Remembering that she had also driven through a fence, Hazel went to the back of the car to see the damage. It was all scratched up and there was a dent, a big one. "Really nice." She knew that there was no way around it, once she found Calvin, he was going to kill her. But she would have to worry about that later. Hazel went to the front of the car and pulled out her two backpacks and put one on each shoulder. Then she looked around Red Diamond hopping that it wasn't going to be the last time she would see it. She took in a deep breath and headed into the forest.

Hazel didn't really have a plan – she just wanted to go straight forward and try to cover as much ground as she could before it started to get dark. She looked around as she started walking. Within a couple feet into the forest she could no longer see Red Diamond. There were a ton of trees and she knew it was going to be a long walk. Hazel looked straight ahead as hard as she could but the forest seemed to go on forever. Hazel was wondering why there was no paths when she remembered that the forest was forbidden amongst the citizens of Red Diamond. A chill ran down her back as she tried to imagine why.

After what seemed like hours of walking, Hazel leaned her back against the tree and sighed. Her clothes were now muddy and her hair had leaves and bits of twigs in it. She was exhausted. Hazel pulled her watch out of her backpack to see how long she had been walking for, she guessed that it had been about three hours.

"Thirty minutes!!" She yelled as she looked at the watch. That was impossible! She got to the forest at around eleven, and her watch said that it was now eleven thirty? She knew that it wasn't broken because it was ticking, and she knew it was the right time because she had checked it with the clocks at the house before she left! It couldn't have been thirty minutes! It felt like such a long time! Yet it didn't look like the sun had moved at all. Hazel sighed and kept walking. A little bit later she took out her watch again because it looked like the sun was suddenly going down quickly. As she looked at the watch she couldn't believe her eyes. "Unbelievable! How could it be six thirty?" Hazel said out loud. "What is up with this place? What feels like three hours is only half an hour, and what feels like thirty minutes is seven hours!" Hazel wasn't sure if she was going crazy or if her watch was broken. She figured that talking to herself was one point towards crazy. But surely she would have been starving if she had walked seven hours straight because she hadn't eaten anything all day!

Right now, though, her main focus was to find somewhere to set up camp before it was completely dark.

Hazel looked around to see if where she currently was would be a good place to stay for the night. She picked up a stick and drew a big circle in the dirt to mark the area she would need to set her camp up in. Then she started removing sticks that were inside the circle. Once she was finished, Hazel knew the first thing she needed to get done was to make a fire. It was getting dark really fast, so she reached into the backpack and pulled out the tube that said Fire Supplies. Hazel figured she should read the instructions on the tube first so it wouldn't blow up on her.

"Step One. Gather up some large rocks and form them into a medium circle. This will be your fire pit," Hazel read out loud. She walked around for a little bit and found some rocks that looked like they would work. Then, she made a circle with them in the middle of her camp site.

"Step Two. Dig out some of the dirt in the pit. Then, gather some dry leaves and spread them out on the bottom of your fire pit. Use only enough to just cover the bottom." Hazel did as the instructions said but, without having a shovel, she was not happy about the amount of dirt that was now on her hands and in her nails.

"Step Three. Get some dry sticks and break them so that they will fit in the pit. When putting the sticks in the pit, place them long ways. Open the can. Place a little bit of the kindle in the sticks. Take some more sticks and lay them crosswise over the previous pile of sticks. Then, put another piece of kindle in the middle of it and repeat this process four to five times." Hazel looked at the can. "Why do they have to make this so complicated?" She thought about just throwing all of the sticks into the pit and lighting it, but she knew she had to do as it said. Hazel opened up the can and dumped the supplies that were inside onto the ground. She saw a box of kindle and matches but then she saw some rope and something that looked like a big sponge. Hazel took her sticks and kindle and did as the instructions said.

"Step four. Set up smoke catcher." Hazel looked through her supplies and saw a piece of paper that said Smoke Catcher. She picked it up hoping that it really would catch the smoke because she just realized that anyone in the forest could see her fire. She read what the paper said.

"To reduce the smoke of your fire, hang the rope above the fire and then put some water on the sponge. Drain out all of the water so the sponge is damp. Tie the sponge to the end of the rope. Make sure that it hangs over the fire. The sponge will soak the smoke up. Sponge should be squeezed every half hour." Hazel sighed. She would need a low-hanging branch to hang the rope from. They should mention this before you set up your fire so that you can set up your fire pit near a low-hanging branch. Hazel looked up to see how near the branches were. There was a perfect branch high up that was right above the fire pit, but it didn't look like she had enough rope. Hazel took some of the extra rope out of her back pack and tied it to the rope that came in the tube. It was practically dark by this point but Hazel found a large rock, tied it really tight to the rope and swung the rock over the branch and got it on the first try.

"Lucky swing," she heard someone say. Hazel swung around but didn't see anyone. She thought that maybe she had just imagined the voice after not having heard anyone talk for almost a whole day. Then she realized just how quiet it was, and how alone she felt. Hazel quickly grabbed the big sponge and dumped a little bit of water on it from her water bottle and tied it to the end of the rope. Then she grabbed the matches. Hazel struck the match and dropped it into the fire. She had forgotten to move the rest of the kindle, and the whole bunch caught fire so fast that it startled Hazel. She went to go take a step back and ran into something that she knew wasn't a tree. Hazel spun around and screamed as she saw a boy who was not much older than herself. She went to take a step back in the opposite direction, forgetting that the fire pit was right behind her. She lost her balance and felt dizzy. The boy grabbed her by the shoulders right as she was about to fall into the fire pit. Hazel figured that he had been sent to take her to Abaddon. Even with as dizzy as she was, instinct still kicked in and she started kicking and punching. Unfortunately, the boy's grip tightened around Hazel's shoulder while he blocked every kick.

"Whoa, calm down," he said as Hazel tried to squirm out of his grip.

"Who are you and what do you want with me?" Hazel asked.

"I'm Scott, and who are you, and why are you trying to kill me?" the boy, Scott, asked.

"Look, you're not going to take me to the king or the king's brother, are you?" Hazel asked. Scott loosened his grip.

"What are you talking about?" Scott asked, but Hazel took her foot and slid it behind his leg and pulled forward. As he lost his balance she lunged at him knocking him onto his back

"What the heck is wrong with you?" he asked, slightly winded.

"How stupid do you think I am?" Hazel asked pinning him to the ground.

"Well, not that stupid because I've never had a girl knock me onto my back, but you are stupid when it comes to *keeping* someone on their back," Scott said flipping them both over so that Hazel was now on her back. Hazel gasped, glad that the wind wasn't knocked out of her. At the same time they both rolled to the opposite side and picked up a stick and pointed it at the other.

"You're not that bad for a girl." Scott lunged forward trying to knock the stick out of Hazel's hand, but she jumped back and hit his stick, almost knocking it out of his hand.

"Well, you're not that bad for a guy," Hazel said as they started circling each other, the unlit fire in the middle of them.

"Now, do you want to tell me why you're trying to kill me?" Scott asked.

"I think you're the one who should tell *me* that," Hazel said. Scott laughed.

"I'm not trying to kill you! I'm trying to protect myself from you! And why would I want to kill you, or take you to the King's brother or whatever you said?"

Hazel took a closer look at Scott. He was tall and slim but he also looked strong. His clothes looked worn and dirty, but not as if he had been wandering in the woods for days. They just looked old. He was wearing a simple red shirt and khaki shorts. She could tell that he was studying her as well. She guessed she looked like a mad crazy girl, dirty nails, wild hair, and scrapes on her face. They got closer to each other and he started to lower his stick. Hazel began to do the same, but she flung her stick up knocking his out of his hand and pointed her stick to his neck. She started walking forward while he walked backward. When she had his back against a tree she moved her stick closer to his neck.

"Who are you?"

"Didn't we already go through this?" he asked trying to make a joke, but Hazel gave him a look that told him that she wasn't playing around. Scott cleared his throat. "I'm Scott, I'm eighteen years old. My mother and father, who were never really quite married, split before I was born. My mother died when I was thirteen. Her sister, who never liked me or my mother, made sure I had food in my stomach every day and gave me a roof over my head until I was fifteen. Then she told me I was old enough to fend for myself. I've been on my own since then. 'bout two weeks ago I went on a camping trip over in Trenton, got back today and there wasn't a person in site. I went to the market square and no one was there either. It looked like most of the houses were beat up. I saw a small piece of paper that looked like it fell out of someone's pocket – it said, 'Take every person to HQ. Bosses orders.' It kind of gave me a clue as to what was going on – er, well, not really, but then I saw you walking into the forest and I figured that you might be able to tell me what was happening and where everybody was."

Hazel took a second to process it all. She didn't quite believe him. He had a good story, but anybody could make up a story like that. Or, he could be telling the truth. But what were the odds that he happened to be camping whilst all of Red Diamond was being abducted? She still had few questions to ask him.

"What made you think that you could trust me? How did you know that I wasn't one of the bad guys?" Hazel asked.

"Well, once I saw that everyone was gone, and you were the only one left, I kind of figured that you were trying to fight whatever we are fighting against." Scott said. "But once you started attacking me, I started to have my doubts," he said with a sly smile. "Can I trust *you*?" Hazel looked at him.

"You can, but how can I know I can trust you? And, wait... did you say what *we* are fighting against?" Scott nodded his head.

"I can be fully trusted. I've fended for myself for three years now and I swear to you that I am not with the bad guys," he said. Then he smiled. "on my honor," he said as he put up his hand. Hazel lowered the stick and sighed. He seemed like he could be trusted.

"Look, um, yeah, I'm sorry – but I really don't know about this whole "we" stuff – I mean, I've got it handled, ok? But, uh thanks though," she said feeling slightly embarrassed. The last thing she needed was someone to come with her and slow her down.

"Excuse me? But I don't think you're able to tell me if I can or can't help bring the people of Red Diamond home!" he said crossing his arms. "And if you don't want to travel together and have help, fine. But I'm going to be traveling right behind you, because you're not the only one who's going to help out. And it's not your forest, and you can't tell me where I can and can't walk," he said as he unfolded his arms. "But I think that we would be able to help each other out, and I think it would be nice to have some company, and I am really helpful. I got a trophy at school for helping out the janitor so much," he joked. Hazel tried not to smile but she did anyway and let out a little giggle. She sighed. It would be nice to have company; she didn't want to go crazy all alone out here.

"How do I know a janitor's helper will be tough enough to help me?" Hazel asked.

"Didn't you hear me? I've been living by myself since I was fifteen! I started off with no money and no house! I think that says that I'm kind of tough! And I've been camping and hiking ever since I was little. My mom would always take me."

Hazel sighed again. It would be helpful having someone who's been camping before. She had only gone camping twice, and the first time, Amber's dad set up the tents and did the fire and made all the food. The second time, she slept in a cabin!

"Ughh! Fine, we can do this together, but I'm the boss! We break when I say we break, we walk when I say we walk, and we settle for camp when I say we settle. And when it comes to fighting, you can't chicken out, not that I can't handle whatever we're going to come across, but it will make me look bad if you run away. And if I say you go, you go. Do I make myself clear?" Scott saluted.

"Ma'am, yes Ma'am," he said with a smile. Hazel rolled her eyes. She looked around and noticed that it was just as dark as it was when she first started setting up the campfire.

"Ok, we need to get the fire going and finish setting up camp. Then, we can have something to eat," Hazel said walking back over to where she had dropped her matches.

"Sure thing, boss!" Scott said walking over to the fire pit. "And just to let you know, that was a lucky swing," he said with a smile. "And you didn't tie the knot around the spongy thing tight enough – it's just going to fall into the fire." Hazel glared at him. She couldn't believe this guy! She allows him to camp with her, and within two seconds he starts criticizing her!

"It was not a lucky shot, I just happen to have very good aim. And, I tied the knot just fine, thank you very much," she said. Just as she was about to light the match, the sponge fell into the pit. Scott laughed.

"Stupid sponge," Hazel muttered. Scott picked the sponge up and tied it to the rope again. Hazel didn't want to, but she had to admit his knot looked pretty nice.

"What kind of knot is that?" Hazel asked.

"It's called the Life Saver," Scott said with a smile. Hazel was starting to notice that he sure smiled a lot.

"I've never heard of it," Hazel said.

"You wouldn't have. I made it up."

"Why do you call it the Life Saver?"

"When I was thirteen, my mom and I were hiking. It was

our favorite thing to do with each other," Scott said as he started to get a distant look in his eyes. "It was just a normal day when we slipped down the side of a cliff. It was probably hundreds of feet to the bottom, but luckily we didn't fall too far because we landed on a ledge. We were laughing about how lucky we were, but then we heard the ledge starting to crack. She told me to get the rope out of my backpack and to tie a rock around the end and to try to throw it around a branch that was above the ledge. I did what she said making it on the first shot. I told her to go first and then lower the rope back for me, but she just shook her head. So I grabbed both ends of the rope and started to climb up.

"Once I made it to the top I told her to grab onto the rope, but she said she couldn't climb up the way I did. She said the branch wouldn't support her. She said I had to tie the rope in a knot on a tree. I didn't really know my knots that well, but I knew that it had to be strong enough to hold an adult. I'm not sure how I thought of it, but I quickly threw together a knot that I just knew was going to be able to support her. But just as I lowered the rope down and she almost had it in her hand, the ledge fell, and so did she." Scott's eyes started to water but he continued. "I screamed in horror, and not just because she fell, but because there was an earth quake. The ground every-where started falling, and the ground I was on just dropped out from under my feet. I began to fall in the same direction as my mom. I looked in horror at where the ledge she had been standing on just moments ago used to be. I was sure I was going to die. I closed my eyes and held my breath hoping that death wasn't going to hurt, but then I noticed that I wasn't falling anymore. And when I opened my eyes I saw that I was still holding on to the rope, hanging from the tree that had managed to stay rooted in the ground up above.

"I tried to climb back up the cliff but I couldn't. I was too upset and tired so I just decided to hold on to the rope until someone came and found me. I held on to the rope for three hours. It was pitch black by then. Just as I was about to give up hope, I heard people yelling my name and my mom's, and I just started crying because I realized that my mom was really dead, and she wasn't here anymore. But I managed to yell out to them, letting them know that I was there.

"They raised me up and asked me where my mother was. I started crying harder and I think they got the idea because I heard someone say "goner." I still can't really remember who the people were that came and rescued me. It might have been the guy my mom was dating or just someone who noticed that we went missing." Scott wiped his eyes a little. Hazel just stared at him not quite sure what to say. Scott stared back at her looking embarrassed.

"Look, I'm really sorry, you just asked me why the knot was called "life saver" and I could of just said that it saved my life once, but I guess I haven't talked much about that day, and it just feels good, you know, to sometimes talk about something sad to just help you move on. Especially with a stranger," he said with a small smile. Hazel nodded even though she really couldn't quite relate to his situation. She had thought her problems were bad, but his were much worse, and now she really wished that she could have made up with her mom and dad before she left.

"Anyway, let's finish getting camp setup," Scott said with a big smile, breaking Hazel out of her thoughts. Hazel lit a match and dropped it into the fire. Nothing happened. Scott laughed.

"May I?" he asked. He took the matches from Hazel, lit one, and touched the flame to several pieces of kindling. Then he began blowing the fire. The fire suddenly jumped to life. Hazel grunted.

"Beginners luck," Hazel said standing up.

"Oh, yes. I agree," Scott said sarcastically. Hazel rolled her eyes.

"Now, I can tell that you haven't had that much camping experience, so please tell me you at least brought some camp- ing supplies."

Hazel rolled her eyes. "Yes, I have these camping um, tube-ish things that have blankets and sleeping bags and all that stuff," Hazel said as she went over to the backpack, which was hard to find because it was now totally dark except for the glow from the fire. Once she found her bag she brought it over to the fire so she could see what tube was what. She dumped them onto the ground. Scott came over and looked at the supplies.

"Didn't feel like bringing a tent?" he asked. Hazel gasped. She hadn't realized that Calvin didn't have a tent with the other supplies!

"Um, yeah, I didn't want to bring a tent," Hazel said looking up. The sky was so clear and there where thousands of stars in the sky. "I thought it would be nice to sleep under the stars," she said, nonchalantly. The more she thought about it, though, it was true; it would be nice. Scott snorted and walked away. Hazel looked back down at her tubes and sorted them. She looked around to see where Scott was and then she saw him on the other side of the fire about a couple feet away from it. He was sticking sticks into the ground. He had two tall ones in the back and two short ones in the front. It looked as if he was making a square.

"Umm...what are you doing?" Hazel asked.

"You'll see," he said with a mysterious smile as he put the last stick in the ground. He walked over to the stack of tubes and started going through them. When he found the one he was looking for, he picked it up and flicked the top off and pulled out a rain tarp. He draped it over the sticks and it looked like a little hill.

"What did you do that for?" Hazel asked.

"Well, I can see you didn't smell the weather today," he said as he walked back over to all the tubes and sat down and started looking at them. "It's supposed to rain tonight...rain a lot. So the rain will fall down the tarp and not get us wet, since you failed to pack a tent," Scott said with a smile.

"Smell?"

"Yup," Scott said, " Hasn't anyone ever taught you to smell the weather?" Hazel ignored him and looked up at the sky again. It was the clearest night she had ever seen.

"Well, I'm sorry that I failed to "smell the weather" while I was trying to figure out where everybody had disappeared to, not to mention also trying to find my way around this stupid forest. And I don't think we have to worry about rain because the sky is very clear."

"Ok, suit yourself, but you will be thanking me in the morning," Scott said as Hazel picked up the tubes that had blankets, sleeping bags and pillows in them. She walked over to the "tent." It was surprisingly big. She took one of the tubes and opened it up and pulled out a small rolled up blanket which, when she unrolled it, was huge and surprisingly fluffy! She looked inside the tube and saw that there was another blanket! She pulled that one out too, and laid both blankets on top of each other so that it wouldn't be too painful to sleep on the ground. She opened up another can and pulled out two sleeping bags and then opened up the Last one and pulled out pillows.

Hazel walked back over to the fire. Scott was just sitting there and looked like he was shivering. Hazel noticed that she was shivering, too. It was as if the temperature had just dropped about fifteen degrees within the last few seconds. Hazel went to her pack and pulled out two of Calvin's sweat shirts. She put one of them on and walked over to Scott.

"Hey, do you want a sweater?" she asked as she handed the second one to him.

"Thanks," he said as he slipped it on. It looked like it was going to be too small, but he managed to get it on, barely. On Hazel, it was really big, but comfy. Hazel's stomach grumbled.

"Are you hungry?" Scott asked, hearing the gurgling noise. Hazel smiled.

"I guess I am," she said as she stood up and walked over to her pack. She pulled out two bottles of flavored water and a box of cereal. "I hope you're hungry," she said as she handed him the drink and then opened the box of cereal.

"I'm starving, and it looks like we'll be having a very healthy and well balanced dinner," he said as he took a handful of cereal and shoved it into his mouth. They both sat there for a while in silence, eating their food. Suddenly, Scott looked over at Hazel with a totally blank expression and asked in a puzzled voice, "Who are you?"

A chill ran up Hazel's spine. *Oh my gosh*, she thought. *He doesn't know who I am. Could Scott have short-term memory loss? Was she traveling with someone who needed to be in the hospital? This Is not good!*

"Um, er... what do you mean?" she asked in a shaky voice.

"Well, I mean, I've told you my whole life biography, and I know nothing about you. I don't even know your name and I don't think I've ever seen you around. Why weren't you captured by the people who took everybody else?" Hazel started laughing.

"Oh, my gosh! I thought you were going crazy on me!" Hazel said. Scott realized what she was talking about and smiled.

"Didn't I mention I have intermittent amnesia? I hit my head hiking one day," he said with a smile. Hazel laughed with relief.

"But seriously, who are you?" he asked.

"Uh, well my name's Hazel and-"

"Wait! Like *the* Hazel?" Scott asked wide eyed.

"Um, I guess?" Hazel said unsure.

"Wow, I mean I've heard of you but I've never actually, you know, seen you. I wouldn't have expected you to be so..." Scott paused as if trying to find the right word.

"So what?" Hazel asked defensively, causing him to blush.

"Nothing, sorry, continue Hazel... your story," he said.

"Umm, well yeah. I'm Hazel, I'm sixteen and obviously not from Red Diamond," she said. Scott stared at her expectantly.

"That's it?! I tell you my entire life story and you're Just going to tell me your name and age?" he asked bewildered.

"What more do you want?!" Hazel asked.

"Your life story! Now speak, we've got a long journey ahead of us and I only think it's fair that I get to know you as well as you know me," he said. Hazel rolled her eyes and then took in a deep breath.

"Fine. Well, my parents are divorced and won't even talk to each other, and when I'm with them they don't even care that I'm there – just that I make them look good. My mom is expecting me to become a lawyer like her, and my dad is expecting me to marry some ambassador person and sit around and do nothing forever and ever. I live with my aunt most of the time. She's a fashion designer and *she* doesn't want to force me to grow up and be a fashion designer, but wants me to do what I want to do. She gives me a lot more attention and support than both my parents together. So, yeah, it's really annoying because when I'm with my mom I have to act like I know everything about the law, and when I'm with my dad I have to pretended I know everything there is to know about being a proper young lady... and act like one, too.

"When I was ten years old my dad gave me a present. It was wrapped up beautifully and I asked him why he had gotten it for me. He told me that he and my mom were getting a divorce, and I was so mad at the both of them for breaking up the family that I never even opened the present for a while. I lived with my aunt for two years without ever spending a night at either of my parent's house. I liked to tell myself that it was my choice, my little revenge at them for breaking up our family. But I knew that wasn't true. My parents didn't want me with them because they needed to 'get their lives restarted' as they put it.

"My aunt made sure I felt right at home, which I did. I remember she got me a really cool bookshelf that had a secret keypad, and when you typed the password in, a secret spot would open in the back wall of the shelf. I remember putting silly little things in there like candy, or pencils. By the time I turned thirteen I had made up with my parents, and that's when my whole life seemed to get a lot more complex. Mom's house on Monday, and Tuesday nights, Dad's house on Thursday and Friday nights. I'm supposed to get to their house after school and stay the nights with them, but they're normally not there. They both work a lot, forget I'm coming, or cancel, so I get to go straight back to my Aunt's. I'm normally at my Aunt's house, which is my favorite place to be.

"Anyway, when I was about fourteen I was cleaning my room at my Aunt's house and I found the present that my dad had given me and decided to open it up. Inside of the box I saw the most beautiful book I had ever seen, and when I opened the book it had lovely blank pages. I stared at the pages, letting my imagination run wild in the sparkles and cream colored pages. But a few seconds later I looked up and saw I was in a forest, still holding the book. I was terrified, but I made my way out of the forest and I saw Red Diamond.

"Someone saw me walking out of the trees and ran over to me. I thought they were going to hurt me – so out of instinct, when they came near me I kicked them in the stomach and flipped them over. I started to apologize immediately because I had no idea how I did it, but the person just smiled at me and said thank you, and said that I had proven that he was right. He asked if I would follow him because he had someone who needed to meet me. Then everything happened so fast.

"He brought me to the King and Queen and they told me about a legend that told of a girl with hazel brown eyes who would travel to and from Red Diamond through a book. She would help Red Diamond when it was in need, and she would be good at martial arts. I thought the martial arts stuff was kind of a random thing to put in a legend but I guess I met all of the requirements.

"It was a lot for me to take in and they asked me if I would like to accept this honor. I thought, why not. It was really weird at first, but I got used to it, and then one day I met Calvin who lives here, and he asked if I wanted him to make me some gadget stuff to use because he was really good at doing things like that. Ever since then we've been best friends.

"So, whenever someone needed help – whether it was getting a cat down from a tree or stopping a bank robbery – I did what I had to do. Whenever there was trouble in Red Dia-

mond, big red letters would appear in the book that said
TROUBLE, and underneath that it would say what was wrong.
The book would start glowing red. I'd close my eyes and in a
moment I'd be in the beautiful world of Red Diamond.

"Right after all this started happening, I told everything to
my Aunt. At first she didn't believe me but then I took the book
and disappeared right in front of her. She sure believed me
then! About a year later I told my best friend Amber, and to this
day, the thee of us are still the only ones who know about this.

"A couple months after I first started coming here, I came
home all scratched up after I had a really bad fall here. My
Aunt hadn't known that I was sometimes in danger when I was
in Red Diamond, and she wasn't quite sure if she liked that
idea, but I told her I would be fine. Once she saw that there
was no stopping me from going back, she decided to sign me
up for simple self-defense and martial arts classes, which was
fine with me. My Instructor was really impressed at how good I
was at martial arts already, and that I just kept on moving up
and up with the belts even though I just started taking classes.
I just got my black belt yesterday. But I got in this really big
fight with my mom and dad because neither of them showed
up for my tournament.

"So today I decide to visit Calvin. I noticed that nobody
was around, but I thought I saw someone following me and I
think I heard them say that it would be a lot easier if I stopped
running. I think they said it through my ear piece. When I got to

Calvin's house, stuff was broken and ripped and it looked terrible, and his grandma – who was dying at the time because she was so sick – said that someone came and took Calvin and his Aunt Page. And when I asked her what was going on, she said that it was a king's feud, and that when King Nicholas died, his last Will and Testament only said who got a few of his things, but didn't say what happened to the rest of the stuff.

"Normally, the king picked his eldest son to be the next king, but it doesn't have to be done like that. So since the last Will and Testament didn't say who was king, they decided that Billamore should be king because he was the eldest. But of course his brother Abaddon thought that was unfair, but no one listened to him, and he left swearing to have his day on the thrown. Calvin's grandma said that the time for his revenge was now, and that Abaddon is holding every one captive in a secret place that only he thinks he knows about, but apparently she knows where it is too. So she gave me a map and told me that once I got out of the forest I would see something, and the first thing that comes to my mind is the right thing I have to do to get to the place. Then she thanked me and told me that she could die without having to worry that her grandson and daughter were in danger and then she passed away.

"I know any normal person would have gone running and screaming from Red Diamond on day one… but I didn't. Because from day one, everyone accepted me for who I was. I was never too young, or not enough for them. Everyone here appreciated me for who I was and what I had to offer. They never asked for anything or excepted me to be something that I wasn't... So, that's how I got to where I am now. Sitting in a forest with a city of people all relying on me to save them and having no idea how I'm going to."

Hazel looked at Scott. He was staring at her with his eyes wide open and a hand full of cereal still in his hand. Hazel wasn't quite sure why she had just blurted out her entire life's story to Scott. Guess he was right about the whole talking with strangers things. She did feel better.

"Wow!" he said with a smile. "Your life is confusing!" He laughed, but then gave a soft smile. "I am sorry about the grandma."

"Thanks, but I think it was her time," Hazel said as Scott nodded.

"You've been through quite a bit," he said.

"Yeah, but I guess it seems a little silly compared to what you've been through. I mean you lost your mom and didn't have anyone." Hazel said quietly.

"Hazel, just because what I've endured was different than what you've had to endure, it doesn't make your problems any less legitimate. We all suffer through things. Just because you have two parents and I don't have any doesn't mean you're not allowed to have it rough," Scott said sincerely. They sat in silence for a minute as they both started eating again.

"So what do you think we're going to have to do to get to the secret place?" Scott asked.

"I honestly don't know," Hazel said as she looked at the sky. TheY fell back into the silence for a moment. "Is it hard?" Hazel asked. "I mean, not having a family?"

"Yeah, it is. But I've lived without one for such a long time that I've just gotten used to it, I guess," Scott said as he took a long gulp of his drink.

"I just wish I could have made up with my mom and dad before I left," Hazel said feeling tears start to come into her eyes. "I can't help but think what will happen if we don't make it back."

Scott suddenly looked serious. It was probably the first time she hadn't seen him smile.

"Don't say that, Hazel. We will get back safely... everybody will. I promise you," he said. Hazel nodded. She looked at her watch to see what time it was – 12:30 am.

"What is up with the time here!? Sometimes it feels like it's been forever and it's only been a minute, and when it seems like it's been a minute it's been like three hours!" Scott started laughing.

"I guess that old cryptic lady didn't tell. Yes this place is forbidden, but it's more by choice. No one really knows why, but time *is* really weird here. For some people it's really long, for other people it's really short, and for some people it's always changing. It's impossible to keep track of time even if you have a watch because it's never really right. And the weather changes in the snap of a finger," Scott snapped his fingers. "We could have walked a whole day today and not even realized it because the sun doesn't always rise and set when it normally would. People have gone crazy in this forest." Scott yawned. "But I think I am going to hit the sack now," he said as he stood up and put his bottle next to the log he was sitting on

"Yah, me too," Hazel said as she put the cereal back into her back pack. Scott walked out of the little circle camp, went a little further, and then disappeared behind a tree. Hazel figured he was going to the bathroom and started to giggle. She stood up and put a little dirt on the fire so that the flames wouldn't be quite so high. Then she picked up her backpack and walked over to the tent, unzipped her sleeping bag and wiggled her way inside of it. She zipped it back up and fell asleep before Scott even came back.

Chapter Eight

Hazel woke up and stretched her arms out. She felt wide awake, but she looked around and saw that it was still dark outside. She turned over and saw a big lump with snoring noises coming out of it. Scott had his head by her feet and had about five pillows under it. Hazel figured he must have opened up more of the tube things. She looked at her watch and saw that it was only two in the morning. She sighed, quietly stood up, grabbed her backpack and made her way to the fire. Luckily the embers were still glowing. She found a stick and started poking the fire so it would start back up. As the fire flared up, it felt like there was a blanket of heat around her. A pleasant shiver ran down her back.

Hazel noticed that she was hungry and took a bag of chips out of her backpack. She looked up in the sky and stared at all the stars. She didn't know why, but all of a sudden she felt safe – shielded by the heat of the fire, by all of the sounds, Scott's soft snoring, the crackling of the fire, the crunching of her potatoes chips – she just liked the way everything felt.

When she was finished, she rolled up the potato chip bag and put it back into her backpack. As she was putting it in, she felt her hand brush up against something hard. Hazel couldn't remember packing anything that felt like that. She knew it wasn't the tubes because they were silver and smooth. This object was rectangle. Hazel pulled out what her hand was touching and gasped. It was the box that Calvin's grandma had given her. She had forgotten all about it. Hazel pulled out the key necklace that she had in her pocket and remembered what Molly had said. *'you mustn't open it until you are safely away.'* Hazel took a closer look at the box. It truly was the most beautiful box that she had ever seen. It was a deep brown wood color and almost had a treasure chest look to it, but it wasn't as chunky. It had an engraved design on it that ran across the whole box, with red diamonds around the rim. There were also two strips of wood that ran from the top to the bottom on both sides of the box. On the front side, the two strips had a lock in each, and the same red diamonds lined the edge. Hazel knew that now was the time to open the box.

She took out a flashlight from her backpack so she could see better and turned it on. Hazel pointed it at Scott to make sure he was still sleeping. Then she held the flashlight under her chin and slid the key into the key hole in the box. She heard a little click, did the same thing to the other lock, heard the second click and knew that the box was open. Hazel put the key on her lap and opened the lid. Inside of the box there were a bunch of letters and newspaper clippings. The first envelope she picked up had 'Molly' written on it in beautiful penmanship. She took the letter out of the envelope and started to read it.

Dear Molls,

Did your day at school stink as bad as mine? I swear Mr. Carter made the clock stop just so we would have to do more history and math! It really stinks that we have to go to separate schools. I sure wish I didn't have to go to the Royal Academy, The School For Boys In Training. Please! All they do is make us read and write and read some more and do some boring math. Then, for about a short hour, we get to go riding. I really wish it wasn't a boarding school. But at least I get to sneak away once in a while to go to our hideout. Let Mom know I said hi! Oh yeah, and I can't believe how much fun it is in the secret room!"

~ Nicholas

P.S. Hey sis, just because I'm at boarding school doesn't mean I'm not expecting my 15th birthday party! Ha, ha, ha.

P.S.S. Always remember, what goes down, will go up!

Hazel gasped. This letter was from a young King Nicholas, who Hazel knew was was King Bilimora's father. Did this mean that Calvin's grandma was King Nicholas's sister? Hazel guessed that the secret room he was talking about was the room that she was trying to find. Hazel read a couple more letters. They just seemed to be King Nicholas' replies to his sister's letters – just things like 'Your performance was great.' 'Sorry I was late for your birthday party.' 'Be careful on your date with Frank.' A couple of them talked about how much fun he had in the secret room. But there were a couple of letters that really got Hazel's attention.

Dear Molly,

I can't believe that Dad is really dead. Even though he was getting old, it seemed like it all happened so fast. A few days ago, he told Joshua that he knew he's been skipping his classes and that he knew Joshua didn't really want to be king, and that he wished Josh could have just told him. He said that he wants me to be king, and I told him that nothing would make me prouder. So now I will be the new king of Red Diamond. But I have to get an arranged marriage. I never really thought that I would have to get married at the age of 19, and I don't know if I want an arranged marriage. I can't wait to see you this weekend so you can help me through this!

With love,
Nicholas

P. S. Always remember, what goes down, will go up!

She grabbed another one and read.

Dear Molly,

I am still terribly sorry that I didn't go to mother's funeral. I know that you have told me many times that you will never for-give me and I don't blame you. It was an unforgivable thing I did and I have no good reason for it. I realized today that I never congratulated you on getting married, and I know the reason you didn't invite me – not only for missing mother's fu-neral but because, as you've said, I have changed a lot since I've become king. I've missed a lot of events that were very important to you, and you are right. I don't think I have ever even mentioned having you as my sister since I became king. I don't know why. I guess I have just turned into a foolish man. Dad told me not to let the power go to my head, but I guess in a way it has. I heard that you had a baby today, and I've heard that she is a very healthy little girl. I don't know if you have a name for her yet, but I think Page is a wonderful name. It re-

minds me of all the letters we've written to each other. I'm not sure if you will even open this one, but I hope you do.

Your brother,
Nicholas

P.S. Always remember, what goes down, will go up.

Hazel saw an envelope that was opened, but had no address on it.

Dear Nicholas,

I've heard that you are very sick so I thought that I would write this to you. I just want to make sure you know how I feel before you move on. I'm sure you know that I did decide to name my daughter Page. Also, my son Eli got married to a girl named Anna. In my opinion, they were too young when they got married, but they thought otherwise. They have a son now. His name is Calvin. They are struggling with money and I thought that you might be able to give them a little something to help them out. I miss you quite much, brother. And I thought that I would let you know that. I was thinking about giving you forgiveness, but the way you just completely turned me away when I came to talk to you today...

I had thought that maybe we could talk things out, but when your adviser came back out and said that you would not see me, I felt so hurt I just couldn't bear it. You have turned into such a different person ever since the day you become king. Joshua agrees with me as well. And in case you can't remember who he is, he is your brother, whom you have also denied. He said that this was part of the reason he never wanted to be king. He said that he was afraid that he would forget who his family and friends were. I thought that maybe you should think about this. I hope your wife and sons are doing well.

Molly

P.S. Even to this day, I still remember the little poem:
Before the evening sun's last glow, always remember where you must go.

Hazel stared at the letter. King Nicholas never got the letter before he died because Molly never sent it! All Hazel knew about Nicholas's death was that he had died really young. Hazel looked at some of the newspaper clippings next. Most of them were clippings about King Nicholas, but Hazel picked up one newspaper clipping that said in big bold letters, "ROBBERY." Hazel read the article:

There was a robbery at the local bakery earlier this week. The two robbers came in and demanded Bread, Muffins, Scones, Cookies and other foods. Police think that it may be the same two people who have robbed different banks and clothing stores over the past couple of years. No one knows why theses robbers have never been caught. Police say they must be very well trained because they seem to rob a place without any commotion. They also have never hurt anyone in the process. While these criminals are on the loose it is advised to keep your doors and windows locked, and to not leave your children alone.

Hazel wondered why Calvin's Grandmother would cut this article out and keep it. She scanned through the other clippings and saw one that had a headline that said,

LARGE REWARD FOR WHOEVER TURNS IN ROBBERS!

Then Hazel saw one that said: *ROBERS CAUGHT!* She read the article. *Today the police have finally found the two masked robbers. It turns out that the robbers were Eli and Anna Rain.* Hazel gasped almost dropping the paper into the fire, but she caught it and kept reading. *Eli and Anna Rain were caught as they tried to rob a new bank that was just opened. They pleaded to not be arrested. They said that they were only trying to pay for their rent and food for themselves and their young son, Calvin. Despite their pleading, Eli and Alice Rain were sent to jail. Their trial is set for a week from today. Their son Calvin, who is nine years old, is to stay with his grand-mother until a decision is made about his parents.*

Hazel quickly found another newspaper clipping that had a big title that said, *ROBERS: Missing? Or Dead?*

And underneath,

Today, when police came to escort Eli and Anna Rain to their trial, they found a hole in the cell wall. Police are unsure as to what caused the hole that allowed them to escape. But they also noted there is no way that the Rains would have been able to survive last night's tornados and violent storms that swept the City of Red Diamond.

Hazel stared blankly at the paper. Hoping there was more about Calvin's parents, she turned the newspaper clipping over and found a piece of paper taped to the back. It said:

Dear Mom,

Anna and I can no longer stay in the City of Red Diamond. It's not safe for us here. I'm not sure where we will be going, but it will be far away. There is no way that we can spend ten years in jail. I hope that you will take care of our dear Calvin.

~ Eli and Anna

Hazel couldn't believe it! Calvin's parents just abandoned him? They would rather leave him behind then do their time for the crimes that they committed? She had never asked Calvin about his parents before, but she understood now why he never brought them up. Hazel saw one last clipping that said Eli and Anna's bodies were found on the side of the road, dead after being caught in a tornado. Hazel felt tears come into her eyes. She felt so bad for Calvin...and Scott! They both didn't have parents, and she was lucky to have two, yet she spent most of her time being mad at them.

Hazel started to cry silently because all of a sudden she felt scared, scared that she would never see her family again, scared that she wouldn't be able to get everybody home safely, scared because she had no idea what to do. Hazel started to feel tired again, but as she began to put the letters back into the box, she saw a big envelope that she hadn't seen before. She wiped the tears from her eyes and pulled it out. It was a very big red envelope and it wasn't even opened. Hazel opened the seal, forcing herself to stay awake. She pulled out two letters. One said, "Open this first," so she did.

Dear Molls,

Boy it feels good to write that again! But I fear this will be the last letter I will ever write to you. The doctors say that these are likely my last hours to live, and that I best finish writing my Last Will and Testament, which is something I have been delaying for days. I'm not sure who I want my wealth to go to, who I want to be king, and all of those kinds of things. But today my advisor told me something that has made me sick to the bones. He said that I have had family members frequently come to visit me, but he has told them that I would not see them. I was devastated when I heard that you had come to see me and he turned you away. When I asked him why he would do such a thing, he simply said that family visits were a nuisance and a distraction to a king. I dismissed him immediately. He's lucky I did not have him executed! I am sorry that I did not know about this sooner. However, that is no excuse for me never reaching out to you.

I have to tell you something I have told no one before. I have a third son. We kept it very quiet, but I divorced my wife Elisabeth thirteen years ago. My advisors insisted that it would be disastrous if the public saw me unmarried, and decided it best to keep the ordeal hidden. They gave me one year to find a new wife. And if I did not, I would have no choice but to re-marry Elisabeth, with the public none the wiser about our divorce. Elizabeth graciously agreed to stay in the castle during that year, lest the public find out about this. Besides which, she wasn't too keen on giving up her queenship. So, we didn't tell anyone - not even our boys Bilimora and Abaddon. They were still at school and too self absorbed to realize anything was different.

During that year, I did in fact fall in love – with a girl whose name was Rose. We loved each other so much. One day I asked her to marry me, and she agreed. Still no one knew of the divorce and we weren't going to tell the public until after Rose and I were married. But only days into the marriage, the night before we were going to tell the public – she left me. She said she didn't want to be queen – she didn't want to live a life like that. I was heartbroken and I tried to talk to her about it but she said that she just wasn't right for me. Then she left. I was out of time and I had no other choice, I had to remarry Elisabeth. Over the years we seem to have worked out most of our problems and have made it work. It was only today that I found out that my advisor had scared Rose off. He had convinced her that if she truly loved me that she would leave, that publicly divorcing the queen would be too disastrous for me. But, a year after Rose had left, she sent me a letter telling me that we had a son. He was nice and healthy and his name was Nicholas Scottery Chapman. She said it would be best if he had her last name so not to cause any trouble for the kingdom. I have missed more than twelve years of his life, and have denied his very existence, but my advisers have told me that he is a wise and compassionate young man. My sons, Bilimora and Abaddon, are too foolish to be kings. They have been *fighting over who will inherit my thrown, and have engaged in other things that do not prove as qualities of a king. I've decided today that Nicholas should be king. Until he is of age to be king, I could only ask of Joshua, my brother, to fulfill my place, but only until the boy is eighteen.*

Therefore, I leave most of my material belongings to my son Nicholas and his mother. I have left a small amount of money to my two sons and a larger amount to you. But I mostly hope that you will open this letter and let my son Nicholas know I am truly sorry for not being a part of his life. I'm sure you are thinking, if you are reading this, why don't I just tell him myself? I guess I just can't bring myself to tell anyone I have a third child, a child whom I have denied for twelve years. I am ashamed. As well, I have mostly lost my voice and can barley move. I am truly sorry Molly.

With much love,
your brother Nicholas.

P.S. Always remember, what goes down, will go up!

Hazel just stared at the letter, unsure of what to make of it. She tried to piece together what she knew so far. Calvin's grandma and King Nicholas were brother and sister, and they had stopped talking to each other when he didn't show up for their mother's funeral. Later in the years, she forgave him at first but when she went to go talk to him, one of his advisors had turned her away. So that's why she never opened this letter! Reading this letter could have solved all of the problems that were going on right now! Now Hazel had to find the king's long lost son! And what was up with the way the ended the letters? The king always ended his with *what goes up must go down* and Molly had ended hers with *before the evening sun's last glow, always remember where you must go*." Hazel had not a clue what it meant! She rubbed her eyes. She wasn't sure how long she had been up reading the letters, but she was starting to feel exhausted. Hazel decided that tomorrow she would think more about what she had to do. But for now, she needed to get some more sleep. Hazel put all of the letters back into the box then locked it with the key, putting the necklace around her neck. She crawled back into her sleeping bag and fell fast asleep.

Chapter Nine

When Hazel woke up, her clothes felt damp, it smelt like rain, and when she looked up she saw that the tarp above her had rain drops dripping down it. She looked over at the dirt and saw that it was all muddy. Suddenly, she remembered that she had left her backpack by the fire. Quickly, she sat up but Hazel saw that it was under the tarp by her feet. She gave a happy sigh. Hazel figured that Scott must have moved it for her. Stretching her arms out, Hazel stood up, grabbed her backpack and walked over to the fire to join Scott who was already awake.

"I told you so! I told you so," Scott sang as he did a victory dance while poking the fire with a stick.

"Sheesh, I don't even get a good morning. You just go straight into bragging?" Hazel asked with a smile.

"Good morning! I told you so, I. Told. You. So! I told you it was going to rain, and did you believe me? Nope! So if I wasn't here, you would have woken up soaking wet! Along with all of your stuff!" he said with a smile.

"Ok, ok, thank you very much for building the tarp tent thing, and thank you for moving my backpack. I guess when I woke up last night I forgot to put it back," Hazel said as she sat down on the log.

"You're welcome. I was up last night too, and as I was heading back to go to sleep again, I saw your backpack," he said as Hazel took out bottled waters, bread, peanut butter, honey, and a plastic knife from the backpack. She started to make Peanut Butter Honey sandwiches – one of her favorite things to eat for breakfast. Hazel handed one to Scott.

"So, what's the plan for today, boss?" he asked before he took a bite of his sandwich.

"Well, I was thinking that we could finish breakfast, pack up camp, then just start walking," Hazel said as she took a sip of her water to wash the peanut butter down.

"Sounds good!" Scott said as he sat down. They ate in silence, and after a few minutes they were both done with their sandwiches. Hazel went to pack up her backpack.

"Do you have any idea how to fit the stuff back into the tubes?" Hazel asked as she walked over to their tent.

"Yeah, everybody here uses tubes for camping," he said as he picked up a tube labeled 'pillow.' He picked up a pillow and pulled a string that Hazel hadn't seen dangling on the side. Then he started rolling up the large fluffy pillow. Soon it was about the size of his wrist. In two minutes he had everything back inside of the tubes.

"How does that work?" Hazel asked as she took the sticks down from their "tent."

"Well you see," Scott said as if he was going to tell her something very scientific, "I really don't have a clue! I think when you pull the rope, it sucks the air out of it or something, but all I know is that it works!" Scott put the last of the tubes in her backpack.

"Ready to go?" he asked. Hazel nodded her head, but noticed that Scott was staring at her in an odd way.

"What?"

"Where did you get that? You weren't wearing it last night, were you?" Scott asked pointing to Hazel's neck.

"This?" Hazel asked holding up the necklace.

"Yeah!" His eyes were fixed on the key, fascinated.

"It was something I brought with me. Calvin's Grandma gave it to me. Why do you ask?"

"Oh, uh no reason... it just looked familiar," he said shaking his head, but he looked distant. Hazel watched him, finding it kind of weird, but she shrugged it off since they needed to get going. The sun was just coming up and already it was turning out to be a bright and sunny day. They both looked around at the empty camp spot.

"I don't think we should leave this area so cleared, just in case someone starts following us. We want to cover up our tracks."

"Good idea," Scott said with his smile back on. They spent the next few minutes putting the sticks back where they found them so it wouldn't look like anyone had been there. After they finished, they started walking, each with a backpack on their back – Scott wearing one of two that Hazel had brought. A short while later, Hazel realized that it was getting extremely dark.

"Hey, why does it look like nighttime? We haven't been walking for that long, have we?" she asked Scott.

"Nope, we haven't," Scott answered. Hazel looked through her backpack to try to find her watch but couldn't locate it in the darkness. She finally gave up, not really caring since time was so weird in this forest anyway. A few minutes later she saw the skies get brighter, as if someone had turned on the lights. Hazel found her watch and it said three p.m. Neither of them were hungry or tired so they found it pointless to break. It kept switching from bright to dark through the day. Hours later, Scott stopped walking and fell to the ground. Hazel dropped down next to him, tired of walking.

"Hazel, I am starving! I need to eat something!" he moaned as he grabbed his stomach.

"Me too," Hazel said as she took her backpack off and dumped all of the stuff onto the ground. She and Scott started grabbing whatever food they could find. They ended up eating some protein bars, cereal, and the leftover honey and peanut butter sandwiches. Hazel fanned her face.

"Why does it feel like a thousand degrees outside?" she asked as she gulped down some water.

"I told you, the weather here is really, really weird," Scott said, slightly breathless. "How long did we walk for?" Hazel started to dig for her watch. "What time did we leave again?" she asked.

"We left at eight this morning," Scott said having another water bottle. Hazel took out her watch then gasped.

"Oh my gosh! Its eight am! There is no way whatsoever that we could have walked twenty four hours without any breaks or food!"

"I think we did, and I don't think it was a very good idea either," Scott said grabbing his stomach. "I think we're dehydrated. We should drink lots water and get some sleep."

"I agree," Hazel said. She lined up the food and water so that whenever one of them woke up and were hungry or thirsty, they could eat and drink then go back to sleep. In minutes, they were sound asleep. They both fell into a trace of alternating between eating and sleeping. Hazel eventually woke up with a shiver and a sore neck. She saw that there was a blanket on her and that she was using Scott's leg as a pillow. She sat up and stretched. She was wearing a sweater that she didn't remember putting on before she went to sleep, but she still felt freezing. It was only then that she noticed that the forest floor was covered in snow. She saw that Scott was waking up. He stretched then opened up his eyes.

"Good morning, afternoon, or evening, I have no idea whatsoever what time it is," he said with a smile. Hazel smiled too.

"It snowed!" Hazel said in amazement. She picked up a handful of the snow and let it fall through her hands.

"Indeed it did," Scott said with a shiver.

"Did you put the blankets on us?" Hazel asked.

"I'm not sure. I remember you waking up and putting a sweater on at some point, and I think I did too, although I don't remember putting one on. And I think I remember dreaming about blankets, so I guess I did," he said as he stood up. They both started stretching their legs. Even though the ground was completely covered in snow, Hazel didn't think if felt cold enough to have actually snowed.

"How long do you think we slept for?" Hazel asked looking in her backpack for some food and her watch.

"I don't know," Scott said with a yawn. "Maybe twelve hours." Hazel found her watch and took it out.

"Oh my gosh! Either we slept for negative three minutes, or we slept a whole twenty four hours!" she said with a small laugh. "I've never even slept in past nine!" Hazel said as she tried to find more food.

"That's this crazy forest for ya! Twenty for hours of sleep and snow," Scott said with a laugh as he started picking up water bottles and food wrappers.

"Scott," Hazel said panicked.

"What?"

"We have a huge problem."

"What?" Scott asked walking over to Hazel.

"The only food we have left is a bottle of water and a protein bar! We must have eaten all of the food during our twenty four hours of being zombies!" Hazel said starting to freak out. "What are we going to do? We're going to die of starvation! What are we going to eat? Who knows how long we could be stuck in this stupid forest! I didn't think to bring so much food! I wasn't planning on feeding two people!"

Scott grabbed Hazel's shoulders and gently shook her. "Hazel! Calm down! We're not going to die! We're going to eat what food we have now, and then we're going to find more food when we get hungry."

"I'm sorry. You're right. I guess that the sooner we get to this secret place the better," Hazel said sitting back down, She took the bar and split it in half then handed one of them to Scott. After a few minutes they had finished the last water and the rest of their food.

"So what now?" Scott asked Hazel who was now lying in the sun.

"I guess we should just head out," she said. The two of them stood and began walking.

◆　　◆　　◆

"How much longer do you think it's going to be until we get to this place?" Scott asked after walking for a few hours. Hazel sighed. The snow had completely melted and had been replaced with a scorching heat.

"Scott, you are like traveling with a little kid! You've asked me that question over a million times. I have no idea how long it's going to take, and I hope just as much as you do that it's going to be soon. But for the millionth time, we'll get there when we get there!" Hazel said, her throat dry from not having any water.

"Ok, ok...you're right, I'm just so thirsty," Scott said.

"I know, I am too. I really wish we had some water. It's so hot out, and I think we've been walking forever. I'm starting to get hungry, too. It looks like the sun is setting, and I want to sleep in a bed...and I feel like I'm going to pass out!" Hazel said, sitting down and leaning against a tree.

"And I'm the kid?" Scott said with a smile. "I'm just kidding. Look, I know this is tough, but we've got to get through it. I know we can," Scott said. He started whistling a happy little song to himself.

"Shhhhh," Hazel said holding her hand up.

"Gessh, someone's a little-"

"Shh, listen..." Hazel said cutting Scott off. She was sure she heard something. She jumped up and started running forward. Scott followed her. She stopped and let out a squeal of joy. "WATER!" she yelled as they came to a lake in the middle of the forest.

"Ok, wait. We have to make sure it's safe to drink," Scott said as Hazel was about to cup her hands into it. Scott took something out of his pocket that looked like a thin white bookmark and dipped it into the water. When he pulled it out, it was a bright blue. He smiled. "We can drink it!" he said as he and Hazel both cupped their hands and started drinking the water. After they were fully satisfied, Hazel laid down.

"I don't think water has ever tasted so good," she said.

"I know!" Scott said plopping down next to her, then sitting right back up. "Hazel?"

"Yah?"

"Have you noticed something about the water?" Scott asked. Hazel sat up and looked around. Then she realized just how large the lake really was, not having paid attention before. She looked ahead and saw that although it wasn't too far to the other side, it stretched out to her left and right as far as she could possibly see.

"Well, you mean besides the fact that it's about two miles to the other side?" she said flopping back down on the ground, frustrated. "What are we supposed to do now?"

"Well, let's hope you know how to swim," Scott said with a smile. Hazel kicked him in the leg.

"Off course I know how to swim! I was on a swim team and I won first place, thank you very much," she said sitting back up.

"Why doesn't that surprise me?" Scott said with a smile. Hazel rolled her eyes. "But we don't even know how deep it is. We could walk right across it for all we know," he said as he stood up and started walking into the water. Hazel watched him gently wade through the perfectly still waters. Each step he got a little further out but the water never passed his knees. He got pretty far, but all of a sudden he was completely under the water.

"SCOTT!" Hazel screamed as she jumped up. Just as she was about to jump in, Scott's head popped up. She couldn't believe it, he was laughing! He was actually laughing!

"I...I...I'm, I'm sssooo, sorry," Scott said between laughs. He grabbed his stomach as he started walking back to her.

"Oh my gosh! I can't tell you how *NOT* funny that was!" Hazel said putting her hand to her chest as if to slow down her heart.

"I'm sssssooooo sorry, it was just too easy. I couldn't help myself," he said still laughing.

"I can't believe you did that! I was so scared! I thought you were going to die!" Hazel said splashing water in his face as he came closer to her.

"Ahh, ok I'm done laughing," he said smiling, running his fingers through it wet hair. "Anyway, the water looks like it gets about eight feet deep once you get past the middle part, but we'll have to be careful because it does actually drop off," he said as he got out of the water. Hazel, whose heart was finally back to its normal beat, tried to see how far they were going to have to swim.

"We're going to want to wear as little clothing as possible," Scott said, "even though the water is freezing. We have to swim fast because we have no idea what kind of animals live in there."

"Ok," Hazel said. She took off the sweaters she was wearing so that she was just in her tank top and shorts. Scott took off his shirt and tucked it into his shorts pocket. Hazel couldn't help but notice his nice frame, but when she realized she was staring, she looked away quickly, hoping he didn't notice and pretended to fuss with her backpack. She felt heat rising up to her cheeks.

"Ready?" he asked.

"Yup," Hazel said, standing up. But as she started to walk into the water, Scott pulled her back.

"What?" Hazel asked.

"Umm, are you planning on swimming with your backpack on?" he asked.

"I guess. Why?" she asked.

"Well, first of all, it will slow you down... a lot! That thing is heavy! And, secondly, everything inside of it will get wet!" Scott said.

"I can't just leave it here! I need the stuff that's inside of it!" Hazel said crossing her arms.

"You can leave it here and we'll get it on the way back, otherwise you're going to ruin everything that's in it!" Scott said. Hazel thought about that. She knew she had to bring the letters. If she didn't, then she wouldn't have the king's Last Will and Testament, and then nothing would happen as it was supposed to.

"What's so important in there anyway?" Scott asked, breaking Hazel away from her thoughts.

"I need to bring the king's Last Will and Testament with me and I need my gadgets!" Hazel gasped and stopped. She had totally forgotten about her gadgets.

"Huh? What do you mean the king's Last Will and Testament? He only wrote a small one that said his sons got a few of his things. He never wrote a larger one," Scott said.

"Ugh, long story short...I have the real one that says who the rightful king is. I'll tell you more later, but right now we need to get a move on. The sun looks like it's going to set and we want to get over the lake before it does," she said looking at the sky. Suddenly Hazel had a thought. She took off the backpack and pulled out the empty water bottles. "I have an idea!" Hazel took out the box that held the letters in it. She thought she saw Scott looking oddly at it but she didn't have time to think about that right now. She pulled out the letters the king wrote to Molly, his Will, and the newspaper clippings about

Calvin's parents. She rolled them up as small as she could and placed them in the water bottle. She turned the cap as tight as she could and hoped it wouldn't let any water drip in. Hazel took out her gadgets to see which ones could fit in a water bottle. She got the invisible bands, the sticking gloves and her mini compass to fit. In the other bottle, she got the string, gum and the lipstick to fit, but the other gadgets were too big.

Hazel took some of the supplies that were in the first-aid kit and put them into the bottle as well. She took one of Calvin's long sleeved shirts and ripped it so it was nice and long. Then she securely tied the bottles around it and tied it tight around her waist.

"Ok, are we ready?" Scott asked as Hazel finished testing to see if any water would get in the bottle.

"Ready as I'll ever be," Hazel said. She winced once she was in the water. It felt like she was swimming in snow. With Scott in front of her they started walking into the cold lake.

"Ok, this is where it starts to get deep," Scott said after walking for a bit.

"Ok," Hazel said as she held her breath and then started swimming.

After swimming for quite a while, Hazel started to get tired. She stopped and started to tread water so she could look around to see how much further they had to go. Scott did the same.

"We're almost there," he said. Hazel knew that was a lie because she could see that the shore was still a ways away. Just as Hazel was about to start swimming again, she felt something brush her leg. When she looked down, she noticed that the water was starting to get murky and thick. Her heart stopped when she saw one of her bottles falling.

Quickly and without thinking, she plunged her head under the water, dove down and started swimming after it, reaching her arms out. Hazel could faintly hear Scott yelling her name, but she knew she had to get the bottle. Hazel felt her lungs screaming for air as she kicked her feet and pushed ahead. She knew she couldn't stay under the water much longer. Her ears were starting to hurt from the pressure. Just as she was almost close enough to catch the bottle, she saw through the dark and mirky water, that it was one of the bottles with her gadgets in it and not the Will. She tried to reach for it but she couldn't, and she knew she had to turn around. She tried to swim back up as fast as she could, but just before she reached the surface she ran out of air. Instinctively, her body took in a big gasp, but instead of air, she just took in a lungful of water. Just then, Scott yanked her up from underneath the surface. Hazel started coughing out water until she could finally take in big gasp of air. She tried to start treading but every bone in her body was limp and weak and she started to go back under. Scott pulled her back up and had her link her arms around his neck so that it was like he was giving her a piggyback ride.

"Are you completely out of your mind?!" he asked angrily. Hazel knew that he didn't expect her to answer, so she didn't. Then everything went black.

Chapter Ten

Hazel grabbed her head. She felt dizzy. She didn't know where she was, and she didn't want to know, either. But deep down she knew the truth – she had died and killed Scott too. Now everybody was going to stay captive forever. She felt around her. She felt dirt. She took that as a sign that possibly she wasn't dead... She took in a deep breath and then let it out. When she opened up her eyes she saw Scott standing above her.

"Are we dead?" Hazel asked as she sat up. Scott laughed. She couldn't take that as a yes or a no because if they were dead, Scott would still laugh.

"Here, drink this. And no, we're not dead... although I suppose we could be. I don't remember dying, and I would have thought that-"

Hazel snatched the water bottle from Scott's hand, interrupting him mid sentence. The bottle looked like it had mud in it, but she drank it anyway. It felt nice to have the cold water going down her throat. Once she finished the water she didn't feel so dizzy any more. Hazel looked down at her waist and didn't see the bottles. She started to panic.

"What happened to the bottles?! Did I lose them in the water?!"

"Calm down, I took them off of you so you could lie down. The bottle with the letters is safe, the bottle with the gum and the first aid stuff is all good, but the other bottle – the one you almost killed yourself trying to get – is at the bottom of the lake."

"Thank you. It must have been hard carrying me and swimming at the same time," she said with a smile.

"Oh, it was nothing. I've got muscles, you know. Cutting down trees with my bare hands. Had to make a house out of something," Scott said, smiling as he flexed his arm muscles. Hazel rolled her eyes and laughed.

"We had better start walking again. We don't know how much light we have left," Hazel said standing up, her legs still shaky. Scott stood up and put on his shirt he had drying in the sun. Hazel shivered and wished she would have brought an extra shirt.

"Yeah, I think we should get pretty far out before we find somewhere to stay for the night," Scott said as he started walking. "Don't know what kind of monsters are lurking in the lake," he said with a mysterious smile.

"How long was I out for?" Hazel asked trying to keep up with Scott, even though he wasn't walking very quickly.

"Well, you passed out when you were on my back, and then you were out for about three minutes when we got to land, so I'm going to say about ten minutes," Scott said.

"Wow, you had to swim with me on your back for seven minutes?" Hazel asked, very glad she had let Scott travel with her.

"Eh, it was nothing," he said with a smile. Hazel smiled back.

"Then you won't mind carrying me on ground then? Because I don't think my legs are ready to walk yet."

Scott turned and saw how far behind she was. "Why of course not. Consider me your noble steed," Scott said walking over to Hazel, then bending down so she could get on his back. When Hazel was situated, they started walking again. After walking for a while the trees started to get thick, and it was getting harder to walk through them. At one point there were a bunch of bushes with thorns on them. Hazel slid off Scott's back so he would be able to walk more easily. The bushes around them were so thick that it almost seemed like night time. Then Scott saw light between the branches. He pushed the branch forward and then gasped and accidentally let it go. The branch flung back and hit him right in the face.

"Oh my gosh! Are you ok?" Hazel asked trying not to laugh, but ultimately failing.

"Yeah, I'm fine, it's just that I didn't expect to see what I saw," he said.

"Well, what did you see?" Hazel asked. Scott pushed the branches aside and walked out into a clearing. Hazel now saw what had taken him by surprise. They were standing on a ledge looking out at what looked like the Grand Canyon.

"Wow!" Hazel said looking around. Everywhere she looked she saw rocky mountains. It was amazing! She looked over the ledge they were standing on then quickly walked back. It looked as though they were hundreds of feet up in the air! Scott looked over the edge too.

"How high do you think we are up?" Hazel asked.

"Five hundred fifty-seven and a half feet," Scott said, backing away from the edge then looking at the ground.

"That's specific," Hazel said. But then she saw the look on Scott's face and understood. "Scott, was this where..." Scott nodded his head. Hazel noticed that he had a little blood on his forehead from where the branch had hit him.

"I had no clue that the whole woods was behind us," Scott said, but the last part of his sentence was drowned out by the sound of rushing water.

"What the heck is that?" Hazel screamed over the sound of waves. They both looked down over the edge and saw a violent whirlpool forming in the canyon waters below. Then it hit her and suddenly everything made sense. She looked up in the sky. The sun was just about to set and she knew they had no time left. She imagined she could hear Molly's voice, speaking the words of her letter to her brother, "*Before the evening sun's last glow, always remember where you must go.*"

"Scott! We're here!" Hazel yelled over the water. "We have to jump before sunset or we're going to have to wait another whole day, and then it might be too late." Hazel yelled. The water below was just starting to spin, rising higher and higher as if it were a tornado.

"I was afraid you were going to say that," Scott yelled back smiling. He grabbed her hand and squeezed it tight. Hazel wanted to push Scott off the ledge right then and there for smiling, but she knew that she wasn't going to be able to jump by herself.

"On three," Hazel said taking a deep breath, the noise of the water getting ear piercingly loud as the sun started to glow brightly. Scott nodded his head. "One, Two..." Then Scott jumped pulling Hazel after him.

Hazel was screaming so loud it was almost drowning out the sound of the rushing water below them. This had been her first thought and Clavin's grandmother said to go with it. Still, she couldn't help but think, what if Calvin's grandma was crazy and Hazel was plunging to her death! What if all of this had been one big mistake. The wind was blowing so hard that Hazel's eyes began to water. Her stomach twisted and turned as she soared through the misty air. She felt a blast of water on her face and she held her breath. Suddenly, they reached the spinning water and splashed into the waves.

She squeezed Scott's hand tighter but then felt a massive pull. All around her the waves tossed her violently back and forth. Her entire body flipped over, and Scotts fingers slipped out of her grasp. She held her breath as she felt herself turning and spinning rapidly in the tornado of water.

Then, all of a sudden she felt a thump. Opening her eyes, she saw that she was on a wet rocky ground. She quickly stood up and looked around. The whirlpool was still spinning around them, but she was standing in the middle of it all in a small clearing. It was like standing in the very center of a tornado. She stared up as it grew larger and taller, threatening to close up at the top and collapse down on them at any moment.

"Hazel!" Scott yelled from behind her. She could hardly hear his voice over the roar of water. She spun around and saw Scott trying to push a large stone block. She ran over to help him. The sun was a bright orange glow and starting to fade away. All around them, wind whipped and water splashed. They pushed harder on the block. When it finally moved, they saw a hole underneath it.

"You first!" Scott yelled. Hazel quickly slipped into the hole and looked up as Scott followed behind her.

She could see the last rays of sunshine as the top of the spinning tower of water collapsed in on itself. There was a large handle on the bottom of the block that they both grabbed onto after Scott hopped in. Hazel watched in horror as the water plummeted down from above. Right as they slid the the rock back over the hole, they heard the muffled sound of the water crashing down on to the rock, and then silence.

"What the heck is wrong with you!?" Hazel whispered as she hit Scott. "I told you on three! Did you not learn how to count when you were in kindergarten?!" Scott laughed.

"Sorry, it's just that I figured you would be really scared on three and might freeze, so if I went on two, you wouldn't be expecting it. Besides, I knew we were running out of time," he said.

"You know, we were about to jump to our deaths and you were smiling! I will let you know that I almost pushed you off that cliff myself right then and there. You *always* find a way to smile in every situation! It's not natural!" she said, smiling her-self and shaking her head as she started walking down the dark slope of the tunnel they were now in.

"Hey, I think it's rubbing off on you!" Scott said following behind her. As they walked to the end of the tunnel they were confronted with three different very large and tall tunnels.

"How big is this place?" Scott asked quietly.

"I have no idea, but I think we should just keep walking straight," Hazel said continuing into the middle tunnel, trying to look confident as she walked into the darkness.

"You'd think it would be darker than it is, seeing as there aren't any lights or anything. I think it's because of the color of the rocks," Scott said from behind Hazel. After he pointed it out Hazel noticed he was right. It wasn't pitch black, but it was still dark enough to stub your toe if you weren't carful. After they had walked for a while, they began to see even a bit more light. Eventually, they arrived at what seemed to be some sort of large door with a circular whole cut in the top of it.

Hazel and Scott peeked through the hole in the rock and saw a huge circular room. The walls and ceiling were, like eve-rything else, stone. She noticed large decorative pillars around the edge of the hall. About fifteen people, wearing white kitchen coats, were busy setting up tables. It looked as if there was going to be a huge party. Then they saw what looked like a big white sheet hanging on one of the walls with a projector not too far from it.

195

One of the tables was on a platform at the front, higher up than the rest of the tables, with two throne-looking chairs. Then Hazel saw someone walk into the room dressed as a king, but Hazel knew he wasn't. He had to be Abaddon. A small crowd of people followed him, taking notes.

"Is everything almost ready?" he asked someone standing next to him.

"Yes sir," the man answered.

"Good. Tomorrow night, I will announce the Last Will and Testament of my father that I," he winked dramatically, "*found,* saying that *I* am the true king. Everybody will see it, and know that I am the rightful leader. They will beg me to be their king. They still all think that Bilimora brought them here, after all. I swear the people who live in Red Diamond are the stupidest people in the world," he said with a look of disgust on his face. "Now, I must get ready for my big night," Abaddon said as he left the room. Hazel and Scott stepped back from the door.

"So what's the plan, boss?" Scott asked.

"Ok... yeah... what I said about the whole 'do whatever I say' thing, that was a long time ago. Things have changed. You've earned a new rank, now you get to make some of the decisions," Hazel said. Scott smiled.

"Well, I think that we should first find a spot to sleep for the night. It doesn't sound like anything is going to happen before tomorrow. Plus, I think both of us are far too exhausted to

accomplish anything. When we wake up, we will find the people, and then come up with the next plan. We just have to take
it one step at a time."

"Good plan," Hazel said smiling. They walked down the
hall looking for a safe spot. Hazel noticed a small stone door.
She pulled it open and found an empty space inside, no bigger
than a closet. She shrugged at Scott.

"I guess this will have to do," she said, walking in.

◆　　　◆　　　◆

Hazel awoke with a start and a kink in her neck from
sleeping on the hard ground. She quickly looked at her watch.
It was already noon. She gasped, shooting up. She pulled her
legs in, which Scott had been using as a pillow, and his head
fell down to the hard ground.

"Ow!" Scott yelled, waking up painfully. "Come on! Can't I
at least have until after breakfast before you start hurting me?"
Hazel rolled her eyes and stood up.

"It's already noon! We need to hurry!" she said, walking
into the hallway.

"Which way?"

"I think we should split up," Hazel said.

"I'm not so sure that's a good idea," Scott responded.

"It's the only way. And if it's been more then fifteen minutes and we haven't run into each other yet, we'll just meet up back here," Hazel said.

"But..."

"No but's! I'm in charge, remember?" Scott rolled his eyes.

"Ok, but just remember that this was your idea," he said with a sly smile.

"I know," Hazel snapped as she turned around and headed in the opposite direction as him. She walked quickly but quietly. Hazel didn't like how dark it was, but finally she saw some light just around the corner. It was a window. She looked through it and saw a huge white carpeted circular room with six long white hallways radiating out from the circular room like spokes on a wheel. Each hallway was also carpeted with doors running along both sides of it's hall. Down below there were about twenty people who were wearing white work coats. Several were pushing what looked like food carts down the hallways. Hazel saw one person knock on one of the many wooden doors against the stone walls of the hallways, and turn the handle to open it up. They walked inside with two trays of food. This must be where they were keeping everybody, Hazel realized. Suddenly her thoughts were interrupted when she heard her name being called. Then she felt someone tap her shoulder. Just as she was about to scream, a hand covered her mouth.

"I told you splitting up was a bad idea!"

Hazel spun around and saw that the hand belonged to Scott.

"What are you doing?! Do you enjoy scaring me to death?" Hazel asked.

"It was *your* idea to split up! I got about twenty feet then I hit a dead end!"

"Ok, I don't think I can take a scare like that again," Hazel said, "so we're going to stick together from now on."

"That is a great idea, oh mighty one," Scott said bowing. "If only I could have come up with such a grand idea," he said sarcastically. Hazel rolled her eyes.

"I found where all the people are staying," Hazel said.

"Good," Scott said looking out the window.

"I figured we could just stay here until they're done serving everyone their food, and then go and find which room Calvin is in. And then we can come up with a plan from there."

"Who's Calvin again?" Scott asked.

"The person who makes all my gadgety stuff," Hazel said.

"The name sounds so familiar," Scott said curiously.

"Hmmm…well maybe as there's all of one school in Red Diamond, maybe you've run into him before!" Hazel said sarcastically.

"Huh…" Scott replied as he searched his memory. After a few moments, the last person hung up their white coat and left the room.

"Ready?" Hazel asked.

"Yup," Scott answered. Hazel looked out the window and saw that there was a narrow ledge that circled around the room. If she climbed out the window out onto the ledge and walked across for several feet, there were some heavy drapes that she would be able to use to climb down. Hazel put one leg out the window and started to rest her weight on the ledge.

"Umm, can I ask what you might be doing?" Scott asked.

"What does it look like I'm doing?" Hazel snapped. "I'm going down there. Do you have a better idea on how to get down there?"

"Well, I was thinking we could take the stairs over there..." he said as he pointed to the staircase that was tucked away in the corner.

"Well, I thought this way would be more fun, but we can do it your way," Hazel said as she climbed back through the window.

"Yeah, sure," Scott said as he started quietly walking down the stairs with Hazel following close behind him.

"Wait!"

"What?" Scott asked sounding slightly annoyed.

"We've got dirt all over our shoes! If we walk across the white carpet someone's going to know we're here!"

"Oh, right." Scott said. Hazel took her hand and started running it down the brick wall.

"What are you doing?"

"Trying to find a hole or something in this rock wall to hide our shoes," Hazel said. She started moving her way back up the stairs when she felt a loose rock sticking out. She slid it to the side making just enough room for them to hide their shoes. "Here, take off your shoes," Hazel said as she took hers off and shoved them into the hole. Scott did the same. Then Hazel started to take off her tank top.

"Whoa, what are you doing?" Scott asked covering his eyes with his hand. Hazel rolled her eyes.

"I have another shirt on rock-head." Hazel took off her blue tank top leaving her with her pink spaghetti strap shirt. They used her blue shirt to quickly wipe off the dirt and mud that was on their hands, faces, and feet. When they had cleaned up as best as they could, they shoved the shirt in with the shoes. Hazel took the Will and other items from the water bottle and put them in her pocket. Scott took out the first-aid bottle and emptied the items into his pockets. He gave the bottle to Hazel who then crammed a bottle into each of her shoes. Hazel shivered as she pulled the rock back into place.

"Ready?" Scott asked.

"Yeah," Hazel said jumping up and down a little on the cold floor. She was nervous, having no idea what to expect.

Chapter Eleven

Scott grabbed the handle that was on the door and pulled it open.

"Alright, stay close!" he said, walking through. Hazel followed him and looked around and saw that there were actually nine hallways sprawling out from the center.

"Ok, let's get those coats and shoes on," Scott said quickly running over to the rack with Hazel right behind him. They both slid on a pair of slippers and a white coat.

"I hate to say this, but... I think we should split up to look for Calvin," Hazel said wrapping the coat tightly around her, just realizing how cold she was.

"You look like a doctor in that coat!" Scott laughed. Hazel glared at him. "Right, always Miss Business. Anyway, *we* said

202

that we *weren't* going to split up anymore because *you* are so jumpy. Also, I don't even know what this Calvin looks like."

"Firstly, you don't look any less like a doctor than I do. Secondly, I'm not always Miss Business. And thirdly, you wouldn't have to know what Calvin looks like, you just have to ask if his name is Calvin. Then you'd come and find me – that is, if I don't find him first. And, I am not jumpy, you always just sneak up on me! Sorry, but we *are* going to split up because it's the best and fastest way to find him!" Hazel said turning around and starting down one of the hallways before Scott could protest.

She walked over to one of the doors. Just as she was about to knock, she jumped as she felt a tap on her shoulder.

"Miss, might I ask what you are doing? We just served the prisoners their snack and we were told not to come back until dinner," a deep male voice said.

"I was just... you see...I wwas ..." She turned around. "I hate you!" Hazel said in a stern whisper as she saw Scott standing there with his arms crossed.

"Awww, I hate you too," Scott said smiling. "See what I mean? You weren't even by yourself for more than two seconds! You could be *expecting* me to do something and you would *still* jump!"

"I would not!" Hazel said crossing her arms.

"Ok, turn around, then I'll do something on the count of three."

"Fine," Hazel said turning around, knowing fully well that he was going to do it on two.

"One...two..." Hazel held her breath waiting for something to happen. She breathed out and Scott poked her sides with his index fingers. She jumped and let out a squeal.

"Ok, so I'm jumpy! I can't help it. I'm freezing and I'm nervous," she said.

"All right. There are doors on both sides of the hall. I'll cover this side and you cover that side," Scott said.

"Fine," Hazel said walking over to the door that was in front of her and knocking on it. She peered inside, opening it up slowly. Behind the door was what looked like a cave the size of a single room apartment. It was slightly damp and cold with uneven rocky walls and celling. A large yellow rug was covering the stone ground and seemed oddly out of place. On each side of the room were two small beds and in the far corner a TV rested on a small wooden table. Carved into the walls were lights that shone brightly. A door, which lead to what Hazel assumed was a bathroom, was placed at the back of the room.

"Yes?" a small voice asked. Hazel noticed a girl, her eyes red and swollen. Hazel saw that there was another girl in the room who looked like she was about eight. More than anything she wanted to rush into the room and hug both of the girls and help them find their parents, but she heard Scott talking to someone and was reminded that she couldn't blow her cover.

"Yes, I am looking for a Calvin or a Page," Hazel said. The girl shook her head.

"No, just me and my sister, Jackie," she said. Hazel stared at the little girl and realized that Hazel had helped her once before when she had gotten stuck in a tall pine tree. Hazel held back the urge to cry.

"All right, thank you," Hazel said as she backed out of the room and closed the door.

"I feel terrible!" Scott said as both of the doors shut at the same time.

"Me too! We have to help them!" Hazel said.

"I had a boy and a girl in there who were both ten! And they have no idea where their mom and dad are!" Scott said.

"I know, which is why we need to find Calvin fast," Hazel said as she knocked on the next door. She opened it up and saw a girl who looked about thirteen. There were three others girls in the room who looked the same age. Unlike the watery eyed girl from the previous room, this one was smiling.

"Hi, I'm looking for a Calvin or a Page," Hazel said realizing she was sounding too polite. "Kings order," she added as sternly as she could.

"No, haven't seen him or her. Is he cute? That's the only thing this place needs is cute boys! But this is still the best place in the world! No school. We get to watch TV and hang out all day! No chores or nagging parents or annoying siblings! This place is great. I told Rachel that my slumber party would

205

beat her slumber party, but she was like, *no way*, and I was like, *um yes way.*" Hazel closed the door on the girl. Scott was laughing. He hadn't knocked on his next door yet.

"That was weird," Hazel said as she knocked on the next door. Hazel and Scott repeated this for eight hallways, each hallway having around twenty five doors on each side. But still no sign of Calvin or his aunt. Each time they opened the door, there were either frightened people, angry people, or some kids who were taking this like it was a vacation.

"We've only got one hallway left," Hazel said.

"Yah, but this one's kind of weird. It only has doors on one side," Scott said looking down the hallway. "I'll start at the far end of the hallway then meet up with you in the middle," Scott said as he started jogging down the hallway. Hazel knocked on the first door. There was no answer. Hazel tried to remember if there was anybody serving food in this hallway. She was sure that there was at least someone down this way. She grabbed onto the door knob and it opened.

There was no one inside – it was an empty room. It was like that for the next twelve doors. Then she met Scott in the middle at the door she was about to knock on.

"All of the rooms have been empty," Scott said.

"I know, same with mine," Hazel said confused.

"Wait, I think I hear something from this room," Scott said pushing his ear against the door they were standing in front of. He knocked. No one came to the door. He knocked again. He put his hand on the door knob and tried to open it, but it didn't turn. Scott reached his hand into his pocket and pulled out a key card and put it into the slot in the door. He pulled it out once he heard it unlock. Scott pushed against the door, but it still didn't open.

"There's someone in here and they're pushing against the door so we can't open it," Scott whispered.

"We'll break the door down on three," Hazel said just loud enough for the person inside to hear them. Hazel noisily took a few steps backward to alert the person inside the room that they were getting ready to charge the door. Scott had his hand on the knob and his shoulder on the door.

"One, Two...." Scott easily pushed the door open a few inches since the person inside still had his guard down, expecting that there was going to be a crash on three. The person in the room furiously tried to push the door closed. Scott tried to heave his body through the small opening, but someone else inside started swatting him with a magazine.

"Go away!" the voice behind the magazine yelled.

"Let us in first!" Scott demanded. With one big push, Scott and Hazel shoved the door open, pinning the person behind it against the wall. The other person with the magazine jumped backward hitting her head against a shelf. Hazel and Scott immediately lost their balance after their final push and fell to the floor in a pile, painfully bumping their heads together.

"Ow!" everyone in the room said at the same time. Scott, who was the first to recover, grabbed his head with one hand and looked around the room. He managed to shut the door with his foot so he was able to see who was behind it. The person was holding his hand to his head to stop the little bit of blood that was trickling down his forehead. Scott stood up and gave Hazel his hand to help her up. He glanced at the woman grasping the magazine.

"Mrs. Change?" Scott said dropping Hazel.

"Owwww," Hazel said as she fell back to the floor. Scott turned around to look at the person who had been behind the door.

"Robber?" Scott asked in amazement.

"Nick?" both people said at the same time.

"Nick?" Hazel asked. She quickly sat up to take a look at the people who had caused all of this commotion, but the pain rushed to her head and she had to lay back down and close her eyes.

"Hazel?" The person who was holding the magazine said. Hazel finally recognized the voice.

"Ms. Page?" Hazel asked sitting up slower this time. "Calvin?" Hazel bewilderedly asked, looking at the person who had been behind the door. Hazel stood up and faced Scott. "Nick?" she asked angrily.

"Hazel?" Calvin asked walking over to her.

"Ok, I think we're clear on the names here...sort of," Hazel said glancing at Scott who shrugged sheepishly.

"How are you here?" Calvin asked in shock.

"Well, it wasn't exactly easy," Hazel said looking at Calvin's head. "You're bleeding! Scott, can I see the firs-aid stuff?" Hazel asked.

"Scott?" Calvin and Page said at the same time. Scott blushed.

"Sure," Scott said taking a bandage out and handing it to Hazel. She put it on Calvin's cut. Then she turned to Scott. "Alright, lets start at the beginning, shall we! Why did you call them Mrs. Change and Robber?" Hazel asked Scott.

"I thought that your description of Calvin sounded familiar. I just didn't think that you would have Robber build you gadgets. I didn't even think he knew how to make gadgets!" Scott said, causing Calvin grimace.

"Why do you keep calling him Robber? And how do you know them?" Hazel demanded.

"Since when did you start going by Scott?" Calvin asked before Scott could answer Hazel's questions. "And why are you with Hazel?" he said accusatively.

"Oh, am I not good enough company for Hazel? Because to me it seems a bit shocking that she would be hanging out the likes of of you," Scott shot back.

"Hello?! What about my question! How do you all know each other?" Hazel asked angrily, sensing that their past wasn't exactly a pleasant one. Page smiled.

"I used to go over to Nick's aunt's house to visit with her. We used to like to have tea and catch up with each other. I would bring Calvin along with me to hang out with Nick. I think Calvin was about thirteen at the time," Page began.

"Ok, my turn," Calvin interrupted. "Why are you going by *Scott*?"

"My birth name is Nick. However, I've been going by Scott since I was like five. It was always the name my mother called me by. But when I lived with my aunt, and was introduced to Calvin, she refused to call me or allow me to introduce myself as Scott. But to everyone else, I'm always Scott," Scott said in one breath with an eye roll. "My turn, how do you know Robber?" he asked Hazel.

"We met in one of my first couple trips to Red Diamond. My turn again," Hazel said. "Why do you keep calling Calvin 'Robber' and Ms. Page 'Mrs. Change'? That's not even her last name!" Hazel said.

"Well, it *was* my last name," Page explained. "I was married once, but my husband and I separated, so for a long time I *was* known as Mrs. Change."

"Oh, I'm sorry. I had no idea," Hazel said.

"Don't worry, it was a long time ago," Page said with a smile.

"And as for your question," Scott began, "of why I call Calvin 'Robber'... well, I think you could tell her, *Calvin*. I mean, a good friend wouldn't keep a secret like that from such a good friend, would he?" Scott sounded angry as he glared at Calvin, who was looking down at the floor. Hazel looked from Scott to Calvin. Why was Scott acting so rude toward him? And what wasn't Calvin telling her?

"Hazel, I know this might be hard to believe, but there is a secret about Calvin you don't know about," Scott said. Hazel assumed that he was talking about Calvin's parents, and she couldn't believe that Scott was bringing that up so rudely.

"Scott, I already know about Calvin's parents. We don't need to discuss it any further," Hazel said giving Calvin a sympathetic glance. Calvin and Page looked at Hazel with surprise.

"I *know* you know. You had those newspaper clippings." Scott responded.

"How did *you* know I had those clippings?" Hazel asked defensively.

"I saw you reading them," Scott said casually. "anyway, Calvin here decided that he was going to take after his parents and became a thief. At school he would steal the other kid's lunches or pens or notebooks. And whenever he was over at my house, he just couldn't resist – so when he saw something of mine that he liked, he would just take it," Scott said looking at Calvin. "Now, I'm not one to hold grudges, but I *do* hold a grudge when someone steals the only thing I have left of my mom's."

Hazel was in shock. She didn't know what to say.

"Calvin, is this true?" Hazel asked. Calvin mumbled some words and shifted his feet.

"I was young. I didn't know any better. My parents abandoned me, and what little they had taught me was that stealing was a good thing. I guess I just thought that it was ok," Calvin said. Hazel gave him a look that said *"you have got to be kidding me!"*

"Ok, so I *knew* what I was doing was wrong," he said with a sigh. "but I couldn't help it! No one ever even gave me a chance! Whenever I went somewhere, or to school, people would always say, "Be careful of Calvin Rain!" They just assumed I was a thief like my parents! So I guess I just figured that since they already had a fixed picture in their mind of who and what I was, that it wouldn't hurt to take a few things here and there!"

"Calvin! I can't believe you would do something like that!" Hazel said, then looking at Scott she asked, "What did he take from you?"

"It was a beautiful brown box with red diamonds on it. And it had a gold key, with red diamonds on it as well. It was the last thing that my father gave my mother," Scott said looking at Hazel's neck. She grasped the key. "When I first saw the box, I figured that you could have just had one exactly like it.

But when I saw the key, then I figured that somehow you had gotten the box from Calvin." Hazel glared at Calvin.

"Ok, ok...so, it was my grandma's birthday, and I knew that she would love it. When she asked me where I had gotten it, I told her I had found it. She gave me this really stern look, so I told her I took it from one of my friends. She told me I had to take it back. I told her that my friend really didn't like it, and that he probably didn't even want it anymore, and I promised her that I would ask if I could have it. She said that that would be ok, but that even if he said I could have it that I still had to apologize for taking it without asking. Obviously I never did, and she never brought it up again." Calvin looked back down at the floor.   "I'm not proud about that period of my life," Calvin continued. "You need to know that who I am today doesn't even resemble who I was back then. When I lived with my Grandmother, she loved me and taught me things that my parents never did. She changed me." He looked pleadingly at Hazel and Scott. Then, just to Scott, "I am truly sorry, Nick... er... Scott. I will make it up to you however I can... I promise. But I especially want you to know... you haven't seen me for a lot of years. I've spent what seems like a lifetime learning about myself from my aunt and my Grandma... unlearning the lessons of my parents and becoming something I can be proud of." Hazel gasped realizing that she had to tell Calvin that his grandma was dead. She tried to swallow, but her mouth was too dry.

"There's something I have to tell you two," Hazel began before Scott could respond. "I went to your house and I saw all your stuff messed up. I talked with your grandma. She was really sick... I mean really sick... and I'm really sorry, but she, umm..." Hazel didn't know how to put it. Page put her hand on Hazel's shoulder.

"She passed away?" Page asked in a quiet voice. Hazel nodded her head.

"She was with us for longer than we thought she would be. I'm sure she's happy now." Page smiled.

"At least she'll be with her brother now," Hazel said without thinking.

"Her brother? She was an only child..." Calvin said confused.

"You know what, I recall her carrying on one day about having a dumb stuck up brother," Page said. "You know how peoples thoughts begin to get confused when they get sick."

Suddenly a voice spoke through a speaker in the room.

"Attention ladies and gentlemen. As you know, today is the Queen's birthday, so we will be having a special celebration," boomed king Bilimora's voice over the intercom, sounding tired and sad.

So he is here as well! Hazel though to herself. The king continued.

"Dinner will be served in half an hour. You will be given appropriate clothing to wear in five minutes. You must wear them and come and enjoy the celebration, or you will have to suffer the consequences."

There was a click and then the voice was gone.

"For Pete's sake!" Page said. "We have been here for two weeks without a change of clothes, and now they have the nerve to have us come eat dinner in *their* clothes, for the Queen's birthday? And I'm pretty sure that today's not even her birthday!"

"Where do you normally eat?" Scott asked.

"Did you just say... two weeks?" Hazel asked ignoring Scott.

"Yes," Page said. "Calvin has been keeping track, since they don't have any clocks or calendars in here. But anyway, we eat in here... in our cells."

"Two weeks?" Hazel asked again, her mind beginning to swirl.

"Hazel, I think we've established that. Two weeks!" Scott said. "How hard did you hit your head?" he asked as he went to put his hand on her forehead. She swatted him away.

"You should know – you knocked your head into mine! But two weeks! My aunt is going to be worried sick! She's going to think I died or something!" Hazel said. Page, who didn't seem to be listening, spoke.

"I still can't believe that King Bilimora would do such a thing!"

Hazel looked at her with surprise. "You think that King Bilimora is behind this?"

"Well, why wouldn't he be? I mean, who would be?" Calvin asked. Hazel was even more shocked.

"Out of all people, you two were the ones I thought would realize that it wasn't King Bilimora! Did you hear how depressed his voice just sounded a moment ago? And why would he do such a thing? It should be obvious that his brother Abaddon is behind it all!" Hazel said.

"Who?" Page and Calvin asked at the same time.

"Hazel," Scott said.

"What?" Hazel asked annoyed.

"You have to remember, they don't know as much as us. We both read the contents of the box – they didn't. No one knows what we know," Scott said.

"You're right. Wait... what do you mean *we* read?" Hazel asked looking at Scott suspiciously.

"Oh, well...you see, after you sort of kind of drowned, I was curious as to what was so important in the bottles. So, I took the papers out and read them. I only read the newspaper clippings and a little bit of one of the letters before I realized I shouldn't pry. But right now is not the time to deal with that! We have to come up with a plan." Scott said slightly embarrassed.

"You're right," Hazel said, letting him off the hook for the moment.

"Did my grandma tell you about the new gadgets?"

"Yah, I got some of them," Hazel said, knowing Calvin wasn't going to be excited about the gadgets she had with her.

"Great! Which ones do you have? The invisible bands? The sticking gloves?" Calvin asked starting to get excited.

"I have the lipstick!" Hazel said excitedly.

"And?" Clavin asked.

"The gum," Hazel said sheepishly. Calvin frowned.

"The gum? What gum?" Hazel gave him an innocent smile. Then realization dawned on him.

"You took the gum! You took the gum! How could you take the gum? I told you not to even touch the gum! Why would you take the gum? I wasn't finished testing the gum! Why did you choose to take the gum? There were a bunch of other gadgets," Calvin yelled.

"Dude, calm down!" Scott said. "We had to swim across a lake and the only gadgets that would fit into a water bottle were a couple of other things and the gum and lipstick. And the other things fell to the bottom of a fifty-foot deep lake! She nearly killed herself trying to get them!"

"And Calvin, I knew you said not to take the gum, but you didn't have that many other gadgets made yet! And I'm sure you got all the kinks worked out by now!" Hazel said.

"The last time I tested it out, it blew up a doll! Just... don't use it," Calvin said calming down and breathing heavily.

"Ok, we need to make that plan now," Hazel said ignoring Calvin.

"All right, first things first," Scott began. "Hazel, you and I need to find where they keep the clothes and put something on so that we don't stick out. Then, we need to find King Bilimora without Abaddon around, and talk to him about what the heck is going on. I know we know some of it, but we need to know why he's going along with it," Scott said.

"Sounds good," Hazel said.

"What do we do?" Calvin asked.

"Just do what they tell you to do and don't cause any trouble," Scott said. Calvin looked as if he was about to argue.

"Oh yeah, and before we leave, why are you guys in this hallway with no other people?" Hazel asked before Calvin had a chance to say anything.

"They weren't going to put me and my aunt in the same room, so I made a big commotion and they finally gave up... but they put us in this room that was separate from everybody else," Calvin answered.

"Why haven't you guys tried to escape?" Hazel asked.

"We have tried – a thousand times. There's absolutely no way whatsoever to leave this place!" Calvin said. Hazel sighed, she hadn't thought about how she was going to help everyone escape.

"Ok, we'll meet up with you guys later then," Hazel said as she and Scott turned around to open the door. It wouldn't budge.

"Oh no," Scott said.

"What?" Hazel asked, already knowing the answer.

"You should have propped the door open! They have it so we can't open the doors from the inside, no matter how many ways we've tried to break it down!" Calvin said.

"Well isn't this just great! You couldn't have told us that before?" Scott snapped.

"Don't go blaming this one on me! You're the one who let the door shut," Calvin snapped back.

"Ok, both of you just shut up!" Hazel said. "We're going to find a way out."

"How?" Calvin asked.

"Look, just because *you* couldn't find a way out doesn't mean that *we* can't," Scott said motioning to Hazel and himself.

"What's that supposed to mean?" Calvin asked, raising his voice.

"You know what it means," Scott said. But before either of them could say another word, there was a knock on the door.

"I'm coming in now," a small voice said. Hazel and Scott jumped behind the door as a small timid woman slowly opened it and pushed a cart in. "I'm here to give you your clothes," she said.

"Why thank you," Page answered in a sweet voice, "but I was just wondering if you could quickly look at something in the bathroom. I think we have a small leak."

"A leak?" the lady asked.

"Yes, but you know, I'm not sure," Page said as she ushered the lady into the little door in the back of the room that lead to the bathroom. Page turned around and signaled Hazel and Scott to leave. They didn't hesitate and ran out into the hall toward a door at the end of the hallway. They quickly reached the end of the hall and tried to get through the passage way, but it was locked. It looked like you needed to swipe a card to get in.

Scott tried to use the card attached to his white coat, but it didn't work. Hazel looked on her coat and found one, but saw that hers was different from Scott's. It was a green card about the size of a credit card but it had a circle on the front with some numbers in it. She slowly put the card in the slot and heard a click. Hazel put her hand on the handle and pushed on the door. They slowly entered the room then shut the door behind them. The room was quite odd. It was painted all purple with a few pictures on the wall and there was a side table with water in a small jar, a small bottle, and a note placed atop it. The side table itself was placed next to a oversized bed with a woman laying in it. As they slowly walked into the room Scott looked as if he was going to start crying.

"Mom?" Sctott said in a quiet whisper as he walked towards the bed. Hazel looked at the woman. She looked just like Scott... same sandy blond hair, same nose, mouth and ears. There was no doubt about it, it was his mother. She rested on the bed with her eyes closed, perfectly still. Her face looked pale. Hazel noticed, though, that she was breathing slowly.

Chapter Twelve

"But how?" Hazel said not really talking to anyone.

"It can't be possible," Scott said now in tears. He grabbed

the woman's hand and started squeezing it. "Mom, Mom it's me, Scott... Mom, come on." Scott was kneeling on the floor. Hazel walked over to her bed stand and picked up the bottle and the note. The note said, "*Give three pills each evening.*" Three pills had been dispensed into a small cup on the night stand. Hazel put the note down and looked at the bottle. It said *sleeping pills* on it. She read the back of the bottle.

"*Not to exceed one pill every 24 hours. Do not continue taking pills after a thirty day time period. Keep out of reach of children.*" Hazel gasped.

"Scott, she's being drugged into sleep!" Hazel said.

"I don't see how she lived," Scott said.

"Don't you see? She must have fallen at sunset!" Hazel said as she put a hand on Scott's shoulder. Hazel heard someone fidgeting with the door.

"I just have to quickly give the woman her pills," a voice outside the door said. Hazel gasped.

"Scott, we have to get out of here," Hazel whispered. Scotts mom turned her head and mumbled something unintelligible.

"Hazel, I can't leave her again."

"Can't we do it later?" a second voice asked outside the door.

"Nah, I've already forgotten to do it for the past couple of days, last thing we need is her waking up," the first voice said.

As Hazel heard him start to shuffle for his key she began to panic.

"Scott, don't be crazy. If we don't leave *now*, we'll never be able to get her and everyone else out of here. You promised me that I was going to see my family again – now I'm promising you that you'll see your mom again, but we have to leave *right now!* Scott stood there for a moment and then nodded. Hazel quickly grabbed the three pills and dumped them into her pocket. Then she took the glass of water and dumped it underneath the bed. Hazel looked around to try to find a way to get out but she couldn't see anything.

"How are we going to get out of here?!" Hazel asked as she leaned against the wall. She let out a yelp as the wall spun around and pushed her into a small hidden room that was only big enough for the bottom of a staircase. The next thing she knew Scott was standing next to her.

"That was awesome!" he said quietly.

"Huh, I guess some one already gave her the pills," the voice on the other side of the wall said. Hazel and Scott quickly made their way up the secret staircase.

"Do you think she's going to be ok?" Scott asked. Hazel reached her hand out and grabbed his and gave it a squeeze then turned around and headed up the stairs.

"I know she's going to be ok," she said.

"Thanks," Scott said. After a bit of walking, Hazel and Scott came to another window and looked in. It was the large banquet room they had come to the first time, but this time there were a bunch of guards standing in a large circle that spanned the entire room.

"That's weird," Hazel said.

"Sounds like this is the first time all the citizens are going to be brought together. They probably don't want them to start a riot," Scott said. They kept on walking until they reached a very dark dead end. They tried to feel around on the wall to see if there were any door handles, but there weren't.

"Wait," Scott said after running his hand across the wall. "It feels like there are a bunch of buttons on the wall."

"What do you mean," Hazel asked, walking over and touching the wall herself.

"There are some rocks sticking out that have a different feel to their surface. I think you have to press them in certain way." Suddenly Hazel remembered something. She took the green key card out of her pocket and looked at the numbers. It was hard to see because there was very little light.

"How many of those rocks are there?" she asked.

"About eight of them, roughly in a circle," Scott said.

"Ok," Hazel said as she held the card up to her face so she could see the numbers better. "Starting at the top and going clockwise, press the first one, the fourth one, the seventh one, the second one, third one, the fifth one, the eighth one, and the sixth one," Hazel said. Scott listened and pressed the

bumps. The wall slid apart and opened up, revealing an entrance.

"How did you know all that?" Scott asked as Hazel put
the card back into her pocket.

"I have my ways," Hazel said with a smile, but Hazel
stopped smiling once she saw inside the room. It looked like a
laundry room filled with clothes on hangers, but there were
also about fifteen people inside who saw them open the door.

"Um..." Hazel said.

"Um?" said a woman whose name tag said 'Carmen' on
it. "You're five minutes late and all you can say is 'um'? Do you
not know how much work we have to get done? Now grab a
cart and get busy!" the lady said taking her attention away from
Hazel and Scott.

"What now?" Hazel whispered to Scott as they walked to
the back of the room where there were a ton of clothes and
carts.

"Just grab a cart and get busy!" Scott whispered mocking
Carman. "When you're done with whatever they have you do, I
guess we'll just meet back here," Scott said as he grabbed a
cart. Right as Hazel was about to grab a cart for herself,
someone grabbed her shoulder. It was Carmen. She frowned
at Hazel then looked down at her clipboard. She looked back
up, annoyed.

"Kimberly, have you forgotten?" Carmen said putting her
hands on her hips. Hazel looked down at her name tag – it

said Kimberly Mist. Carmen continued without waiting for an answer.

"It says here that you are supposed to give the King, Queen and their bratty little children their clothes," she said pointing to a cart that was separate from the others.

"Right. How do I get to their room again?" Hazel asked.

"Ha, very funny. Now move along," she said turning her back to Hazel and looking at her clipboard again. But as she turned, Hazel saw a map hanging on the wall. She quickly walked over and spotted exactly where she was - the laundry room. As she studied the map, she saw that there was a secret door, behind what looked like a picture frame, which lead straight to the King and Queen's room. Hazel tried to look around for Scott but didn't see him, so she just grabbed the cart and headed to the back of the very big room. When Hazel finally reached the end of the room she saw a huge painting on the wall of someone dressed in King's clothes – but Hazel noticed that it was not King Bilimora, but the king's brother; Abaddon.

Hazel put both hands on the corner of the picture frame and then slid it over just enough to be able to get the cart and herself through. Once she was in, the picture frame slid itself back into place. Hazel couldn't see a thing it was so dark. She didn't have a clue where she was going, but just kept on walking forward. She was starting to get creeped out that it was so dark and quiet, so she started to pick up the pace and walk a little faster. Then she started to jog a little. All of a sudden her cart hit the wall and the handle shoved painfully into her stomach. She let out a little groan. Looking ahead, Hazel saw some light coming from a crack at the bottom of the wall. She walked closer to the wall and pressed her ear against it to see if she could hear anything.

"Now make sure you do as I say, or else!" said a male voice that Hazel didn't recognize.

"I really think there is a better way to do this," a female voice said that Hazel recognized as the Queen's.

"Oh really? How do you think we should handle it, hmm? My brother is going to see what it feels like to have something stolen from him after having worked very hard to get it!"

"Abaddon, you don't deserve to be king, nor will you ever!" Hazel heard King Bilimora reply.

"Just because I'm the youngest? Just because you think you're the better one? Or just because our stupid father didn't write in his Last Will and Testament which of us was going to be king? You think any of those things really makes you king?" The voice, which Hazel assumed was Abaddon, asked furiously. Hazel heard shattering glass. Nobody said anything.

"Now, your formal-wear should be arriving very soon. You are to put those on and wait until I call for you," Abaddon continued. Hazel heard his feet walking to where she was standing. She jumped back from the wall, grabbed her cart and wheeled it over to the dark conner and crouched behind it. The rock slid into the wall and Abaddon charged into the darkness, walking right past Hazel. Hazel waited until she was sure Abaddon had made it out some other door before she slowly pushed the cart away and stood up. She pushed on the door and it opened.

As Hazel made her way through with the cart she let out a small scream as a book just barely missed her head and hit the wall.

"What in the world!" Hazel said looking at the King and Queen's faces.

"Oh, sorry. We thought you were someone else," the Queen said quietly.

"We'll just take our clothes and you can leave," the King said. Hazel was confused, but then she realized that they didn't recognize her. She quickly shut the door behind her, and then looked the Queen and King in the face. She barley recognized them herself because she was used to seeing them both dressed in such grand attire, but today they were both in what looked like dull grey pajamas.

"It's me!" Hazel said. They both looked confused. "Hazel."

"Hazel!" they both yelled out. The Queen ran over and gave her a hug.

"We didn't even recognize you!" the Queen said. "How did you find us? Are you alright? Does anyone know you are here? Have you seen the kids? You look thin, have you been eating enough?"

"Darling..." the King said. "I think you should give her a little breathing room."

"Right. Sorry," the Queen said starting to blush.

"You're probably wondering what's going on," the King asked, looking into Hazel's eyes.

"No, I know exactly what's going on. Abaddon is trying to overthrow you to become king because your father never left a Will and Testament," Hazel said. The Queen and King both looked shocked. "But what I don't get is why you're going along with him and making it look like you're the one keeping everybody held captive," Hazel said. The King sighed and the Queen looked like she was about to burst into tears.

"Well, as you know, Abaddon never let it go that my father didn't say who was King, and he swore to me that he would get his day on the throne. At first I thought that he would eventually get over it, but evidently he didn't. We were at the castle when we heard screams and yells from outside. I ran to my window and saw dozens of black cars with men coming out of them, weapons in hand. They were coming toward the castle! Just then, one of my advisors and two of my guards entered the room saying we were under attack by Abaddon and that he was taking families captive. Before I could even utter a word, Abaddon's men had poured into the room. Several of them were my own men, whom he had convinced to overthrow me! I couldn't believe we were being betrayed by some of the people we trusted most.

"Two of them grabbed Emily and James. Out of nowhere they gave each of us an injection of something and everything went black. We woke up here. Abaddon told us of his plans and said that if we didn't go along with them, we would never see our two children again. I'm not sure how far Abaddon would really go, but I simply can't take that chance." Hazel nodded. She knew what the King meant.

"Ok, that's all I need to know," Hazel said. "I'm going to come up with a plan, and I'm going to make sure that your kids are safe. Just keep doing what you're doing and everything will be fine," Hazel said, trying to convince herself just as much as the King and Queen.

"Is there anything you need us to do?" the Queen asked.

"No, but do you know where your kids are being kept?" Hazel asked hopefully.

"No, I'm sorry. We don't, we haven't seen them since they brought us here," the King said.

"Ok, don't worry. I'll find them," Hazel said confidently. "But I'll have to be quick, so let me give you your formal-wear," Hazel said quickly taking the extremely nice but heavy clothes off of the cart.

"Thank you so much, Hazel," the Queen said as Hazel started to head back the way she had come.

"Any time!" Hazel said as the door slid closed, leaving her in darkness. Hazel sighed. Now all she needed to do was to find the twins.

"Hazel," she ever so faintly heard someone say. Hazel shook her head. She was starting to feel a bit faint. She should have seen if she could have found some food. She wasn't even quite sure when the last time she ate was.

"Hazel." the voice said harsher this time. Then she felt someone tap her shoulder. Hazel spun around, her heart racing. She could make out someone standing in front of her but she couldn't tell who it was. She started to run away but a hand grabbed her. She was about to put up a good fight when the person spoke.

"It's Scott!" Hazel took a deep breath.

"What are you doing here?" she asked.

"I tried to get your attention without scaring you, but I guess that didn't work," Scott said laughing.

"I mean, why did you follow me? We said we would meet up back in the laundry room!" Hazel said.

"I know, but I thought it would be too risky, so I grabbed a tuxedo and grabbed you a dress and I figured that you would have found the King and Queen by now and we could change once we found the twin's room," Scott said.

"Well, I did find the King and Queen, but I haven't found the twins yet. By the way, the King is only doing what his brother says because if he doesn't, Abaddon said he wouldn't ever see his kids again," Hazel said, thinking about the awful position the King was in right now.

"It figures. Ok, well it's good you at least found the King and Queen. Are they well?" Scott asked.

"They are now."

"Let's go talk to the twins. I think I might just have a small plan," Scott said.

"Wait, I don't know the plan! And we don't know where the twins are!" Hazel said.

"But I do," Scott said. Even though it was dark, Hazel knew that he was smiling. Scott grabbed Hazel's arm and started pulling her so they wouldn't get separated. After a bit of walking they came to a door. Just as Hazel was about to give it a push Scott stopped her.

"What?" Hazel asked.

"Just a warning, I saw Abaddon trying to go in there and they started throwing things at him. He didn't even go in all the way, he walked right back out. I think he just wanted to make sure that they were still alive," Scott said.

"Ok," Hazel said thinking that the twins had much in common with their mother. "We'll open the door, wait a moment, and then we'll charge in. You can quickly close the door and I'll block the stuff they throw," Hazel said. Scott nodded. Hazel gave the door a push. As the door was opening she shoved the cart into the room then jumped back so the twins couldn't see her. She could see them both holding up stuffed animals and toys in their hands. Both Hazel and Scott ran into the room. Scott pushed the door in place as fast as he could as the twins started throwing the stuffed animals and anything else that they could grab at them. Suddenly they stopped.

"HAZEL!!" the twins both said at the same time. They dropped the things in their hands.

"Hey you guys!" Hazel said as they both ran up to embrace her.

"We thought you were our father's stupid brother, or one of his helpers," Emily said, hugging Hazel.

"You sure look like one of the helpers," James said suspiciously as he stepped back. "And so does he," he said pointing at Scott.

"Well, you see, it's our disguise," Scott said sounding mysterious. The twins gasped.

"Really?" they both asked.

"You bet ch'ya!" Scott said nodding his head. "Now, we have a very super duper important mission." The twins looked at him with big eyes. "And we need your guys' help." The twins looked surprised. So did Hazel. What was Scott doing?

"Our help?" James asked amazed.

"Yup. But you see, you are the only ones who can do it. Nobody else can do it, not even Hazel!" Scott said. The twins looked shocked beyond belief. They looked at Hazel to see if this was true. Trying not to laugh, Hazel put on a serious look and nodded her head.

"Wow," the twins both said at the same time.

"It must be big!" Emily said.

"You bet it is! I mean, without your part, Operation: Free Everyone would be a disaster! Now I understand if you don't want to do it," Scott said with a sly smile.

"No! We want to do it!" they both said.

"Are you sure?" Scott asked. The twins nodded their heads. "You're going to have to be brave and strong, and you're going to have to work together." They nodded their heads again.

"We promise!"

"Ok, so listen up – here's the plan," Scott said pausing for suspense. "When I give you the signal, you both are going to start fighting at dinner, ok?" Scott paused till the twins nodded their heads. "I don't care what it's about, but at first it has to be kind of small. Then, one of you has to do something that makes it bigger, and then when I give you the signal again, you can start throwing food and being wild and crazy!" Scott said throwing his hands up in the air. "And the thing is, other people are going to join in. And then you're going to start fighting with all of them, got it?" They nodded their heads. "Any questions?" Emily raised her hand.

"Yes?" Scott asked.

"What's the signal?" she asked. Scott stroked his chin for a moment in thought. "I'm going to pull my ear," Scott said demonstrating by tugging on his ear. James raised his hand.

"Yes?"

"Do we get disguises like yours?" he asked eyes wide.

234

"Why of course! They're right here!" Scott said taking their clothes out of of the cart.

"What's so special about these? They look like normal clothes," James said. Scott seemed at a loss for words.

"Well of course they do," Hazel said, chiming in. "That's why it's called a disguise. You have to blend in with the other people. Because if you stuck out, well then everybody would know what you're up to!" The twins smiled and nodded.

"Got it!" they said at the same time. Scott gave her a thankful smile.

"Now, Emily – come with me and I'll help you get dressed. Scott, you help James, and you can get dressed as well," Hazel said as she walked over to the cart with Scott. "A food-fight?" she whispered.

"A diversion!" he whispered back, Hazel raised and eyebrow. "Alright, a food-fight! But I figured if the guards are busy trying to keep peace, we'll have more time to find an exit!" Scott said with a sly smile as he swooped his clothes off the cart. Hazel rolled her eyes, unsure if Scott's idea was genius or disastrous. She picked up her dress and underneath she saw a makeup pad. She was probably supposed to have given it to the Queen. She shrugged and picked it up as well. Once Hazel was in the bathroom she looked in the mirror and gasped. She could tell why nobody recognized her! Her hair was not only crazy from not being brushed for a quite a while, but she had streaks of a brighter brown on top of her dark brown hair from the mud. Her face looked older, her skin was tanned and dirty, and she definitely looked like a completely different person.

"I can't get my disguise to stay tied!" Emily said interrupting Hazel's thoughts. Hazel turned around. Emily had put her pink dress on. It was tight around her torso and then pooffed out. It looked more like something a five year old would wear. Her hands were tangled up as she tried to zipper up the back of her dress and tie the bow. Hazel laughed.

"Maybe I can help with that," Hazel said as she zipped up the dress and tied her bow. Emily looked at herself in the mirror.

"I hate this dress, it makes me look like I'm a little kid!" She complained as she picked up a brush and started to brush her blond hair, Hazel resisted the urge to laugh as she started to put on her own dress. Luckily Scott had gotten her the right size – and she knew it was just pure luck because Scott probably grabbed the first thing he saw. But the dress itself was really nice. It was a silk sparkling purple dress with a halter top, and once it got a little bit past her knees, the dress cut off and fell down in a ruffled diagonal. Hazel looked at herself in the mirror. The dress looked amazing on her!. Hazel looked herself up and down and spun around. She looked great from the neck down, but her face and hair were dirty and messy. Emily also saw the dilemma.

"Wow! I love the dress, but the hair and the face...got'a go," Emily said. Hazel laughed.

"What do you mean got'a go?"

"You know what I mean! We need to clean you up so you can look good for your boyfriend," Emily said turning the faucet on. Hazel was a little bit shocked at the last part.

"Who? Scott? He's not my boyfriend," Hazel said.

"I'm not talking about him, and you know who I'm talking about. Now put your head under the sink," Emily said.

"Wait, what do you mean you're not talking about..."

"Sink!" Emily said pointing at the running water. Hazel obediently stuck her head under the water, and with Emily's help, she managed to get all of the dirt, sticks, leaves and mud out of her hair. She then cleaned her face, arms and legs, which were more tanned than dirty.

"Do you have a hair dryer?" Hazel asked while drying her hair with a towel.

"No," Emily answered.

"Oh well, I'll just leave it like this then," Hazel said putting the towel down.

"You can't do that!" Emily said.

"Why?"

"Because they only let us shower on certain days, and today wasn't one of them. If people see your hair wet, then they'll know that something is up!" Emily said wiping her hands on a towel.

"Oh, then what are we supposed to do? We can't leave it wet, and we don't have time for it to dry," Hazel said.

"No, but I know how to make it look like your hair is dry," Emily said making Hazel sit on the ground. "Hand me the brush," she ordered. Hazel handed the brush to Emily.

"How do you know so much about this stuff? You're only like seven and you know more than me!" Hazel said as Emily yanked on the brush.

"Um, firstly, I'm nine, almost ten years old and I have gone to about ten thousand balls. I like playing outside with my brother, and it drives my nannies crazy at how fast I get muddy! So they're always quickly washing my hair in the sink if we don't have time for a shower. And over the years, they've found certain ways to make my hair look dry when it was really wet. So I guess I just picked up a few things," Emily said as she yanked a piece of Hazel's hair.

"Ow," she complained.

"Oh stop your whining! It's your own fault for getting yourself dirty!" Emily said sternly. "I also picked that one up from my nannies, too! They say that to me a lot," Emily said laughing. "Now, I'm almost done, give me your watch."

Hazel obediently took off her watch and handed it to Emily. "Now I'm going to just..." Emily tugged at Hazel's hair and used the watch strap to tie it back. "Ok, we're all done!" Hazel pushed herself off of the ground to look at her hair.

"Emily, I love it!" Hazel said as she looked at her hair. Emily had taken Hazel's hair and wound it up into a nice bun. She left a piece in the front hanging out that looked curled. You couldn't even see the watch! It looked like she had just gotten her hair professionally done!

"Thank you!" Hazel said as she picked up Emily and spun her around. Emily giggled as Hazel put her down. Hazel quickly put on a little makeup then gave herself a final look in the mirror.

"You look great!" Emily said, and Hazel could not deny it.

"We both look great!" Hazel said. Hazel then took the letters, gum and lipstick out of the pockets of her shorts which sat on the floor. Hazel sighed – where was she supposed to put them? She checked in her back pockets of her shorts to make sure she didn't forget anything, and then smiled when she saw that she had a gadget band in one of the pockets. She couldn't believe she hadn't noticed it before! The gadget band looked almost like a thick black stretchy band, but it had little zippered pockets where you could fit small gadgets. Hazel took the letters, gum and lipstick and put them each in a pocket, then she took the band and slid it up her leg so it was little higher than her knee. It was easily accessible, but still hidden. Hazel looked once more in the mirror to make sure you couldn't see the band.

As the girls walked out of the bathroom they saw both boys immersed in a video game.

Chapter Thirteen

"You rock at this game!" James said as his fingers zoomed across the controller.

"You're not too bad yourself," Scott said laughing.

"Ehemm," Emily said. James sighed loudly as Scott turned around.

"You look nice," James said.

"Thank you," Emily said with a curtsy.

"I was talking to Hazel," James said with a giggle, "but I guess you look ok, too."

"You do look nice," Scott said looking at Hazel.

"Thanks, you look good too," Hazel said as she admired how he looked in his tux.

"I was talking to Emily," Scott said with a smile as he nudged James. "but you don't look half bad either." He smiled and gave her a wink.

"Well you made it easy with this dress that you picked out," Hazel said. "Now all I need are my shoes," Hazel said walking over to the cart.

"Uhh...shoes?" Scott asked. Hazel turned around expecting Scott to be laughing and then to say he was just kidding, but he was standing dumbstruck. Hazel closed her eyes, took in a sharp breath and then let it out.

"You didn't get me a pair of shoes," Hazel said through clenched teeth.

"Uh, well that thought didn't really cross my mind," Scott said.

"Scott!"

"What? I'm sorry, I didn't think of shoes!" he said. Hazel looked at Scott's feet and saw that he was wearing a nice pair of shiny black shoes.

"How could you get yourself a pair of shoes and then not get me a pair?"

Scott thought about it. "I guess it just slipped my mind?" Scott said with a shrug and looking sorry.

"Ugh! Well this is perfect! What am I supposed to do now?!"

"You could wear your slippers?" he suggested.

"Oh, like that won't attract any attention!"

"Barefoot?"

Hazel glared at Scott.

"What size do you wear?" Emily asked just as Hazel was about to lunge at Scott.

"Thank you, Emily, but I don't think I will fit into your shoes," Hazel said, then turned back and glared at Scott.

"No! You see, one time the lady brought shoes that were too big for me," Emily said "Way too big!" she added.

"I'm a size eight and a half," Hazel said. Emily walked over to a closet and pulled out a pair of black high heeled shoes that had a laced front with scattered diamonds on them.

"The lady was going to have you wear those?" Hazel asked surprised.

"No, she brought the wrong cart, but I took the shoes off to cause some trouble," Emily said with an evil little smile.

"What size are they?" Hazel asked hopefully.

"Seven and a half," Emily said. Hazel grunted as she grabbed the shoes out of Emily's hand. She tried to push her feet into them. After a bit of squeezing she finally got them in.

"Hey! They fit!" Scott said with a smile.

"Hey! I can't feel my feet!" Hazel said rolling her foot. "I don't think I can wear these shoes! They're cutting off my circulation!"

"Oh, come on! Aren't girls supposed to suffer for beauty?" Scott asked.

"Oh, shut up!" Hazel said as she kicked Scott in the shin.

"Ow! Come on, you're wearing heels, that hurt!" Scott said rubbing his shin.

"Seriously? Aren't boys supposed to be all tough and strong?" Hazel asked mocking Scott's voice.

"Hello!" James interrupted. "Do we not have a mission?"

"You're right! Thank you, sergeant," Scott said, saluting James. "Now let's go over the plan again. Like I said, you guys just do what you'd normally do, and then at dinner when I pull my ear, that's your cue..."

"...to start fighting!" Emily said finishing Scott's sentence.

"We start off small, and then we get really big!" James said.

"Wow, you guys know the plan better than I do!" Scott said laughing.

"Ok, we're going to split before someone comes to get you guys!" Hazel said walking back to the picture on the wall. Scott slid the picture to the side and held it open for Hazel.

"Good luck!" Hazel said before slipping into the dark.

"I never thought you would be so good with kids," Hazel said after a bit of walking.

"What... does that surprise you?" Scott said trying to sound offended. Hazel knew he wasn't.

"Why, yes it does," Hazel said. She knew Scott would be able to get along just fine with the rudest person in the world. "I mean... since I met you, your people skills have been terrible!" Hazel said with a laugh.

"Well then!" Scott said with a smile. After a couple of wrong turns they finally made it back to the main hall.

"My feet hurt so bad!" Hazel said quietly as she sunk down the wall.

"Come on! They're not that small!" Scott said.

"Scott! They're one whole size too small!" Hazel said rubbing her feet. She didn't want to take them off in fear of not being able to get them back on.

"Can we please go back so I can get a pair of shoes that fit my feet? I'm not going to be much help if I can't walk."

"For the ten billionth time! It's too risky and we can't go back! You're just going to have to suck it up for a little bit longer!" Scott said.

"I really hate you," Hazel said as she crossed her arms. "So what's the plan? We cause chaos, and then what?"

"I don't know yet! I already came up with half the plan, I think it's time you start coming up with ideas!" Scott said. Hazel stood up and peeked her head out of the window and down into the main hall. There was food on every table now and the same guards were still standing in a circle around the room. Hazel noticed that behind the guards there seemed to be a strange stream of water that was going around the perimeter of the room, except for in front of the doors in the room. It re-minded Hazel of something you would throw pennies into.

"I still don't see why the guards are standing in a circle," Hazel said.

"Like I said, probably so nobody tries to make a run for it," Scott said.

"But they're not standing in front of the doors, just in front of the-" Hazel was silenced by the sound of a door opening. Hazel and Scott both slowly and quietly looked down below to see who it was. It was the King and Queen with Abaddon.

"Now, let's just make sure everything goes as planned..." Abaddon said to the King.

"You're a terrible man," the King said stiffly.

"Oh really? I'm not the one that cheated his brother out of the crown!" Abaddon said with an evil smile. "Really makes you think, doesn't it? What if we had worked it out.." Abaddon said in a mocking tone, imitating his brother's voice, "...and I hadn't been a selfish fool, would I be where I am now?" King Bilimora glared at him. Abaddon continued in his own terrible voice. "And it doesn't look like that stupid Hazel girl is going to save the day this time! She's probably still wandering in the forest, starving and lost and if I'm lucky - dead." The Queen and King said nothing.

"Now... I'm going to have the people brought in, and then I will go get my part of the evening ready!"Abaddon said laughing. He ushered the King and Queen to the raised table at the front of the room.

"Richard! Steve!" Abaddon yelled. Hazel almost laughed in surprise as Richard and Steve entered the room – the stupid criminals whom Hazel always caught. She wondered if Abaddon was the "boss" who always sent them on their missions.

"Yes, your highness?" they said as they came running into the room, both dressed like everybody else, wearing a white coat and white slippers.

"You may go get the people now. And I'm feeling generous tonight, so you can let them sit wherever they would like!" Abaddon said with a smile as if he was the nicest person in the world.

"Yes, your highness," they said, taking a deep bow before leaving.

"Ahhh, you know I think I like that… your highness," Abaddon said looking at the King. "Your highness," he said again as he left the room.

"Ok, we need to get down there so we can blend in with the people," Scott said quietly. "Make sure we sit about three to four seats away from Emily and James," Scott said. " He started walking down the hallway, his back pressed against the wall. Hazel followed.

"Do you think anybody will recognize me?" Hazel asked, knowing that if they did the whole plan –which they still didn't have yet – would be ruined. Scott stopped walking and turned around and smiled.

"No, they won't. You're much uglier now," Scott said with a laugh. "I'm just kidding, you look a lot different now. Older. Your hair is a different color from all the sun. You just look... different," Scott said with a smile.

"Thanks... I think," Hazel said, still unsure about the "different" thing, because different was not always good.

"And with all that makeup..." Scott said as he turned with a smile towards the stairs, but then he stopped. "But we should probably go by different names when we're sitting with everyone," Scott suggested.

"Ok, that's a good idea," Hazel said.

"I'll just go by my real name and–"

Hazel had glared at Scott causing him to stop short. "That's right! I forgot you *lied* to me about your actual name!" she said. Scott rolled his eyes dramatically.

"I didn't *lie* to you, my name is Scott. My mother didn't really think through the whole "naming thing" and we both hatted it, so we changed it when I was younger." He said.

"Ok, whatever. I'm going to go by Amber Claire Jones," Hazel said, thinking of her aunt and best friend back home.

"That's a nice name!" Scott said. "Maybe you should really change it to that!"

Hazel gave him a punch in the arm. "I *like* my name, thank you very much."

"Ow! Ok, we better get a move on," Scott said seriously. Once they reached the stairs, they quietly crept down them. They quickly opened the door that was at the bottom, went through and shut it, looking around. There were a bunch of people in front of them walking into the room. Luckily nobody noticed them coming down. They quickly blended in with the crowd and sat down at the table where James and Emily were sitting. If Emily or James saw them, they certainly didn't show it.

"I still don't believe it!" a lady said as she sat down in front of Hazel. "I just don't see why the king would bring everybody here!"

"I don't know. But I heard someone say that the king and queen are in debt! So they're going to keep us here for a while and then only let the people who pay leave!" a man said as he sat down in front of Scott. The couple started talking about other things but Hazel wasn't really paying any attention. She looked around the room. She still couldn't figure out why the guards were in front of the moat of water that surrounded this place but not in front of the actual doors. If they didn't want anyone making a run for it or starting trouble, it seems like their primary concern would be to guard the doors. It was almost as if they didn't want people to go near the water. It certainly didn't look that deep if someone were to fall into it. And then Hazel heard the words in her head that she had read in the letters - the same ones Molly had spoken before she died, "*What goes down, will go up!*"

That was it! That had to be the way out! You had to go down through the water to get up and out of this place! Hazel felt a kick on her leg that brought her back to reality. She looked up to see the lady who was in front of her staring at her as if she had just asked a question.

"I'm sorry, what was that?" Hazel asked.

"Would you like some mashed potatoes?" she asked. Hazel saw that she was holding a large bowl in her hands.

"Sure, thanks," Hazel said as the lady started scooping some onto Hazel's plate.

"Go somewhere?" Scott asked Hazel quietly as he took the bowl of mashed potatoes from the woman.

"I think I know how to get out," Hazel whispered as she started taking some food and then passing it along. "But I'm not positive – I'll need a distraction to see if it's the way."

"Just let me know when," Scott said excitedly.

"Well, I suppose the only good thing about this place is that this food isn't half bad," the woman said, digging her fork into her plate. Hazel nodded her head as she put some food into her mouth. Even though she hadn't eaten properly for days she could barely taste the food. She was too preoccupied with looking for just the right time to make her move.

"Why, I don't think we've met before," the woman said. "I can't believe my manners! I'm Mabel Pat Bloomer, and this is my husband Dan Patrick Bloomer," she said pointing to the man sitting next to her."

"Howdy!" Dan said through a mouth full of food.

"Nice to meet you. Umm, I'm Amber Claire Jones," Hazel said wondering why they were using middle names.

"And I'm Nicholas Scottery Chapman," Scott said with a polite smile. Hazel started choking on her mashed potatoes when she heard Scott say his name.

"Are you ok?!" Scott and Mabel both asked. Hazel coughed and drank some water.

"I'm fine, thanks. Sorry, guess it went down the wrong tube." She looked at Scott. *Nicholas Scottery Chapman?* He was the one! Scott was who was supposed to be king! Did he know? She was going to kill him if he knew that he was King Nicholas' son!

"What was that about?" Scott whispered.

"I thought you said your name was Nick!" she hissed. Scott stared at her in confusion.

"Yes, short for Nicholas, why does that matter?" he asked.

"Never-mind, I'll tell you later," Hazel replied. There was no time right now. Just as Hazel was about to tell Scott she needed the distraction, the grand doors swung open with a bang. Everybody turned to look to see who had opened them. Standing in the door was a person wearing torn and dirty clothes.

"Ladies and gentlemen. That is not the real king!" the person shouted waving a piece of paper and pointing to King Bilimora on the other end of the room, sitting at the raised table with his wife. Everyone in the room quieted down to listen.

"You all know that King Nicholas never left a Last Will and Testament stating who was to succeed him as king. So because of age, they went with Bilimora. But I have here in my hand the real Will! Bilimora had found it then stole it and hid it! Then he made up his own Will! What you don't know is that Bilimora wasted the money he inherited, and so he kidnapped everybody here and plans to keep you here until you pay your way out!" At this point people were starting to whisper angrily. Hazel didn't have a clue who the person speaking was.

"Well then who's the real king?" someone bravely yelled.

"The king, the real king..." He paused for dramatic effect. "Is his brother Abaddon!" Everybody looked shocked. The speaker continued.

"He is the true heir to the throne." People gasped. Then out of a table in the middle of the room, Abaddon popped up. He was no longer wearing the big gold and blue robes but was wearing a tux like all of the other men in the room.

"Me?" Abaddon said acting surprised. Hazel tried to hold in a laugh.

"Now wait one minute," the King said with no emotion in his voice, though no one seemed to notice that. "And what proof do you have?" he asked, robotically reciting his lines.

"This!" the person in the door said waving the paper again. "I will show you all!" he said walking over to the projector. At this point, Hazel was biting her tongue so she wouldn't start laughing. Nobody, not one person, looked like they knew that this was all a setup! They all looked so into it and believed it all! No one even seemed to question why there just happened to be a projector conveniently in the room! The person put the letter on the machine and turned on the projector. He stepped back, waiting for it to come up. Hazel studied the person. He looked quite familiar. Then she let out a small laugh, quickly disguising it as a cough. It was Steve! She never knew that he could act! Finally, the projected image of the paper appeared on the wall.

"I, King Nicholas, being of sound body and mind, fully pass forward to the next generation, my position as King, after my death, to my son Abaddon William Brendon, along with the property, horses, stables, and all of my other possessions, including all of my money. And to my son, Bilimora Barthelme Brendon, I give nothing. For, before I died, he showed no loyalty or trust whatsoever. Signed, on this day, Nicholas Steel Brendon." Steve dramatically read out loud even though everyone could clearly see it and read it on their own.

"So, my father left me to be king? And you took that from me?" Abaddon said to Bilimora, putting his hand over his heart.

"You always got what you wanted! You never had to work for anything. For once, I wanted to have something you had," Bilimora recited without any emotion again.

"Well then. As King, I banish you, Bilimora Bartholomew Brendon, from Red Diamond... forever!" Abaddon said. To Hazel's surprise people actually started clapping. She couldn't really blame them – after all, they thought that their king was a lying kidnapping maniac! Hazel knew she had to do something before things got totally out of control. She bumped Scott's knee. Getting the hint, he pulled his ear, sending the twins their signal.

Chapter Fourteen

Hazel held her breath hopping that at least one of the twins saw the signal, but nothing happened. They just sat there listening to Abaddon drone on and on. Then suddenly out of nowhere, James took the drum stick off of Emily's plate and licked it then set it back down again.

"Hey!" Emily said just loud enough so that only a few people turned their heads. "You're so disgusting!"

"What are you going to do about it?" James said, followed by a loud burp. A few more people turned their heads to see what was going on. The Queen looked like she was going to faint. Hazel realized that she probably should have clued them in.

"This!" Emily said as she took her water and dumped it on James' food.

"I wasn't done eating that!" James said louder. More people were looking now, but Abaddon hadn't noticed yet, he was still droning on about the promises he promised to fulfill as new found "king".

"Too bad," Emily said. Scott pulled his ear again letting them know to bring it up a notch.

"Sweetie, I'm sure she didn't mean to," the lady sitting next to James said trying to calm him down.

"Yes, she did!" James said picking up his water. As he went to dump it on Emily, he instead dumped it on the lady next to her, as if by accident. Emily ducked as the lady let out a scream and hopped up. Everybody suddenly turned as she shrieked, soaking wet. Everyone was watching. Abaddon looked confused and annoyed that nobody was paying any attention to him anymore.

"Missed me, missed me, now you have to kiss me!" Emily said scooping up mashed potatoes with her hands. She threw them at Scott but made it look like she had been aiming for James.

"What the heck!" Scott said wiping it off of his jacket and then swinging his arms so that he knocked over Hazels water onto her lap.

"Jerk!" Hazel yelled pushing her chair back and standing up as well.

"See what you did!" Emily yelled at James.

"No, you did it!" he yelled back throwing a drumstick at her. Emily ducked so that it hit the person behind her.

"Ungrateful little brats!" the man yelled.

"They're just children, give them a break!" the lady next to him yelled. Emily and James started throwing more food at people but made it look like they were just missing each other. Soon everybody in the room was mad at someone for doing something, and food was flying everywhere. People were yelling and screaming, and some of the kids were even laughing. Before anyone had a chance to do anything, the entire place erupted into one huge fight.

"Guards!" Abaddon yelled. Just as Hazel hoped, the guards who were surrounding the water ran into the crowd of people, trying to calm them down. Hazel looked around. She didn't see Scott anywhere, but she couldn't wait any longer. Just as she was almost to the water, she heard Emily scream "Take this!"

Hazel quickly turned around and saw each of the twins and Scott holding fire extinguisher and shooting the foam into the crowed which was causing even more screaming and confusion. Hazel ran straight for the water. Without even thinking about it she jumped in and closed her eyes. She felt herself sinking down into water that was much deeper than it should have been, and then the next thing she knew, she was standing up on solid ground.

Hazel opened her eyes. She was in a spacious area, standing in dark water that rose up to just below her waist. There was ladder in front of her, so she climbed up it. After about five feet, she climbed out of whatever she had been in and found herself standing in grass.

She looked around and saw that she was on the castle grounds! Looking to see what she had climbed out of, she saw a pretty white well with vines and flowers growing on it. There was a little roof above it, but where there should have been a bucket and rope, there was just an empty space. This must have been how Calvin's grandma got out of the secret spot when she was young. Then Hazel's heart stopped.

"Oh no!" she said out loud. "How am I supposed to get back now!?" She had no idea what she had been thinking. She didn't have time to find her way through the weird forest! But then again, she realized, neither did Molly. Wherever the king went to school, he must have had access to where the forest let out and jumped in there. But Molly wouldn't have that luxury. She looked down the well. It couldn't really hurt if her idea didn't work.

"Always remember, what goes down, will go up!" Hazel said, remembering the other words from the letters. She took a deep breath and jumped into the well. A moment later, she opened her eyes. She was back in the grand room in the secret spot and people were still going crazy.

"Stop them! Stop them now!" Abaddon was yelling over the noise. Hazel had to act quickly. She figured she'd take four kids and three adults at a time. Hazel ran into the mess of people and randomly grabbed one girl and two boys who were throwing foam at each other. They let out a small yelp as she scooped them up.

"Stay!" Hazel ordered them as she put them down by the water. She ran back into the crowd and dragged out two adults.

"What in the name of..."

"One at a time, you guys are going to jump into this water. Once you open your eyes you will be in a well. Climb up the ladder and then help any other people who come up behind you. Do not go back to your houses, just stay put! You go first," she said pointing at the girl. Then she turned to the boys. "Count to five, then you jump in," she said pointing to one of them. "Then you do the same. Climb up as fast as you can." Then she turned to the adults. "Got it?" They all shook their heads. "Go!" she said. The girl who was surprisingly brave jumped right in.

Hazel ran back to get more people. After bringing several people over to the water, she grabbed someone who didn't seem to want to come with her. The twins were spraying more foam so it was hard to see who it was.

"What are you doing!" the person yelled.

"Just come with me!" Hazel said trying to drag the person. "Let go of me," the person yelled.

"Look, I'm going to take you to safety!" Hazel said losing patience with the lady.

"Hazel? My goodness, I thought you were a – I'm so sorry!" the woman said. Hazel still couldn't tell who it was but dragged her away. Once they were over by the water, she saw that the woman was Page.

"Do you know where Calvin is?" Page asked.

"No, I don't. But I'll find him and send him to you," Hazel said. She then explained the rules on what they all needed to do. Turning around, she realized that it was going to take a long time to get all of these people out just by herself. Running into the crowd looking for Scott, she spotted him fighting with a guard. It looked like the guard was winning. Hazel ran over and kicked the guard in the back of his leg. He collapsed to the ground in pain.

"Hey, what's up?" Scott asked casually with a smile.

"I need you to grab ten people at a time – five kids and five adults. Bring them over to the water, and then have them jump in two at a time, adult and child together. Make sure they wait about three seconds before the next pair jumps in. Tell them to climb the ladder but not to go to their houses after climbing out. Tell them to wait there until everyone is out! Once everyone is gone, leave with Calvin. I can handle the rest here alone," Hazel yelled over the noise.

As Scott opened his mouth to protest, Hazel looked him in the eyes. "Please," she said sincerely. Scott nodded and ran back into the crowd.

Hazel was getting people out as fast as she could, but it was starting to get obvious that people were missing. Abaddon finally noticed people jumping into the water.

"Guards!" he screamed.

"Jump!" Hazel yelled at the people lined up. Guards began running towards them. Hazel yelled to the line of people waiting to jump in. "As soon as someone jumps in, go in after them. Do not stop the process for any reason!" Someone behind her grabbed her wrist. She spun around and kicked them in the stomach.

"Oh my gosh! Scott, are you ok?" Hazel asked. Scott was holding his stomach.

"You are crazy!" he said and groaned with a smile. Hazel wasn't sure but she thought she might have cut him with her heel.

"I thought you were a guard," Hazel said.

"I thought that might happen," Scott said as a guard came up behind him and grabbed both of his arms.

"Duck!" Hazel yelled. As Scott ducked, she round-house kicked the guard in the face. She felt slightly bad for having heels on, but only slightly. Turning around, she saw that there were plenty of guards still coming. Some of them were trying to stop people from jumping into the water, but they weren't having a lot of success with that. By now, news had spread on how to escape from this place. Some of the guards were even jumping into the water as well. Hazel was trying to fend them off as well as she could and Scott was doing the same.

"Oh, no. I hope you don't need stitches," Hazel said to Scott between kicks. Blood was starting to stain his white shirt from where she had kicked him.

"I don't think..." Scott jumped out of the way as two guards ran into each other. "...it's that bad..." He spun around and punched a guard in the stomach. "...just bleeding a little..." he said with a smile. Hazel looked around the room. They had gotten almost all of the people out. It looked like there were about fifty people left, including the King and Queen who had two guards standing in front of them. Hazel made her way over to those guards, trying not to let anybody see her. She pinched a vein in the side of their necks, causing both of them to drop to the floor. She had learned that little trick in her self defense class.

"We're almost out of time," Hazel yelled at the Queen and King. "Get over to the water and jump in now!" Hazel turned away and tried to dodge the fighting people. She felt someone grab her hand. Thinking it might be Scott she turned around without swinging and came face to face with Abaddon.

"You!" Abaddon said angrily, gripping her tighter. Hazel tried to pull away, but the harder she tried the tighter he held. She swing her leg to kick him, but he grabbed her foot with his other hand. He was obviously no stranger to the martial arts himself. "You are the stupid little girl who messes everything up," he said getting closer to her face.

"And you are the king's brother who lies," Hazel said angrily pulling her leg free and taking a step back.

"I do not lie. Just because our idiotic father neglected to choose a king, they think they can rule me out. Why? Just because I'm the youngest? I think not..."

"Or maybe your father thought that you and your brother were acting foolishly about becoming king and he picked someone else entirely!" Hazel said. Adaddon chuckled and shook his head.

"You really are a stupid little girl. Everybody knows that when you are King you must pick one of your own kin. You cannot pick some random peasant – it has to be a blood son."

"Maybe it was," Hazel said tauntingly.

"And what would give you such an idea as that?" he asked, starting to get irritated.

"A hunch," Hazel said with an innocent shrug.

"Stupid girl, don't you think the people would know if the King had *another* son?" he asked losing his patience. Hazel opened her mouth to say something but then changed her mind.

"I thought so." Abaddon smirked. "I knew that the only way I would rule the kingdom was if the people turned against my brother. Then it would be *I* who would save the day. Everybody would hate the King and who else would they turn to to be their new leader? Me! And now I have succeeded. Now I shall become crowned King. I'll go to the forest, find that book of yours, shred it to pieces and burn it along with the entire forest so you can never return here again. That is, if I let you live," he said with a sly smile. Her heart stopped. For the first time, Hazel was scared that he might actually kill her. She stared at him, trying not to show her fear.

"How'd you get people to help you?" Hazel asked, trying to keep him talking as long as possible. She could see that the people were still leaving. She needed more time. "It's not as if you were able to accomplish this all on your own."

"It really wasn't that difficult. You would be surprised what people will do when promised more power or wealth. And you forget, I grew up with most of these people. Quite a few of them are my close friends. Convincing them was hardly any effort. As for the rest of my followers, I had to do a little traveling here and there. It took hardly any time to gather the people I needed. Of course, there were a few difficult ones who needed a bit of... persuasion. Though, we always seemed to come to an agreement in the end," Abaddon said with an evil smile. Hazel didn't even want to think of the things Abaddon might have done to force people to help him.

"What about Scott's... I mean, what about the lady you have drugged? The one at the end of the very last hallway? What does she have to do with any of this?" Hazel said trying to grow her distance between Adaddon and herself.

"Rose is her name. When I first discovered this vast underground place, I had come across her and learned that she had been living here for quite some time, apparently unable to find her way out. Had it been anyone else, I would have demanded her death on the spot, but her beauty persuaded me otherwise. I kept her comfortable for a few years, though she was constantly complaining about needing to get back to her son or whatever. She's actually been quite a drag. However it will all be worth it when I command her to serve me as my queen." Hazel looked around the room. There were about five people still left to jump into the water. She wasn't sure if Abad-

263

don was completely unaware that people were escaping or just didn't care, but she had to keep him talking. Fortunately, evil schemers love to babble about their grand plans and achievements.

"But when I saw her, she was drugged. How long has she been like that?"

"Oh not long now, only once I started bringing in the prisoners. I couldn't risk having her escaping and spoiling my years of hard work. She's been given sleeping pills and food to keep her alive and beautiful. I'm sure you noticed how angelic she looked resting there on the bed, a perfect queen she will be."

Hazel did remember her looking like an angel. "So what are you going to do now?" Hazel asked as she saw Scott and Calvin lead the last person into the water.

"What do you mean?" Abbadon asked, confused.

"I mean, everybody is gone. Nobody is here." Hazel saw over Abaddon's shoulder that Calvin and Scott were now arguing about something.

"Yes, that may be the case, but everybody still hates the King. I have no doubt that I can still make this work." He looked as if he was planning his next actions. Calvin and Scott were still both fighting. Hazel couldn't quite tell what it was about, but then she saw Scott point to the water. Hazel kept herself from groaning. She realized that they were fighting about who was going and who was staying. She could kill them both!

"But then, there is you," Abaddon said, saying each word slowly as if to make Hazel more frightened, which it actually did do.

"I could just *JUMP IN TO THE WATER!*" Hazel said hoping that the boys would get her message. Calvin and Scott looked at her.

"Then you wouldn't have to do anything with me and we could *BOTH JUST GO* our own ways," Hazel said looking at Calvin and Scott. They looked at each other for a second, confused, and then they got it. Hazel rolled her eyes. She didn't need either of them to stay here with her. She couldn't let either of them get hurt - especially Scott. With him being the actual heir to the throne and all.

"Yes, but then you would tell everybody what was really going on, and that wouldn't work well, now would it?" Abadon said, brushing his finger against her cheek. Hazel took a step backward, a lump forming in he throat. She looked behind her and saw a few of the remaining guards, but she didn't see Calvin or Scott anymore. She was relieved that they had finally left and were both now safe, but she also felt terrified because now she was all alone.

"So then what are you going to do with me?" Hazel asked, her voice cracking slightly. She figured it would be better to know than for it to be a surprise.

"Well, I was thinking about bringing you back to the palace to let you be my personal servant."

"You mean slave?" she said as she stopped walking.

"Well, we don't need to complicate things with fancy titles. But unfortunately that would never work. You are so loved in this pathetic city. The people would see you and know that I'm the bad guy. I could just kill you..." Hazel gulped. "...but what fun would that be? Hmm, what about this. I can just keep you here! It would be best! You would have food and entertainment... it would be great! It would be just... like... camp!" he said with a wicked grin on his face.

"Camp is with other people. You get to send letters to your parents to let them know how you're doing, and you're not kept at camp against your will!" Hazel said. If only she had her bracelet that Calvin had made for her – she could shoot the magnet up to the metal chandelier and swing out of here.

"Oh, don't worry, I'm not that heartless. I wouldn't want your parents to worry - a letter from "you" will be sent to them letting them know you ran away." Hazel realized that would actually be the best way – make her parents think she ran away. After all, they knew she was unhappy with them. It was better than them thinking she had died. She just wouldn't be able to stand it if they thought she was dead. Hazel didn't say anything. She held back tears.

"And as for company, you would have your shadow and could play patty-cake with it on the wall. You'll love it here, Rose did." he said with a terrible toothy smile.

"I think I'll pass on that plan," Hazel said sternly, not even wanting to imagine what the years Scotts mom had been trapped here had been like.

"I'm afraid that *that* is not an option," he said with a fake sympathetic smile. He snapped his fingers. Before Hazel could react a guard grabbed her around her waist.

"Let go of me!" Hazel screamed as another guard went for her feet. She kicked him in the face.

"Ooh," the guard groaned as he grabbed his bleeding nose. The guard holding Hazel around her waist tightened his grip. She tried kicking him but he lifted her up in the air so her feet couldn't reach him. Hazel couldn't move her arms at all. The guard was squeezing them so hard she was afraid that he was going to break them. She tried kicking her legs once more but that was doing nothing but making her tired.

"Now, now... let's be a nice girl. No need to be naughty, because naughty girls get punished," Abaddon said with a purely evil smile. Hazel swung her head back hitting the guard squarely on the chin.

"AHH," he yelled. The back of Hazels head throbbed. He loosened his grip a bit, but not enough to get out. She opened her mouth and bit his hand. He yelled and dropped her on the cold earthy ground. Abaddon lunged for her but she rolled over, quickly got up and started running. Dodging the guards who were trying to grab her, she raced ahead. Abaddon and the other two guards were coming for her on all sides, trying to stop her from going into the water. She turned around and headed through the doors and right out of the room, without putting up a fight. She looked behind her to see if someone was following her, but she couldn't see anyone. She then heard Abaddon yelling out.

"Catch her! And bring her back! Dead or alive," he roared. Hazel started running faster. She knew exactly where she was going. She stopped and quickly turned her head around. She was in the room with all the hallways running off it. Hazel remembered that she still needed to get Scott's mom out, so she ran down the hallway with her room at the end of it. When she got to the door she tried to open it but it wouldn't budge.

"Come on..." Hazel said quietly. She didn't have a key for the room anymore. Looking through the small circular window, she could see that Scott's mom wasn't on the bed. Hopelessly, she knocked quietly on the door. She heard it click. Confused, Hazel put her hand on the handle and turned it. It was unlocked. She pushed the door open and walked into the room.

Chapter Fifteen

Something flew at her head as she entered the room, and Hazel ducked.

"I have a vase too and I am not afraid to use it," a voice yelled. Hazel turned her head slowly and saw Scott's mom. She looked just like him. Hazel stood back up quickly.

"Oh my gosh! You're ok! The pills wore off quicker than I expected – perfect!" Hazel said.

"Who are you? And where the heck am I?"

"My name is Hazel. I'm here to help you. You do know who you are, right?"

"Of course I know who I am! I'm Rose Chappman. And I've been held a prisoner here for years! And you're going to tell me how to get out!" she said raising the vase threateningly.

"I am here to help you, I promise, but we have to hurry."
Rose didn't looked convinced. "Look, I came here with your
son, Scott. We're going to help you escape!" Rose dropped to
her knees letting the vase fall.

"Scott! He's ok?" she said starting to cry.

"Yes! He's fine. But *we're* not going to be unless we
hurry!" Hazel said pulling Rose up.

"Ok..." she said getting up quickly and wiping her teary
eyes. She followed Hazel. Hazel grabbed Rose's hand and
leaned back against the wall. Rose gasped as the wall quickly
spun around.

"Sorry, I should have warned you," Hazel said with an
apologetic smile. Hazel spun around, hearing a nearby voice.

"Hazel..."

Out of the darkness, someone tapped her shoulder. She
started to let out a scream but a hand covered her mouth. She
bit down then turned around to make sure Scott's mom was
still there. She was, but she looked confused.

"Ow! Gosh, Hazel, I'm starting to think that I'm going to
have to wear a suit of armor if I want to continue being your
friend," Scott said as he came out of the darkness with Calvin
following behind him.

"Scott!" Hazel said, her heart still beating. "Why do you
always sneak up on me? What have I ever done to you?"

"I think it would be quicker to say what you haven't done
to me!" Scott answered. Hazel laughed, and then she remem-

bered Scott's mom. She turned around and saw Rose with tears in her eyes. Scott noticed her as well, and ran over and gave her a hug.

"I thought I would never see you again!" he said, his voice trembling.

"I, I wasn't even sure if you survived the fall," Rose said while crying and hugging her son lovingly.

"I think she went in here," came a voice from behind the wall. Everybody froze.

"Yes, it's great that we're all alive and well, but I think that we should get going!" Calvin said.

"There's nobody in here!" they heard one of the guards say angrily. Hazel could barely see anyone in the darkness, but she heard Scott whisper in her ear.

"Quickly, let's go," he said quietly. She felt someone grab her hand.

"Grab Scott so we don't get separated," Calvin whispered. Hazel obediently grabbed onto Scotts arm. She felt almost like she was flying because of how fast the boys were running.

"We have to find away to get out of here!" Calvin said, louder now that they were out of ear shot of the guards.

"Thank you, Captain Obvious," Scott said as they pulled Hazel round another corner.

"I was just saying, maybe we should stop running and find somewhere to exit!" Calvin said, starting to slow his run.

"No. Keep running. We're not there yet!" Scott said speeding up. Hazel's arms started to hurt because they were now being tugged in two different directions.

"Sorry, I didn't know you had a map of this place!"

"Who said I had a map?" Scott said, running faster.

"Well, if you know where to stop, then you must—"

"I never said I had a map! I just said that we needed to—"

"Who died and made you king?"

"Stop fighting!" Hazel said tugging her arms back as she stopped running. Calvin, Scott and Rose tumbled forwards.

"Sorry," both boys mumbled at the same time.

"Now, I'm in charge, remember?" Hazel said. In the little bit of light, Hazel could see Calvin nod, but Scott looked unsure, as if he should point out the fact that Hazel had said he got to make plans too.

"I changed my mind!" Hazel said impatiently. "Now, just stop talking and let me think!" Hazel put her hands on her head and paced back and forth. She had to make sure that everyone was safe, and then deal with Abaddon. She also knew that she had to prevent people from being brought here, ever again. But there was no way to do that unless...

"It has to be destroyed," Hazel said quietly.

"What?" Calvin asked. "You want to destroy this place?"

"It's the only way to keep people from abusing it!" Hazel said.

"And how do you suppose we do that?" Scott asked.

"I don't know!" Hazel said, throwing her arms down. She tried to think out how you would go about knocking a rock fortress down. Then she remembered an experiment she did in school once. They had made a bunch of little rock towers, and then tried to see which way worked best for tumbling them down. Knocking them down was the best way, fire did nothing, but surprisingly, water was strong enough to ruin the rock towers. Hazel remembered the watch she had put in her hair. She squinted her eyes to see the time – six forty-five p.m

"I've got it!" Hazel said as she started walking towards something she hoped was a wall. "We're going to have to split up."

"What?!" everyone said at the same time.

"Hazel, we've been through this multiple times - splitting up is not a good idea!" Scott said trying to follow her footsteps.

"Just listen to me," Hazel said as she started patting the wall. "Cal, start thinking of something that I can travel in, that goes really fast, with the simple supplies we'd be able to round up." Calvin nodded his head, already searching his brain and having a pretty good idea of what he was going to need.

"Scott, get your mom back to the dining hall and have her jump to safety." Scott didn't argue with that.

"Abaddon will probably still be in there with a couple of guards, so you'll have to be quick. Calvin, once you make your thing, you're going to give it to me. Then, you're going to go back to Scott. You'll only have about one..." Hazel felt a hole in the wall. "...minute to convince Abaddon to jump with you, along with the guards, or else they are all going to die. Don't let anyone get too close to you. If he doesn't go within a minute, then jump by yourselves. Calvin, what are you going to need?" Hazel asked as she slowly pushed on the wall, which to her pleasure opened up and led her back to the main room with the hallways leading off of it where the citizens had been kept.

"I need a cart and some stuff," he said as he quickly started sorting through the supplies the new room had to offer.

"Hazel, what are you up to?" Scott asked. Hazel didn't answers as she headed towards the hidden stairwell - Scott traveling behind her.

"Hazel!"

"Rose, can you see if Calvin needs any help?" Hazel asked as she pulled open the door and started climbing up the stairs. Scott followed her.

"Hazel! What is your plan here?" he asked sternly as she kept walking up the stairs. Then he stopped in his tracks, realizing what she was going to do. "Are you out of your freak'n mind?!"

"Scott, don't start with me! It's the only way!" She walked back to the wall where Scott and her had first come in. She walked up to the wall and sighed, hoping that everything would work out.

"Hazel! I'm not going to let you do this! No one is! You can't do this – it's too risky." Scott turned away and stomped off. Hazel chased after him.

"Scott!" she yelled after him, but he was already with Calvin.

"Stop making that thing! She's suicidal!" Scott was yelling.

"What are you talking about?" Calvin said, not stopping.

"She's going to flood this place, and she plans on using that cart to get her out before the water gets to her!"

"You're going to do what?" Calvin yelled as he backed away from the cart.

"Look you guy's, we don't have time for this!" Hazel said, frustrated. Calvin didn't look like he was done with the cart, and now he didn't look like he was going to finish it.

"You can either finish it, or I can run," Hazel said evenly. Calvin reluctantly started on the cart again.

"So let's go over the plan – and no talking until I am finished!" Hazel said, looking at her watch. "The guards are probably going to be here soon, but this place is so big, and they already checked this area, so we've got a bit of time. You three are going to have to go through that hallway and take a right," Hazel said pointing toward the hallway. "Scott, get your mom in the water, then talk to Abaddon about going too. Sixty seconds tops. If he doesn't come along, then jump into the water yourself. In..." Hazel looked at her watch "...exactly five minutes, I'm going to push open the rock where we first entered through. I'll still be able to get a head start, but I won't have much time, so I'll use the cart to get myself to the water in the main dining room." She looked over at Calvin who had stood up, finished working with the cart. It looked as if he had just tied a fire extinguisher to the back of it - but Hazel knew he had done more than that.

"Questions?" she asked.

"Hazel, you can't—" Scott began.

"I said questions, not comments!"

"Mom, tell her she's crazy and it's not going to work!" Scott said turning to his mother who hadn't said anything.

"Scott, she's made up her mind and she doesn't look like she's going to change it. I think that it might be a good plan," Rose said. Scott stared at his mom with his mouth wide open.

"That's the drugs talking!" Scott said. "Moms don't let kids do stuff like this!"

Hazel winced. Her mom and dad wouldn't even care if she went volcano swimming.

"Scott, you are not my parent! I don't even have normal parents! I've made up my mind! I'm doing this and you can't stop me!" Hazel said loudly. Before Scott could say anything, Calvin pushed the cart forward.

"All you have to do is sit on this top part and pull the strap when you're ready to go," he said quietly. Hazel went over and grabbed the cart.

"Go," Hazel said evenly to Scott as she started pushing the cart towards the stairs.

"Hazel," Scott yelled as he turned and grabbed her by the shoulders.

"Scott-" Hazel started, she didn't have time to argue this anymore.

"God, just be careful, please. Please be careful," Scott pleaded sincerely, cutting her off. "You're the craziest person I know. And if your hair band falls off, or if you drop... I don't know... anything, just do not get off the cart, no matter what." Hazel looked at Scott's face. It was the first time she'd seen him without a smile on his face.

"I'll be careful. I promise," She said looking him straight in the eye. He pulled her into his chest and wrapped his arms around her.

"If anything bad happens to you," he started, his voice slightly cracking.

"Scott," Hazel said wrapping her arms around him, wishing that she could stay in the safety of his arms forever. She knew there was no point in telling him that everything was going to be ok, because they both knew that it might not be. "Go get your mom to safety," she said breaking their embrace. Scott nodded then kissed her softly on the forehead and turned to go grab to his mom.

"Go help her get set up and then come back here with us," Scott said to Clavin. He nodded his said solemnly and grabbed the cart from Hazel and started pushing it up the stairs. Hazel followed behind him. Hazel and Calvin pushed the cart up the stairs to the hallway and back down to the spot where she and Scott had first entered the underground world. She looked up above her at the handle on the great stone that was guarding the entrance and keeping the water from coming in.

"Ok, you're only going to have about two minutes to get down to Scott and his mom and get out - make sure you leave that door open for me!" Hazel said to Calvin.

Calvin looked down the hallway, calculating the distance she was going to need to travel.

"I don't think it's going to work, Hazel," Calvin said as he pushed the cart into place.

"Calvin..."

"You're not going to have enough momentum!"

"Then I'll give myself some momentum! I'll make a sling shot or something," she said looking away from Calvin.

"Out of what?" Calvin asked, thinking of what she could possibly use. His eyed widened as he realized what her plan was. "You can't use the gum!"

"Calvin, just stop it! Ok? I have to! I don't have any other choice! Red Diamond is just as much a home to me as it is for you! And if I didn't have my aunt back home, I would be living her full-time in a heartbeat! I will do whatever it takes to make sure it stays safe! I have to do this," she pleaded. As Calvin looked at her, his eyes started to water.

"Hazel, I've lost my Grandma and my parents. I'm not going to lose you, too. You're my best friend, and if something happened to you, or if..." Hazel wasn't sure what made her do it – maybe it was the fact that she might die in the next couple of minutes, or maybe because she had always, deep down, liked Calvin, but she leaned over and kissed him. When she pulled her head away, Calvin's face turned a deep red. She gave him a quick hug.

"Nothing is going to happen to me," she said, sounding more sure than she actually felt inside. Calvin, who was still in shock, just nodded and gave her a funny smile.

"Now go! We don't have much time!" she said as he turned away and started walking toward the others. Hazel pulled the gum out of her dress and held it in her hand. She took out one of the pieces and put it in her mouth. It felt like she was sticking her tongue to a power outlet! Her entire body tingled with electricity. She wanted to spit it out – the pain in her mouth hurt so much she couldn't stand it – but she chewed on it for a couple of seconds more and then pulled it out of her mouth, feeling as if all the energy was drained from her body. It looked like a ball of electricity, and it was burning her hands. With her mouth feeling numb, she quickly stuck the gum to one of the walls and then stretched it to the other side of the room.

She clenched her teeth so she wouldn't scream out in pain, her body starting to shake as she grabbed onto the sparking sticky gum. Then she secured the center of the gum against the far wall, forming a slingshot – and finally, she pushed the cart firmly against it. Her hands were burned and bleeding. Hazel ignored the pain knowing she only had a little time left. She was about to get into position on the cart, but her dress was too tight. She took the lipstick out and cut slits in the side so she would be able to move her legs far enough apart to straddle the cart.

"Much better," she said, but gasping for air because it hurt to talk. As she climbed on to the cart, Hazel looked at her watch - six fifty-nine. If she had calculated correctly, sunset would be at seven o'clock sharp and the water would come crashing down moments later.

She held her breath, reached up above her, and used what strength she had left to slide the stone off of the entrance. Looking up above her, she could see the water rising upward higher and higher, swirling viciously. She knew she only had seconds before the water would come crashing down and in through the hole. She had one hand ready to pull the cloth on the cart, and one hand holding the lipstick above the gum, ready to cut it and have her make-shift slingshot propel her down the hall. She prayed that Calvin, Scott and his mom had made it out ok.

Hazel held her breath and cut the gum from the cart, dropping the lipstick in the process. The cart flung forward and her hair whipped behind her. Hazel heard the water rushing in. As the flow of water rushed through the small entrance, she heard a gigantic crack as it burst through the rock and into the opening, forcing the ceiling to break apart. She held onto the cart to keep from tumbling off as it rattled down the tunnel. She leaned slightly so the cart would turn toward the hallway. On the back of her neck she could feel drops of water splashing her. The water crashed into the walls, and Hazel heard rocks crumble as the giant waves charged ahead. To her left, a large break forming in the stone suddenly shattered and the wall crumbled to the ground. Ahead of her, the ceiling broke apart in large pieces and crashed onto the floor. She swerved around the debris as the entire place collapsed all around her. Hazel pulled the cloth on the back of the cart causing the fire extinguisher to ignite. She had expected the white foam to stream out but Calvin had other plans. A stream of purple flames shot behind her, propelling her to even greater speed as she shot down the hallway. As Hazel's cart sped through the entrance way of the main dining room she looked to see if Abaddon had gone with the others, but there he was, the only one in the room, standing on one of the tables and waiting for her. He jumped into the air and landed on the cart, nearly knocking Hazel off. The water was getting louder and louder, chasing behind her.

"Stop this cart!" he yelled at her over the roaring waters as Hazel shifted her weight, dodging the tables and making her way toward the end of the room.

"No! Give it up, you lost!" Hazel screamed at him. She rolled to her side and off the cart, landing onto one of the tables. Hazel screamed out in pain as the glass cups she landed on shattered. She saw Abaddon sliding around on the cart, trying to hold on. He slipped to the front, and suddenly the cart drove full force into one of the large pillars. A large crack slowly ran up the entire beam before it shattered near the top with a loud bang. Slowly, the entire column leaned forward and fell down. It crashed into the ground with an explosion of dirt and tableware.

Before Hazel could even think, the gigantic wave of water came crashing into the room. She watched as it rammed through the opening sending the doors flying and racing over the grand hall. It forced its way to the rest of the pillars, snapping them like toothpicks. The floor shook and the chandelier on the ceiling jingled as the stone it was fastened to broke while everything else around it collapsed into ruins. Hazel took one last final breath as the water crashed down on her, pounding her to the ground. She tried to fight through the pain and swim through the water but it was pointless. The current was too strong and she was too weak. Hazel was tossed around, along with the tables and chairs which still littered the hall. She was running out of air and her chest was screaming with pain from holding her breath. The force of the water slammed a large piece of rock into stomach, pushing her downwards. Hazel yelled in pain, taking in a mouthful of water.

She knew she was going to die. She thought of Calvin, Scott and everyone else in Red Diamond. She loved them all so much. Then she remembered her aunt and Amber. And most of all, she remembered her mom and dad. Emotions stirred around inside her as she realized that she would never get to see any of the people she loved again. Hazel felt herself falling, and then suddenly she felt like she was flying. She opened her eyes and then shut them immediately as she was sent upward, crashing through the wood roof on top of the well on the castle grounds. She flew through the air, water pushing her higher. Everything went white and she couldn't see, hear or feel. Then, just as suddenly, it felt like she had run into a wall and all of the pain, plus more, came shooting back. Every inch of her body was in agony. She felt dirty water in her mouth, and then felt someone shaking her – which only made the pain one hundred times worse. Someone was yelling her name. She could barely open her eyes, but when she did she saw Scott hovering above her pumping her chest. She opened up her mouth as water came spilling out. She knew she wasn't dead. She could see people were surrounding her. She felt like she couldn't breathe – probably due to all the water in her lungs, but she managed to choke out a few words.

"Is everybody safe?" she asked Scott, so quietly that everybody had to stop talking to hear her.

"Yes, Hazel. Everybody's fine. Everything's going to be just fine! Just hold on, we're going to get help," came Scott's soothing voice. Hazel closed her eyes. She had done it. She had saved the people of Red Diamond. As she remembered something, her eyes slowly fluttered open.

"Scott, one last thing..." Everybody pressed forward to hear her. "...you are the real King," she said so quietly that only Scott heard. She saw his eyes fill with confusion, then everything went black.

Chapter Sixteen

Every inch of Hazel throbbed with pain. Her eyelids felt too heavy to move but she opened them up anyway. Her vision was blurry at first but things started to come into focus. Everything was white. She sighed. She didn't think you were supposed to feel pain once you died. Her head felt like it was spinning.

"Hazel?" she heard a voice ask. Hazel slowly turned her head. Scott was sitting in a chair next to her.

"Am I dead?" she whispered. Scott didn't say anything because he hadn't heard what she said, but he had a sort of an '*I'm so sorry*' smile on his face. Hazel turned her head up to the ceiling. She felt like crying but it was too painful.

"Great!" she said out loud. "I died!"

"What makes you think that?" Scott asked, hearing her this time.

"Because you're smiling!" Hazel said turning her face back to Scott.

"You think I would be able to smile if you were dead?" he asked, sounding surprised and upset.

"You smile through anything! You were even smiling when we could have been jumping to our deaths!" Hazel said, tears in her eyes. Scott laughed.

"Ah, well, I promise you that you are not dead. After all, wouldn't that mean that I would be dead, too?"

"I don't know. You have blood on your shirt. So, maybe someone could have killed you without you knowing! Maybe we are dead." Hazel said, still feeling slightly hysterical.

"That, my friend, was from you," he said, pointing at Hazel. "You were such a mess, and you looked disgusting too, I might add. Still kind of do! You ruined the dress and everything!" he said laughing. Hazel gave him a weak smile, even though it hurt. She was glad she wasn't dead. She had a thousand questions to ask but was still too exhausted.

"I'm tired, I'm going to sleep," Hazel said as she closed her eyes. "And I need a sign or something to let me know that I'm not dead. This whole white-room thing creeps me out. Every time I look at it I think that I'm dead," she said through her closed eyes.

"You got it. Now some sleep," Scott said softly.

When Hazel woke back up again, she felt wide awake, which must have meant that she had been sleeping for a very long time. She felt stronger, and nothing hurt, but it still felt good to have her eyes closed. She realized though that she still had several questions she needed to ask Scott. When she opened her eyes she saw that she was in a sky-blue room with bright pink signs, hanging from each of the walls, with purple writing that said "*HAZEL! YOU ARE NOT DEAD! I REPEAT YOU ARE NOT DEAD! – Scott*"

Hazel laughed and sat up, looking around the entire room. Calvin, Page and Rose were sleeping in chairs facing Hazels bed, and to her left Scott was sleeping in a chair. There was a tray of food attached to the side of her bed. On the tray there was a half eaten ham and cheese sandwich, some chicken noodle soup, a half eaten chunk of bread, an empty pudding cup, and the reminders of a muffin wrapper.

Hazel looked over at Scott. He hadn't changed his shirt yet, but there were crumbs on his face and a little chocolate on his lips. Hazel laughed. She looked up at the clock - it said that it was ten am. She figured it wouldn't hurt to wake him up.

"Scott," she whispered quietly. He didn't move. She took the chunk of bread and started ripping pieces off of it and throwing them at him. He shifted a little in his seat. She threw the rest of the bread at him and he sat up quickly, looking around the room to see who had thrown something at him. When he saw that it was Hazel he laughed, then yawned and stretched.

"Ah, trying to hurt me. Glad to see that you're feeling better. Anything still in pain?" he asked with a smile.

"Nope!" Hazel said, which happily was true.

"Good," he said, wiping off his face.

"What happened last night?" Hazel asked. Scott gave her a small smile.

"That was more like last week," he said. Hazel gasped.

"I was sleeping for a whole week?"

"You were pretty banged up. You came to here and there but mostly you slept. You would say something that wouldn't make sense, then you would go back to sleep. Sleep talker!" he smiled. "But anyway, regarding the night that you were asking about, after Calvin came back with that stupid look on his face..." Scott said, stopping to wiggle his eyebrows, causing Hazel blush. "...we immediately started running. Once we were in the great room, I quickly got my mom in the water before anyone could do anything. We told Abaddon what you planned on doing and that he had sixty seconds to jump into the water so he could get out. Most of the guards started jumping into the water the second they heard me say that, although some of them stayed behind with Abaddon. Then Abaddon sent a couple of them to find you. He said that he wasn't leaving until you were dead. Some other guards tried to jump on us, but we ducked out of the way and then ran back to the water and jumped in. Once we got out of the well, we waited. The sun had set, so I knew the water had to be flooding in. We were all waiting, but nothing happened. I can't even tell you how it felt – waiting to see if your were dead or alive. It was terrible.

"Everybody was holding their breath, and then the water came shooting out of the well with you on top, and you crashed right through the top of it and then landed on the ground in front of me. You were a mess with blood every where, especially your head! I started to go give you CPR, and then you coughed up water and started breathing on your own again. People were running around trying to get help. I scooped you up after you started talking and ran to the hospital where they fixed you up. Well... the best that they could. I asked them to do something about that face of yours but they said it was no use." Scott said jokingly. "They had to put you into surgery, because like I said you were really banged up, but after about five hours later you woke up and started talking to me, and..." He pointed to the signs he had made and put on the wall. "...I did as you requested." Hazel laughed.

"Thank you for that, by the way," she said. "I'm sorry for what I put you through. My plan was working so well, and then Abaddon jumped onto my cart and the waves came crashing in, and... wait! Did Abaddon and the guards ever come back up?"

Scott shook his head. "No," he said quietly.

"So I killed them." Hazel said, feeling he heart drop, her eyes began to water. "I killed all those people."

"Hazel! Do *not* blame this on yourself. We told them they had to leave with us, but they didn't listen. They made their own choices. You knew what you had to do, and you did it. You are not the bad guy here, they are. If Abaddon hadn't been so power hungry, then none of this would have happened," Scott said sincerely. Hazel nodded and took in a deep breath and let it out, knowing that he was right.

"What kind of crazy things was I saying in my sleep?" she asked wanting to get off the subject of Abaddon.

"Well, first you were going 'Calvin, Calvin!'" Scott said in a gushy way, putting his hands over his heart and batting his eye lashes. Hazel gasped.

"I did not!" she exclaimed mortified.

"Oh, yes you did!" he said laughing. "And it was quite entertaining! Calvin's face turned so red!" Hazel could have died of embarrassment. Scott gave her a playful shove. "But after you'd been sleeping a little longer, you started saying 'I'm in charge' like you were scolding me! Which is very offensive, I might add. But then, and this is really funny, you started saying 'Scott the king, Scott the king', which was hilarious, but a little weird, and then..." He stopped talking when he saw Hazel's face. She wasn't laughing with him anymore. Hazel suddenly remembered what she had told Scott right before she had become unconscious.

"Scott, hand me my gadget band." She said, looking over at the table where it sat. Remarkably, it had stayed on her leg during the entire water ordeal.

"Gadget band? What, are you going to break out of the hospital?" Scott joked, but Hazel could hear the uncomfortable tone in his voice.

"Just hand it to me," she replied. Scott handed it to her. Hazel pulled the plastic bag out of one of the pockets. She noticed that her fingertips were still raw from where she touched the gum. Hazel took the papers out of the bag and set the empty bag on the table next to her.

"Read them." she said. She handed Scott the last letter that the king had sent to his sister before his death, along with the real Last Will and Testament. Scott took the letter, confused, but started reading it. While he was reading, Hazel started eating what was left of her sandwich, taking each item off, one at a time, and eating it separately. Once Scott was done reading he just looked at Hazel.

"Is this real?" he asked blankly. Hazel nodded.

"The box that Calvin took from your house... he gave it to his grandma and that's where she put the letters that her brother sent to her. She told me to take them with me before she died."

Scott smiled meekly. "Who would have ever thought? Me, King?" At this point, Rose opened her eyes. She had been listening to the whole conversation, but neither of them realized it. She sighed.

"I'm sorry, Scott," she said softly. "I was planning on telling you who your father was when you were older... But I never got the chance. I was so in love with him. I could hardly wait to start our life together. But one of his advisers who was against our marriage told me that by staying with him, I was only causing him trouble – that people would think he had been cheating on the Queen and think that he was an untrustworthy King. I was very young, and he was able to convince me that I would be responsible for that, and that if we had kids, they would have to live in the shame of it all. He made me believe that I was being selfish and inconsiderate. So I told Nicholas I couldn't take the pressure of being queen and that I wasn't right for him.

"It hurt me to see how much I was hurting him, but I left, and a couple months later I found out I was pregnant with you, Scott. Nicholas and I had often talked about our future children. He said he wanted to name one of them Nicholas Scottery, after himself and his father, so I did. Once you were born, I wrote a letter to Nick to let him know. I told him that he shouldn't be a part of his son's life because it would just complicate things.

"When you got older, the sophisticated name of Nicholas didn't really fit with your lively personality. And you looked so much like your father – every time you were upset, it reminded me of the day I told Nicholas I was leaving him. So I suggested we change your name to Scott. You really liked that name and I liked it much better too, not having to be reminded of your father every time I called you." Rose had tears in her eyes. Scott got up and hugged her.

"Mom, it's ok," he said as he was hugging her. By this point, Page and Calvin were starting to wake up, hearing the commotion.

"Hey, you're awake!" Page said. Calvin just looked a Hazel and smiled.

"I'm awake!" Hazel said.

"Did we miss something?" Calvin asked, looking over at Scott and his mom.

"You missed a lot," Scott said looking at Hazel and smiling.

"What could we have possibly missed? We were sleeping for what – an hour?" Calvin asked. Scott held up his hand.

"Excuse me, peasant, but nobody is to argue with the new King." Calvin looked from Hazel to Scott.

"Ok, whatever," he said, assuming they weren't going to let him in on their inside joke.

"Have a look!" Scott said, handing the papers to Calvin. Page leaned over Calvin's shoulder to read as well. Their mouths fell open while they were reading. Hazel laughed.

"Oh my word," Page said. She got up and hugged him. "Scott, congratulations!"

Calvin rolled his eyes. "So now we have to report to you?" he asked in disbelief.

"That is correct! I am King, and I rule you all!" Scott said laughing. "But I am, however, forever in debt to you!" Scott said kneeling by Hazel's bed. "What might your first request be? Off with the peasant's head?" he said, pointing to Calvin. Hazel laughed.

"First, thou must getteth me a new pudding cup! Then, I banish thee from my room." Scott looked confused. Hazel laughed.

"Scott, you haven't left my bed for a week! You need to go home and change because you look gross, and shower because you smell bad, and eat some food so that you'll stop eating mine...and then come back! And then we'll tell the king your the king... I guess?"

"Fine, fine... but you're one to talk," Scott said, looking Hazel up and down. Hazel wondered how bad she looked.

"Give me a mirror," Hazel quickly said.

"I don't think that you should," he said somberly.

"Scott, give me a mirror!" Hazel said. Scott picked up the mirror that was on the counter.

"Ok, but just to let you know, seven years of bad luck if it breaks." He handed the mirror to Hazel. She closed her eyes and held it up to her face, expecting the worst – large scars and missing eyebrows. She opened her eyes. She let out a relieved sigh. Her hair looked as if someone had washed it for her and her face had a few small scars... nothing major. But she looked a lot older for some reason.

"Did anybody ever tell you, by the way..." Scott said looking at Hazel, "...that you're not a freak'n mermaid?! And did you ever really learn how to swim, because you and water don't really mix. I mean, you must think that you can breathe under water, because you sure do try to a lot!"

Hazel threw the empty pudding cup at him. "Go home!" she said laughing.

"OK, ok…I bid my subjects a fair-well!" Scott said as Rose smiled and waved goodbye. The two of them left. Page looked at the clock. "Well, I should probably get home. Calvin, Hazel probably wants to sleep," Page said, gathering up her purse.

"Actually, sleep is far from what I feel like doing right now! I've been sleeping for seven days. Do you mind if Calvin stays to keep me company?" Hazel asked.

"Of course not. I'll see you later, Calvin" she said as she walked out of the room. Right as she left, the doctor came in.

"Look who's up, Sleeping Beauty!"

Hazel gasped. It was the lady she had sat next to during the King's dinner the other night, Mabel Pat Bloomer.

"You're a doctor?!" Hazel asked.

"Sure am! I should have known it was you!" she said as she started flipping through paper. "Anything hurt, dear?"

"Nope, but how did I recover so quickly? And what needed recovering?"

"Well, you needed a lot of stitches, you broke your ankle and your right foot, and your chest had three broken ribs. Your head had some serious damage and a cracked skull. Your left arm had a cracked bone and a torn ligament. We preformed a small surgery on you when you first arrived. And you sure did a lot of sleeping."

Hazel's mouth dropped open. "How did I heal so fast?"

"We have this stuff called MediFoam. Calvin here actually helped invent it. It helps injuries heal faster than normal, so let's just say you practically took a bath in it!" she said laughing.

"How long do I need to stay here for?"

"You can leave whenever you want - you're all fine now," she smiled sweetly.

"Do you guys have showers here?" Hazel asked. Though it seemed as they cleaned her up a little bit, she still felt pretty dirty.

"Sure do! Just come with me and we'll see if we can't get some clothes for you to wear as well," she said. Calvin just sat there in his seat and waited.

"Don't leave, I'll be right out," Hazel said as she swung her feet out of the bed to follow the doctor. She led her to a room that had about five shower stalls in it, and then left Hazel to wash up. Taking a shower had never felt so good to Hazel. She made the water steaming hot and just soaked it all in. After scrubbing herself clean, she turned the water off. When Hazel opened up the curtain there was a nice white fluffy towel for her to dry off with and a pile of clothes.

Someone must have given her the outfit, and they had good taste. There were purple sparkly flip flops, with blue jeans that had flowers on the pockets, and a light blue t-shirt that had a butterfly on it, with a black stretch hooded sweat shirt. Hazel slipped into the clothes and ran the towel through her hair.

There was a disposable tooth brush on the sink with tooth-paste already on it. Hazel ran it under the water then brushed her teeth for longer than her normal two minutes since her teeth hadn't been brushed for quite a while. Hazel threw the tooth brush away in the garbage and walked out.

"Thank you so much, Doctor Mabel," Hazel said. "And thank you for the clothes! It feels so good to be clean!" Mabel laughed.

"Of course! Now, I'm sure you're starving, but I know you want to get going, so go ahead and stop at the foodstation. Use the code 44579 and you can get on out of here!" she said.

"Thank you," Hazel said as she turned and walked back to her room, not quite sure what the foodstation was. Calvin was still sitting in the chair. He smiled as she walked into the room. "Ready?" he asked, standing up.

"Yup, just going to quickly stop at the foodstation?" Hazel said questioningly. Calvin laughed.

"This way," he said as he lead her down the hall. The foodstation pretty much a nicer version of a vending machine. The machine itself had a pole running down the middle of several large circular trays where the food was placed upon. Hazel was glad to see that instead of gross processed food, it was all freshly baked and packaged. Hazel typed in the code the doctor had given her and got a bag of chips, cookies, a sandwich, and two bottles of water for her and Calvin. They quietly made their way out of the building while Hazel dug into her food.

"Do you know where Scott's house is?" Hazel asked, realizing that she wasn't sure how to contact him to let him know she left the hospital.

Calvin frowned and looked at the ground. "Yeah, it's this way. We can take the long way if you want, just to get some fresh air."

"Sure, that'd be nice." Hazel took in a deep breath of air. It smelled nice – the leaves, the smell of smoke in the chimneys, fresh cut grass. Hazel and Calvin walked in silence.

"Hey, Hazel, could I... er... ask you something?" Calvin said looking at Hazel.

"Sure, anything," Hazel said in between bites of potato chips. Calvin looked at the ground again.

"I know it's not really any of my business, but I was just wondering if... well... are you and Scott like…" he paused. "Together?" he finally said.

Hazel started laughing so hard that she started choking on her potato chips. She opened up her water and took a sip. She looked at Calvin's face to see if he was kidding. He wasn't. Hazel couldn't even imagine if she and Scott were to date! It would be so weird that she didn't even want to think about it.

"Calvin, Scott is like my older brother! What would give you an idea like that?" she asked, taking another sip of her water.

"I don't know. I mean, you spent all that time together in the forest, and he always seems so protective of you, and he wouldn't leave your side at the hospital to even go home and change, and he made the signs for you, and... I don't know, he just seemed like a boyfriend to me." Calvin didn't take his eyes off the ground.

"Calvin, I mean it. He's like my brother! And I don't have siblings, but I'm sure we act like them. We're always teasing each other, and he's always making fun of me. Yes, I do really like him, but I really like you, Calvin. I don't need a boyfriend right now, or even for a while. All I want is best friends who I can hang out with, be myself with, and they can do the same." She said sincerely.

Calvin looked up and smiled. "Really?" he asked.

"Really," Hazel said. He smiled and stuck his hand out.

"Best friends?" he asked. Hazel laughed and shook his hand.

"The best of the best!" Hazel said. They both smiled and continued walking.

"But would you pick me over him? I mean, he's older and better looking, and he's going to be the King!" Calvin said.

"Calvin," Hazel said warningly.

"I know, you're not looking to date anyone, but theoretically if you did want a boyfriend, you would pick me, right?"

"Cal, drop it," Hazel said.

"Ok, fine, fine," Calvin said with a smile. She smiled back. The sun was up and the skies were blue. She had one of her best friends with her and everyone she loved in Red Diamond was safe. She smiled as she linked her arm through Calvin's and walked through the field to Scott's house. After a bit more walking through the warm sun, Calvin stopped.

"Here we are!" he said. Hazel looked up at two very large and expensive houses.

"Wow! Which one is his!?" She asked, finding them both equally as impressive.

"That one," Calvin said, pointing in between the two houses. Hazel cupped her hands above her eyes to ward off the sun and spotted a small little stone and timber shed back in between the two large houses, a little stone pathway leading up to it.

"You've got to be kidding me! This is where he lives?" she asked. Calvin laughed.

"Now you can see why you'd pick me!"

Hazel hit him on the arm.

"Ok, I'm dropping it!" Calvin said quietly, a wide grin on his face.

Chapter Seventeen

Hazel started down the pathway. When she got to the Stone shed, she knocked on the door. Scott opened it. He was wearing a clean T-shirt and pants, and looked freshly showered.

"I thought we were going to meet you back at the hospital!" he said hurriedly, blocking the door so Hazel couldn't see inside.

"This is where you live?" Hazel asked. "Oh my gosh, I feel so bad for you!" Hazel went to give him a hug. When he lifted his arms up she pushed past him and into the small house. There was one main room that was a little bit bigger than your average dining room, and pushed up against the wall there was a small bed that Scott's mom was sitting on.

On the same wall there was a small fridge with a very small stove next to it. The fridge was actually bumping up against the bed. There was a small table that would fit one person comfortably, sort of, and there was a small TV on a table across from the bed. Next to the small table there was a sink. Hazel saw a small door she thought must be the closet, but when she opened it she saw a toilet and a shower that was so small you would hardly be able to stand up straight in it. And you had to practically climb over the toilet to get in it.

"Look, don't say anything about it. I've lived in it for three years and it works for me. Nobody said it was perfect. The people who own the houses next to me let me stay here for cheap – and I do some yard work for them here and there," Scott said with a shrug. Calvin gave a cough to cover up his laugh. Scott glared at him.

"It's, well, hmm... cozy wouldn't be quite the right word," Hazel said, and then started laughing.

"Did you just come over to torment me or was there some other reason?" He turned back to his mom who was trying to shuffle the magazine to cover up her laugh.

"I'm sorry, sweetie. It is very nice how you did this all by yourself!" she said turning back to the magazine.

"Ok, I'm done." Hazel replied, pulling herself together. "We did have a reason for coming over. We have to decide what we want to do next." Hazel looked around the room and then gently sat down in the chair at the table. She didn't want to move anything too much because it all looked like it might break at any second.

"Well, what do you think we should do?" Scott asked, on the bed next to his mom.

"I was thinking we could go see the King," Calvin said sitting on the floor next to Hazel.

"Hello, he's right here!" Scott said gesturing to himself, chuckling at his humor. Calvin rolled his eyes.

Hazel agreed though. "Calvin's right, we do need to go see the..." (Scott cleared his throat.) "...the *old* king, let him know what's going on, then call the whole town for a meeting and let *them* know what's going on." Hazel said. Scott nodded his head. "Do you still have the letters?" Hazel asked getting up from her chair slowly.

"Ughhh no! I needed a tissue and I couldn't find one!" Scott stood up. "Of course I still have the letters!" He took the papers out of his pocket. "Oh, won't you hold them, oh mighty one?" he said giving the papers to Hazel.

"Ok, then we should probably head up there," Calvin said. Rose got up off the bed.

"Ok, you guys can go get a head start," Scott began. "I'll catch up with you there."

"What?" Calvin asked.

"I need to change! I want to look nice if I'm going to talk to the King. You might not care what you look like, but I do," Scott said defensively.

"Hazel, why don't you stay back with Scott until he's ready, and I'll head up there with Calvin," Rose said.

"Sure, no problem," Hazel said before Calvin could object. They must have planned that out earlier so Scott would be able to talk to Hazel alone. Scott disappeared into a small closet that Hazel hadn't seen before and Rose ushered Calvin out of the house. Hazel started to wonder what Scott could possibly need to talk to her about. Then she started to get a bit nervous. She wandered over to the bed and took a seat. After a moment Scott came out of the closet wearing the same outfit he had on before.

"Out of clean clothes?" Hazel asked.

"Oh...yeah, I just needed an excuse so that we could stay behind and talk," he said with a smile.

"Sure." Hazel said, her heart beating quickly. What if Calvin was right? Did Scott *like* her liker her? What would she say if Scott told her he liked her as something more than just a friend? Scott pulled the chair over from the table and sat in it across from the bed and sighed.

"Look, I don't know how to say this, but I've been thinking..." He stopped. Hazel didn't breath.

"I don't want to be king," he said quickly.

"What?" Hazel said, partly relieved and partly confused.

"I've been thinking, and I don't want to be king... at least not yet. I want to at least wait until I'm a bit older. I mean, I just found out my mom's alive! I would like to spend at least some time with her – maybe do some stupid teenage stuff. I don't know... I just feel like I'm letting you down because you went through all that trouble to find out who the true king is, and now he's just walking away." Scott looked at the ground, ashamed.

"Scott, you don't have to be king ever if you don't want to! I was just trying to find out who was king just to prove that it wasn't Abaddon... so people could get things straight! I know that *I* wouldn't want to be in charge of an entire city of people! But I do know that *you* could...if you wanted to," Hazel said with a smile. "And although everyone might just flee the city once they hear that you're the new king, that shouldn't stop you from at least trying!"

Scott laughed. "Well, I think I might be good at it, too. But I just want to wait until I get a little bit older."

"I think that would be fine, and I think that would be fine with Bilimora. But you have to promise me one thing..." Hazel began.

"What?"

"You can't be going around saying '*Is that any way to treat your future king?*' and stuff like that." Hazel and Scott laughed.

"It's a deal!" Scott continued, but now he looked even more serious. "Hazel, I wanted to thank you for letting me come with you to find everybody." Hazel laughed.

"Like I had a choice?"

Scott smiled. "I mean it! It was the most fun and the biggest adventure I've ever been on, and probably ever will be on! At first I thought it was going to be a pain, but after the first couple of days, hours, seconds... however long it actually was... I started actually liking you!"

Hazel stopped breathing and looked panicked. Scott started laughing.

"Don't worry, not like that! Best-friend, sistery kind of way! I mean, you seemed so much like me. We both were going through tough times, yet we were surviving. And you're easy to talk to, fun to hang out with – although dangerous to hang around with sometimes! But you're the only real friend I've ever had, and I really want to keep being your friend... if that's ok with you." Hazel didn't know what to say. She was so touched her eyes began to water.

"That's the nicest thing anybody has ever said to me." She wiped her eyes. "Scott, I feel the exact same way about you. Even though you're still a pain in the butt, and you smile too much, you're like my brother now, and one of my best friends! And I want to stay friends with you, but… I don't think I'm ever going to see you again, or Red Diamond for that matter." She tried to stop the tears from coming down her face.

Scott looked shocked. "What do you mean? You're not coming back?"

Hazel gave a short laugh. "Like my aunt will even let me touch that book again. Scott, I've been gone for god knows how long. I feel so bad because I know she's worried sick right now, and she's probably blaming herself thinking that I'm dead or something. She won't ever let me come back here again," Hazel said feeling sick thinking about the pain she must be putting her aunt through, and feeling even sicker because what she said was true – her aunt wouldn't let her come back.

"Don't worry, we'll figure something out, Sis," Scott said with a smile as he nudged Hazel with his foot. Hazel laughed. "We better get going. They're probably wondering where we are." Hazel stood up and wiped her eyes again.

"We can take my car," Scott said. Hazel laughed.

"Oh, yes, please. I've got to see that!"

Scott stuck his tongue out and grabbed a pair of keys off the top the refrigerator. He walked out of the house with Hazel behind him.

"Were do you keep your car?" Hazel asked looking around.

"The person who owns this house has an extra garage, so he lets me uses it for my car, along with storing some knick knack stuff I've collected over the years." When they got to the end of the pathway, they walked past the second house and kept walking to a small little garage that looked barely big enough for a car. Scott had painted his name sloppily above the door. When he pulled the garage door up, Hazel could see there was a car with a protective cover over it.

"Hazel, meet my baby!" Scott whipped off the cover and Hazel gasped.

"Oh my gosh! Scott, you stole a car!" Hazel exclaimed, looking at the car. It was a jet black, shiny and very expensive looking sports car. Hazel knew nothing about cars, but she knew this one must have cost a fortune!

"I did NO such thing!" he said defensively.

"Scott, this is like Batman's freak'n Bat Mobile..."

"Well, I don't mean to brag, but Batman and I are pretty close! He gave this to me for Christmas!" Scott said, not even knowing who Batman was. "No... seriously, the guy who owns this house – his wife died and this was her car. It needed a lot of repairs, and he said it hurt too much to look at the car in his garage. So he gave me the stuff I would need to fix it up and said if I could work on it, I could keep it. And I did! I actually just finished a few weeks ago."

Hazel ran her hand across the hood of the car.

"You live in a doll house and you own a fancy sports car?"

"Excuse me, not just a "fancy sports car" but a Lagoona Dianadi!" Scott said as he clicked a button on the keys, making the car give a little beep.

"Now, if you don't say you're sorry to my car for calling it a 'sports car' – because this is far better than a sports car – you're going to have to walk to the King's palace." Scott got in the car, and before Hazel could open the passenger seat he locked the door.

"Scott, come on, open the door," she said. Scott put his had to his ear. He was really going to make her do it.

"Scott's car, I'm sorry," Hazel said without any emotion in her voice.

"Like you mean it!" Scott yelled from inside the car." Hazel sighed. "Lagoona Dianadi, I am so sorry for calling you a sports car. Please forgive me and let me in!" The car clicked and Hazel opened the door.

"Now, was dat so hawrd?" Scott asked in a voice like he was talking to a two year old. He pulled out of the garage, stopped, and then got out of the car to shut the garage door.

Hazel was still struck by how beautiful the inside of the car looked. When he got back in, Hazel asked, "Tell me though, why do you own this wonderful and beautiful car, yet live in a house that is smaller than my bathroom? Do you know how much money you would probably be able to get from selling this car?" Scott looked shocked.

"Sell my baby? Do you know how much work I put into this car!? Do you know how much time I put into this car? Do you know what the guy who gave it to me would do if he found out that he just gave the car to me for free and I sold it? He would pull out all my teeth." Scott and Hazel laughed. "I'll be honest, my first thought was 'how can I sell this car'. But after I fixed it up, and the first time I put the key in the car and I heard that purr, it was love at first drive! And then I couldn't even imagine selling it!"

Hazel laughed. After driving for a while, Scott sighed. "I never thanked you, Hazel, for bringing my mom back to me. We've done nothing but talk since we got home. It's still so hard to believe! I really thought that she was dead! And to have seen her there, held captive, so helpless, but then to see her there with you, finally free and coming home.... I don't know how I can repay you."

Hazel smiled. "Ok, can you stop thanking me and going all mushy on me? It's fine. I'm glad you're back with your mom. But there is one small thing you can do to repay me..." Hazel said looking at the steering wheel and raising her eyebrows.

"Ha! That's a funny joke. You? Drive my car?"

"You're right, it's silly to ask. It's not like I am the one who brought your mom back, and am the one who found out that you were king, and am the one who made sure that everybody was safe in Red Diamond, and it's not like I'm the one who—"

"Do you even have a license?" Scott asked interrupting her. "Aren't you like twelve?" Hazel rolled her eyes dramatically.

"Drivers permit, license in two months," Hazel said holding up her hand.

"Have you ever gotten in any accidents? Even a scrape on a car? A ticket for speeding?" He asked.

"N-O-P-E! Nothing! Nada," Hazel said. Scott muttered something that Hazel was pretty sure was a curse word, as he pulled the car over.

"How much driving practice have you had?"

"Thirty five hours of it," Hazel said matter-of-factly, not mentioning the fact that she still gets nervous when she gets behind a wheel. But this car just looked so fun to drive!

"One scratch on this car and I swear I will kill you... slowly."

"Understood," Hazel replied, getting out of the passenger seat.

"I know I'm going to regret this," he said as he got out of the driver's seat. Hazel gave a little squeal of delight as she hopped into the driver's seat. "Seat belts buckled..." Hazel clicked hers down then waited for Scott's click. "...check!"

"Please don't go over the speed limit," Scott said as Hazel put her hands on the steering wheel. For some reason she didn't feel nervous at all. Maybe it was Scott, or maybe it was the car – who knows, but she knew that she was ready to drive! She gripped the steering wheel and pressed on the gas pedal and shot forward. But it wasn't a jerk, it was smooth... so smooth! Everything outside the window was just flying by, similar to what it looked like as you quickly flipped through the pages of a book.

"Hazel, slow down!" Scott yelled.

"Ah, ah, ah! Don't distract the driver," Hazel said with a smile. "This is the best car in the world!" Hazel said as she turned the corner. She looked over at Scott. He looked like he was going to be sick. "Try not to throw up in the car please."

"If I do, you're cleaning it up! NOW SLOW DOWN!"

Hazel ignored him and pressed down on the gas pedal a little more. Eventually, she slowed the car down as they approached the palace and pulled up to the front where Calvin, Page, and Rose were standing. Calvin didn't look too pleased. Hazel stopped the car and took the keys.

"Now that was the best drive I've ever had!" Hazel said as she got out of the car. Scott spilled out of the passenger door and fell to the ground.

"LAND! LAND!" he said while on his hands and knees, looking like he was going to kiss the ground.

"Oh, stop it! I didn't run a single stop light or stop sign," Hazel said.

"That's only because there weren't any!" Scott stood up.

"What's up with you, Mr. Grouchy Pants?" Hazel asked Calvin as she started climbing the stairs. Page and Rose rolled their eyes and shook their heads.

"Don't get him started," Page said. Calvin glared at Hazel.

"What?" she asked, slightly annoyed. She thought he had gotten over the whole 'her and Scott' thing.

"You!" he said pointing at her accusingly.

"What did I do?" Hazel asked defensively.

"You WRECKED MY CAR!" he yelled.

Hazel put her hands over her mouth. She had completely and totally forgotten about Calvin's car.

"Oh my gosh! Calvin! I am so sorry about that! I was under a lot of pressure! I just found out that I was responsible for making sure that everybody got home safely. Wouldn't you have been a little jumpy, too? And I swear the car was in drive, not reverse, but it went backwards anyway! And it kind of was your fault, too! I mean, who the heck puts a turbo button on a car! But I swear I'll bring back money for you to get a new one. I can get you a Lagoona Dianadi," Hazel said pointing to Scott's car. Scott glared at Hazel.

"YOU WRECKED HIS CAR!?" Scott yelled. Calvin looked pleased that Scott was mad at Hazel for a change.

"Well..." Hazel began.

"OH, COME ON! You said NO accidents, NO speeding tickets, not even a scratch on a car! And I let you drive my car!" Everybody looked shocked at that. Hazel gave a small nervous laugh.

"Your car?" they all asked in unison.

"YES! My car! MINE, MINE, MINE!" Scott did a quick check-over to make sure that there weren't any scratches. "You are so lucky!" he said pointing to Hazel.

"Look, now's not the time for this. We have to go talk to the King," Hazel said, running up the steps toward the door.

"You are never driving my car again," Scott said while running after her. Rose and Page were laughing now, following right behind in the chase.

They were greeted by the king's guards who walked them straight to the end of the hallway toward the family suite. That was normally were the King was at this time of day. Hazel came to a big door and knocked on it.

"Come in," the King's voice answered. Hazel opened the door and saw the King and Queen reading books while lounging on a long black couch. The twins were playing a card game on the floor. Seeing them all together made Hazel homesick, thinking of when she was sitting at home with Claire and Amber.

"Hazel!" they all said as she walked into the room.

"And you brought some guests – how nice! Would you like anything to eat or drink?" the Queen offered as she stood up.

"No, thank you. We actually came because we have to talk to you about something very important," Hazel said. The King and Queen looked confused. The twins jumped up and ran over to Scott.

"How did we do on our secret mission!? Did we do well?" they asked at the same time. Scott put a hand over his heart.

"I couldn't be prouder of the job you two did," he said. Both of the children beamed.

"Sit down," the King said. Everyone took a seat. Hazel could tell that the others felt awkward since, other than Rose, none of them had ever been in the Palace before. And they were sitting in front of their king, getting a private audience with him, it wasn't exactly something every citizen got to do. The twins took a seat by their parents.

"Ok, there is really no easy way to say this, so..." Hazel took the letters out of her pocket and handed them to the King. Looking very confused, the King took the letters and started reading them. The Queen was reading over his shoulders, and like everybody else who had read the letter, their mouths dropped wide open. When they were done reading them, nobody said a word. Finally, the King cleared his throat.

"Do you know who this Nicholas child is?" he asked.

"Yes, Scott's real name is Nicholas Scottery Chapman. And this is his mother, Rose Chapman, King Nicholas' second wife. She's the one who was being held prisoner by your brother for the last couple of years. Scott changed his name from Nicholas to Scott when he was younger."

It was quiet again.

"So, you're the rightful heir to the throne?" the Queen asked.

"Yes M'am, but..." He looked at Hazel. She gave him a look encouraging him to go on. "I don't feel ready take on the throne yet. I would like to, someday, but with me just being back with my mom, I feel like there's more I want to do and see - and maybe even fall in love and get married before I become king. And over all I just don't feel ready yet. So, I was wondering if you would continue to be king until I was older, and then we could take a look at it again then," Scott said to the king.

Calvin and Page looked a little shocked at the news. Everybody held their breath to see what the King's response would be.

"I think that is a wonderful plan," the King said with a smile. Everybody in the room let out their breath.

"And this palace – it's pretty big! We have plenty of space. I think it would be a good idea if you and your mother lived here. We could even start preparing you, while you are young, for taking over the kingdom. If that is alright with you, that is."

"Yes!" Rose said before Scott could say anything. Scott looked at her, surprised.

"I'm sorry, sweetie, but I am not living in that little house of yours!" she said quickly. Everyone burst out laughing.

The twins, who had just finished reading the notes, smiled.

"Does this mean you two are brothers?" James asked. The king chuckled.

"I guess we are!" Scott laughed.

"So you're our uncle!" Emily said.

"Uncle Scott!" they both yelled at the same time, bursting into giggles.

"Well, I guess we should let everybody else know what's going on," the Queen said with a smile. She and the king stood up, and per tradition everyone else stood up as well. But before they had a chance to bow, the King and Queen bowed to Scott, the future King. Every one else in the room did the same.

Chapter Eighteen

Shortly after meeting with the King, the officials and citizens of the City of Red Diamond had been gathered in the palace courtyard. There was a little podium set up were the King would speak.

"Leaders of Red Diamond!" the King said into the microphone. "Thanks to Hazel, we are now all home, safe and sound." Everyone applauded and cheered. Several people around her patted her on the back. After a few moments, the King held up his hand to quiet them.

"Now, I know you all thought I was the one who brought you down to that awful place, and thank goodness we got it cleared up that it was my brother as part of his plan to overthrow me as King. As you know, key to that plan was to convince people that I was not the real king. As it turns out though, he was right."

The crowd broke into whispers of muffled and worried conversations.

"I know what you are thinking, but it is not him either. Hazel found my father's one and true Last Will and Testament. He had sent it to his sister. Due to some unfortunate circumstances, it was never opened. But fortunately, his sister gave it to Hazel before she passed away. So now, I stand here before you, with the real Will. And it was not me who was meant to be king... it was this young man."

Scott stepped forward and gave a nervous little wave. Everything was very quiet.

"To make a very, very long story short, today I found out that I have a second brother – this gentleman. Through his bravery while assisting Hazel in saving the citizens of our city, my children, my wife and myself, he has already proven his worthiness for assuming the thrown."

Everybody was shocked and couldn't say anything.

"But by his request, I will stay on as King until further notice, giving him time to mature and learn the ways of a king, and then he will take his rightful place on the throne." There was a brief moment of silence before everybody started clapping and cheering. Scott smiled.

"Thank you, everyone, very much," the King concluded, stepping down from the podium. The King had wanted Scott to say a few words to the people of Red Diamond, but Scott had told him he didn't feel ready to do that yet.

Hazel looked around to find Calvin. She looked into the crowd and saw family members hugging and laughing and talking. More than ever, Hazel felt homesick. She turned to Scott.

"Help me find Calvin. I want to go home now."

Scott nodded. He grabbed Hazel's hand so he wouldn't lose her in the crowd, though as they walked past, the people parted for them and cheered. Several people whistled and clapped them both on the back. When they made their way out of the courtyard, they saw Page, Calvin and Rose talking.

"That was nice," Rose was saying to Page.

"I'm going to go home now," Hazel began. "It was really nice meeting you," she said, giving Rose a big hug.

"Oh it was so nice meeting you, too! I don't know how I'm ever going to thank you," she said.

Hazel laughed. "Bye, Ms. Page. I'll miss you." She gave Page a big hug too.

"We'll miss you too. Come back soon!" Hazel felt a lump in her throat and just nodded because she knew that she wasn't going to be able to come back. She was having trouble speaking.

"Do you want to come bring me back?" she managed to choke out to both Calvin and Scott who nodded. Since Scott's car only fit two, they had to walk to the woods. Hazel was walking faster than normal because she wanted to go home quickly. But inside, she was torn because she also wanted to stay. When they got to the forest, the boys followed her to her chest. She leaned down and pressed her charm to the chest and it opened up to reveal her book. She stood back up.

"I'm really going to miss you, Calvin." Hazel felt tears coming to her eyes. It seemed unfair that she wasn't going to be coming back. Calvin looked confused.

"What do you mean you're going to miss me? You're not going to be gone that long, right?" he asked, worried from the emotions Hazel was showing.

"Calvin, I'm not coming back My Aunt's not even going to let me look at that book, let alone come back here, after I've been gone for so long. I'm sure she's worried sick. And I don't blame her if she never lets me see the outside of my bedroom again."

"So you're not coming back, ever?" Calvin asked shocked.

Hazel nodded. "I'll miss you," she said. She gave him hug. "Don't forget me, ok?" she said half joking, but a part of her was serious. Calvin nodded somberly. Then Hazel turned to Scott and gave him a hug. Hazel smiled.

"Hopefully every time you look at your mom, or pull up to the castle in your Lagoona Dianadi, you'll remember me." He smiled back.

"Or when I look at all the scrapes and scratches and bruises I have on my body, I'll remember you, too," he joked. Hazel laughed even though she was crying. Calvin handed Hazel her book. She looked at Scott and Calvin for the last time and thought of home.

Hazel felt a chill run down her back and heard a loud scream. Opening her eyes, she saw that she was in her room, but she wasn't alone. Her dad was sitting in her chair, Amber was sitting on her bed, her mom was standing by Hazel's closet, and her aunt, who had come to the sound of scream-ing, was standing in the doorway. Hazel's mom and dad had looks of horror in their eyes. Amber and Clair had looks of sheer relief. Clair ran over to Hazel and gave her a hug, and they both started crying.

"Where have you been? Do you know how much you scared me? How could you run away like that? Are you ok?" Hazel started crying even harder. Her aunt thought that she had run away. After all the beautiful things her aunt had done for her, how could she have thought Hazel was so unhappy that she would run away?

"I...I... I'm so sorry!" Hazel started hiccuping which made her aunt laugh a little. Hazel wiped away her tears and sighed.

"Aunt Clair, I could never, ever in a million years, run away. That's not at all what happened. You see, when I got to Red Diamond, there were no people, they had all been kid-napped – every single one of them – and I had to get them back. I ran into a boy named Scott, and there was a weird for-est, and there was the King's brother and..." She stopped talk-ing realizing that she wasn't making any sense.

"Hazel," her dad said, still shocked that his daughter had just appeared out of thin air right in front of him. "What did you just do, there, and what...and how?" he stammered. Hazel looked at her dad. He was wearing jeans and a t-shirt and by the looks of it hadn't shaved in days. She looked at her mom who had her phone's ear piece in her ear, was dressed in black pants and a nice, but simple, white shirt - which was dressed down for her.

"Daddy, I'm so sorry." Hazel ran over and gave her dad a hug. He hugged her back. Hazel couldn't remember the last time she hugged her dad. He let go and cupped her face with his hands.

"No, I don't want you to apologize. I need to apologize. I know that everything you said to me that night was true, and I know you weren't just upset about me not coming to the tournament – you were upset about everything. I'm the one who is sorry. I really have been a terrible father and I really want to fix things. I really do." He gave her a kiss on the forehead. Hazel knew that her Dad really meant it, and she hoped that they could fix things.

"Hazel, your father's right. We haven't been good parents. I haven't been a good mom. I would like to fix things, too." She came over and gave Hazel a hug. While it wasn't as sincere as her dad's apology, Hazel knew her mom was never one to get mushy and she meant it just as much. Hazel looked over at Amber who was awkwardly sitting on the bed. Hazel gave a laugh.

"OK, we're done with our mushy family-moment," Hazel said as her best friend jumped off the bed to give her a hug.

"Good! Because I was about to strangle you if you didn't tell me where the heck you've been for the last three weeks!" Amber said laughing.

"Would someone like to fill me in on how my daughter just appeared in the middle of the room?" Hazel's dad asked. Hazel sighed.

"Dad, it's a long story, so get comfortable."

Hazel told her parents the whole story, starting from when she first opened the book and went to Red Diamond to when she came back there to all of them, not leaving out a single detail. She even got so wrapped up with everything that she even accidentally told them about her kiss with Clavin. Causing some not so pleasant looks from the adults and a cheer from Amber.

When she was finally done, nobody said a word at first. Though, of course, it was Amber who was the first one to speak.

"Wow, you did all that in three weeks? The only thing exciting that happened to me during all that time is that I became an intern at your Aunt's Shop!"

"Hazel, you are not allowed to go back into that book!" Hazel's dad said firmly.

"But dad—" she started, but knew it was no use. She had been expecting this.

"Hazel, do you know how much danger you put yourself into?" Clair asked, cutting Hazel off.

"You could have been killed!" her mom interjected.

"I know, I know! But I didn't die, and everybody there helped me, and I helped all of them. And I know how to protect myself!" Hazel paused for a moment. "I have great friends there. Can't we at least think about it, or talk about it!?"

All of the adults began talking at once. Hazel could only make out bits of it like "too young!" and "could have killed yourself!" and "I don't care if you saved the people!" and "I'm going to sue someone!" Hazel couldn't quite make out who was saying what, but she knew her mom was the one who said she was going to sue. She waited, and finally, they all stopped talking.

"Hazel, we can't let you go back into that world. I know how much the place means to you, I really do. But it's become far too dangerous for you to *ever* go back," her Aunt said in a tone that told Hazel she wasn't going to change her mind, no matter how hard she tired.

"Hazel, I know you're upset" her father started, "but there's really no way that ahhh!" Her dad suddenly jumped out of his chair.

Everybody was looking at Hazel in horror. She knew someone was behind her. Had a burglar just climbed in through her window? Suddenly she felt someone from behind grab her wrist. She quickly reached behind with her other hand, found the person's arm and flipped them over to the ground. A split second later, she was straddling the person, her knee pressed firmly against his throat.

"Scott!?" Hazel said in amazement as she got up off of him.

"That's the last time we settle anything with Rock-Paper-Scissors," he said to Calvin, stretching his back. Hazel turned around and saw Calvin standing there. She was excited beyond imagination to have them both here with her.

"How are you guys here?!" she asked. She had never thought of anyone from Red Diamond coming into her world.

Calvin smiled impishly at Hazel. "A page must have gotten ripped out of your book when I handed it to you," he started. "And-"

"And, we knew that we couldn't let your parents and Aunt not let you come back to Red Diamond," Scott said cutting him off. "So we took the page so we could visit you. The first time we tried to think of what your world would be like, it didn't work. So then we thought of you! And we appeared... in your interesting room that doesn't have anything in it," Scott said looking around the room. It was still empty from when Hazel had cleared it out in anger. Everyone stood in silence again. Staring at Scott and Calvin.

"Hi, I'm Scott. You must be Hazel's Aunt Clair," Scott said, breaking the silence, and shaking Clair's hand. "And you must be her parents. I've heard so much about you," he said shaking their hands, both of whom were shocked beyond speech that two boys had just appeared in the room – not to mention that Hazel had flipped the larger of them over as if he was a bag of feathers.

"Did she just knock you to the floor?" Hazel's dad asked. Scott gave a small smile.

"One of many times, sir. And you must be Amber!" Scott said shaking her hand. Amber gave him a flirty smile.

"Hi!" she said mesmerized as she walked over to Hazel and whispered, "You get Calvin and I get Scott." Hazel laughed and shoved her, playfully.

"And I'm Calvin," Calvin said, taking Scott's lead and shaking hands with everyone.

"So you're the boy who's dating my daughter?" Hazel's dad asked when Calvin got around to him. Her dad didn't loosen his grip on Calvin and stared into his eyes. Hazel could have died on the spot.

"Dad! He's just a friend!" Hazel exclaimed, her cheeks reddening. Hazel wished that Page or Rose or even Emily or James had come with them, because she suddenly realized that it didn't look so good having two cute teenaged guys asking if Hazel could keep coming to their world.

"So, this is Scott, the one I was telling you guys about, and this is Calvin who I was also talking to you about." Hazel said, gesturing to the two of them. They smiled and waved.

Scott spoke to the room. "Ok, well I'm sure by now Hazel has told you everything, and I can't blame you for not letting her come back... ever! Because you're her family. But I *can* blame you, too! Hazel has been a great help to Red Diamond, and I don't know what we would do without her. Like you probably heard, she rescued a whole town of people! And she is very capable of handling herself, as you can clearly see. And when she can't, there is always someone there to help her out. Everybody in Red Diamond loves Hazel! And she always has

Calvin's awesome electronic gadgets to help her out." Scott paused. "She's been like my sister over the past few weeks, and she's both of our best friend," he said, pointing to himself and Calvin. "And while you're her family, she's apart of the Red Diamond family too."

Hazel smiled. She knew that when Scott was king that he would be great at it.

"And if she can't ever come back, can she at least come back for my Grandma's funeral? My Grandma would die if Hazel wasn't there!" Everyone looked at Calvin oddly. "Um... you know what I mean," he said awkwardly, looking down at his shoes. He clearly wasn't as good at public speaking as Scott.

Nobody said anything for a moment. Then Hazel's dad cleared his throat.

"Clair, Carol could we please go and talk in the living room?" he asked. They both followed him out, shutting the door behind them. Hazel turned back to the boys. "I can't believe that you guys are here! I never even thought about that!" Hazel said happily.

"We weren't sure it was going to work..." Scott began.

"...but it did! I can't believe it either." Calvin finished.

"Would Hazel be able to bring me with her sometime when she visits?" Amber asked, batting her eyelashes.

"I don't see why not," Scott said with a flirtatious smile.

"That is, if Hazel's parents let her come back," Calvin said.

"I hope they do," Hazel began. "But they did leave the room to talk, so that must be a good sign. If it was a definite *no*, they would have just said so. I think my flipping you over didn't hurt my case any," Hazel said, giving Scott a shove.

"I'm glad my pain could be of service!" Scott said, cracking his back. Amber and Calvin laughed, and the others joined in, too. The adults walked into the room and everybody got quiet.

"Hazel," Clair began. "What are the odds of something dangerous like this happening again in Red Diamond?"

Hazel wanted to jump with joy. "Never!" Hazel, Calvin and Scott said at the same time.

"Hazel, I know how happy you are when you come out of that book. You always have a smile on your face, and I would hate to take that away from you, but-"

"We have to think about your safety!" her mother said, cutting off Clair. "After all, we had no idea where you were for the past couple of weeks, and your aunt wouldn't let anyone call the police. We just don't want that to ever happen again."

"But after seeing you flip that young man over," Hazel's Dad began, "I think you showed us that you are alert and able to handle yourself. And it's obvious you have friends there who care about you very much. BUT... until we're completely comfortable with this, you are required to be home every night before six o'clock – unless you tell us beforehand that you're going to be staying later. And you have to tell someone when you

329

are going to this place – no more leaving notes," he said firmly. "And your grades can't go down either," he added awkwardly. Hazel assumed that was part of the "new and improved" father.

"So, that's a yes?" Hazel asked. They nodded.

"Thank you, thank you, thank you!" she said giving her aunt, dad and mom a hug. "I promise, nothing like this will ever happen again!" She ran over and hugged Calvin and Scott. "Thank you guys so much for coming!"

"Ok, we're going to go talk about what to have for dinner. Are you guys hanging out here?" Clair asked as she started to leave the room with Hazel's parents. Amber looked at her watch and gasped. "Oh my gosh! It's six thirty! We have to go Trick or Treating!"

Hazel gasped. She had forgotten all about Halloween. Amber ran into Hazel's closet and came out with the two costumes she had designed. Hazel laughed.

"You made my costume and I wasn't even here?"

"Well of course! I knew you were going to be home by Halloween! And if you weren't, I was just going to show you the costumes every single day and make you feel guilty for the rest of your life!" Amber said with an evil laugh.

"What's Halloween?" Scott asked, staring at the funky outfits in Amber's hands.

"You're kidding, right?" Amber asked.

"And what's Trick or Treating?" Calvin chimed in. Amber jumped up and down excitedly.

"You guys have to come with us!" she said running out of the room.

"Where'd she go?" Scott asked.

"You don't want to know!" Hazel answered. Clair had a room full of knick knack stuff – things from her job that they didn't want anymore. Most of the things were really crazy and weird – dresses, shoes, hats, or feather boas. Amber came back in to the room with a pile of stuff. She handed Scott and Calvin matching neon orange dresses with bright blue polka-dots and big ruffles at the bottom. She gave them both a huge pink hat with a green feather boa around it and bright pink high heel shoes. Scott and Calvin just stared at her while Hazel laughed hysterically.

"Did we miss something?" Scott asked looking at the dress that was in his hand.

"Halloween is when..." Hazel stopped to laugh. "...is when everybody dresses up in a costume, and then you go door to door saying *Trick or Treat!* And then they give you candy. Amber and I are going as matching disco girls, and you guys are going to go as matching girls!" Amber and Hazel started laughing again.

"We're going to go change. You guys hurry up and get dressed!" Amber said as she left the room.

"I call my aunt's bathroom, and I'll bring down her makeup when I'm done," Hazel said running up the stairs and laughing.

"Ok, I'll let the adults know we're going out Trick or Treating!" Amber called after her. Hazel figured that they probably already heard them, as loud as they were being.

When Hazel looked in the mirror she loved her costume! It was just like the one in Amber's sketch book, but better! It was purple and silver mixed together, with the off the shoulder sleeves that got big at the bottom and the slits that ran down the side. She even had the white shorts, and Go Go boots – it was perfect! Hazel took her hair and piled it on the top of her head letting a few pieces fall down. She looked great. Then she scooped up her aunt's makeup bag and ran back downstairs. Amber was just coming out of the bathroom with her hair looking just like Hazel's. They laughed.

"Great minds think alike!" she said. Hazel laughed.

"Amber! These are the greatest costumes ever! I can't believe you made them!"

Amber laughed. "I can't either! But it's so cool that I'm now an intern at your aunt's work. Not the store, but where she actually makes the clothes. I do errands for people, but in my free time I'm allowed to sketch out designs and make clothes with the leftover fabric. It's perfect because that's exactly what I want to do when I'm older! And a lady there was so nice. She helped me make the boots! And other people were saying how good I did on the costumes, and gave me tips and advice!" Amber knocked on Hazel's door where the boys were changing. Hazel smiled. She was glad Amber was doing what she loved.

"Come in!" Scott said in a high girly voice. Hazel and Amber opened the door then fell to the floor laughing. Both Scott and Calvin were wearing the costumes, and even though the colors were all different, it all seemed to still look kind of good. Both boys were posing.

"Are you sure people dress up like this, or are you just trying to humiliate us?" Calvin asked, looking mortified at himself in the mirror. "And does this dress make me look fat?" They continued laughing, all four of them. Once they were finished, Amber and Hazel gave themselves some wild makeup and then did the same for Scott and Calvin.

"Hazel, I almost forgot," Amber said as she was tying a head band around Hazel's head. "If you see anyone you know, let them know your chicken pox went away this week." Hazel laughed.

"Got it," Hazel said, glad to know that her friend had her back while she was away.

Once everyone was finished getting dressed up and ready to go out and get some candy, they went to show the adults. The laughing just started all over again. Clair took pictures and then, after they all grabbed a bite to eat, all four of the "girls" left for Trick or Treating.

The night flew by for Hazel. When they got back, they had some dinner and candy and then Scott and Calvin went back home. Amber spent the night and Hazel's parents slept in the guest bedroom and on the couch. In the morning, Amber went home so that Hazel could talk with her parents a little more.

Hazel let her parents know how she had felt every time they canceled or missed something of hers, or when they didn't care that she was with them – and they really listened. Her dad promised that he would not schedule anything when Hazel was with him unless it was a meeting that he absolutely had to go to. And in those cases, she would just spend an extra day, not go home early. Her mom said she would try, but said it might be difficult, being a lawyer and all. That was perfectly fine with Hazel. That was all she wanted, for her try. They had both decided that they would spend more time with her, and go places like on vacations, to the movies, shopping... bonding stuff like that... and Hazel knew that her life was going to be different from now on. Different, but good. Just the thought of it made her happy.

◆　　◆　　◆

"Hazel." Hazel jumped at the sound of her name. "Would you like to read us your report?" Mrs. Madison said. Hazel smiled. Until just the night before, she had forgotten about the paper she was supposed to write, talking about where she wanted to be in fifteen years. So far, most of the reports were kids talking about how they wanted to be a famous singer, have lots of money, be a fashion designer, teacher, or what not. The J girls all did theirs matching. Hazel could see that her paper was going to be way different from the rest. She stood up, grabbed her paper and walked to the front of the room.

"When Mrs. Madison gave us this assignment, it really got me thinking. Where do I want to be in fifteen years? But more importantly, what do I want to do with my life now? And I really had no idea! And how can you decide what you want for the future when you don't even know what you want to do in the present? So for the last couple of weeks I've been doing a lot of thinking. I am glad to say that I finally found out what I want now, and although I still can't say *exactly* what I want for the future, I can say that I want it do be a little something like this – I want to have a husband whom I love, and who loves me back. I want to have two kids whom I will also love dearly and with all my heart, and who will be spoiled by their loving grandparents and my wonderful Aunt. I want to have a much closer relationship with my parents. I want to continue being great friends with the friends I have now, and to make great new friends along the way.

"I know lots of people know exactly what they want to be when they are older, but I am not one of them. I don't know if I will work, or stay home with my kids, or maybe even homeschool them like my best friend Amber. Sure, I may not know *what* I want to be, but I do know *who* I want to be. I want to be a great daughter, a great wife, a great mom, a great friend and a great person. Now, I would say a perfect daughter, a perfect wife, a perfect mom, and a perfect friend, but we all know that nobody is, or can be, perfect. I'm good with shooting for great." And Hazel knew that was true.

She knew that life was never going to be perfect. In fact, it was her life's imperfections that led her to Red Diamond in the first place. After all, her dad would never have given her the book if her parents hadn't gotten divorced. Hazel knew there wasn't any way she would be able to avoid having fights with her parents, her aunt or even her friends. People were always going to have their own opinion about her and what she did, but that was them and who they were. There was nothing Hazel could do to change them, and she wouldn't try to. Hazel knew that being herself was the most important thing she could do, and the first step in making the most out of any situation. Whether it was arguing over where to spend the holidays or dealing with a crisis in Red Diamond, Hazel knew that she would be able to handle anything with her friends and family at her side. And that, Hazel realized, is how it's supposed to be.

19590682R00202

Made in the USA
San Bernardino, CA
04 March 2015